WHAT BE[...]
BROKE[...]

Alan Duff was born in R[...]n Havelock North with hi[...] published two previous novels (*Once Were Warriors* and *One Night Out Stealing*), a novella (*State Ward*) and a non-fiction work (*Maori: The Crisis and the Challenge*). *Once Were Warriors* won the PEN Best First Book for Fiction Award and was made into an internationally acclaimed film for which he wrote the original screenplay. *Once Were Warriors* has been published in numerous countries. His works have been critically praised as 'powerful'. Alan is a full-time writer and has a weekly newspaper column syndicated nationally. He has also written screenplays.

WHAT BECOMES OF THE BROKEN-HEARTED?

Alan Duff

RANDOM HOUSE
AUSTRALIA

A Vintage book
published by
Random House Australia Pty Ltd
20 Alfred Street, Milsons Point, NSW 2061

Sydney   New York   Toronto
London   Auckland   Johannesburg
and agencies throughout the world

First published 1996

Copyright © Alan Duff 1996
The moral rights of the Author have been asserted

All rights reserved. No part of this publication may be reproduced, stored in a retrieval system, or transmitted in any form or by any means, electronic, mechanical, photocopying, recording or otherwise, without the written permission of the Publisher.

National Library of Australia Cataloguing-in-Publication data

Duff, Alan, 1950– .
   What becomes of the broken hearted?

   ISBN 0 09 183420 1.

   I. Title.

NZ823.2

Cover painting by Sheila Pearson
Cover design by Yolande Gray
Author photograph by Richard Brimer
Typeset by DOCUPRO, Sydney
Printed by Griffin Paperbacks, Adelaide

I (Who Have Nothing): Lieber/Stoller reprinted with kind permission of Campbell Connelly (Australia) Pty Ltd.

To my father, Gowan.
My grandfather, Oliver.
And to love mending most things.

Thanks to G.K. and K.K. *for childhood memories.*

ONE

JAKE HEKE WOKE from a dream in his sheetless bed, what he'd been born to, and never had all those years of being married to Beth (oh, Bethy) managed to change his ways; he had never been able to understand why she didn't prefer the feel of blanket — man, it's the feel of the wool, like my own fucken sheep keeping me warm, I like. A man'd cracked her once over her telling him he was a filthy animal just for not bothering about sheets when she'd been away for a few days to a funeral and come back to the house she said was a mess, which it was — 'cept a man'd had some of the boys still there, out in the kitchen finishing off the keg even though it was near flat, long's the party kept on (but that was in them days, years ago) — so he told her why don't you fucken clean it up, and when she went upstairs and saw the bed got no sheets (I don't know what I did with them, I musta thrown them off when I was drunk and got into bed with my sheep — hahaha! — an' flaked) that's when she came back down and called me what she did front of the boys. Well, naturally a man gave her one, and I ain't talking a root, eh, boys! HAHAHA! had to laugh, and not as if it was a hiding, just a backhander to let her know, don't talk to me like that front of my mates. Or a man'll never be able to show his face again. But that's how a man thought back then, 'bout, what, five, six years ago? No, longer'n that, the sheet incident, that musta been ten years, the six is how long we been apart. (That long? We been apart that long? Well I'll be: a man's been hurting for her that long?) Now, he wasn't so comfortable about — well, a lot of things.

Rubbing a hand over the back of his processed sheep (there, there, boy, Jakey's here) and giggling inside that he thought of the blanket in its original, living form, and while his hand was down there he may as well get rid of that; and he thought of Rita, even though he'd had her heaps of times, because she was the best and she was still available, and she did it with a kind of instant intensity. Jake couldn't quite come up to the same level — not the act nor his understanding of her own part in it (I just lap it up!) that in his more clear moments of thought he saw as a tap Rita turned on — of love but with a capital L. Yeah, Love it was. For not just himself, Jakey, but — and this confused him even more — herself. (So how does she fuck so good if she's loving herself?) Ah, fuck it. He was finished with himself in a few minutes anyrate and then nothing about sex gave him a bothering thought and as for love or Love, well that was different after a man'd shot. For a while anyway. And anyway Rita Bates was one of those strong women who decided her relationships on her terms, so a man knew he had to ring first (from the next door's phone) and not just turn up when he felt like it, and sometimes she might say no, not this week Jake, I'm busy, meaning she had someone else, or her period, or she was just showing a man he needed her more than she needed him. Yet when he did get the yes from her she acted like he was the only man in her (comfortably) over-weight life. So he thought he may as well get up, now he'd had her in his mind. But then somewhere in his head he felt a kind of grabbing. It was the fucken dream. A man's mind is trying to grab what the dream meant. And then it hit him, it was an actual physical jolt.

It was this picture, with these groups of people spread across a rocky landscape of all sorts of things you see in ordinary life, and some things you didn't, 'cept in dreams, like plants talking to each other and changing between being talking plants and people you knew, and colours that went with music, both of which you knew and yet you didn't; they were big groups, small groups, in clusters and talking (urgent talking) or busying (fucken cunts hurrying everywhere yet still somehow connected) and what they had in common was, humming. Mmmmmmmmm-uhhhhhh like that, like an engine going on quiet but steady idle. (And me, I'm up on this low rise of hill, Jake The Muss like I used to be, looking down on these cunts — well, they weren't cunts, only if they were gonna try me on, or only if they were out to hurt me when I wasn't out to hurt them, not to start it, ask anyone: Jake The Muss never started the scraps. I finished them!) And these groups became engines, or each one's centre did, how things evolve in dreams, and a man's smiling to himself cos he's back where he belongs, on top. Till it occurred to him the reason he wasn't down there with them, one of the groups, was he didn't know the tune. Even if it was tuneless. The note then; a man didn't know the note and had never known it. That was the physical jolt he felt in recalling the dream: that he didn't belong nowhere.

For some reason the largest group were Chinese — fucken chinks, never give up trying to take one lousy spare rib out of a man's feed even after all these years a man'd given the slits such loyal whatsitsname, custom. Changing their car every year for another brand new one, as if I fucken care what kind of car they drive. There were several groups of honkies, and yet they were humming the same one-note constant as the Chinese. And a man was looking around, to find a group of his own kind, which (thank God) he did, it was a wonder he hadn't spotted them first for their humming was musical and so he started off down the hill toward them, till it came to him that though they were making something musical, melodic, of their humming, they were distracted by it. That's what his eyes back into the dream were telling him: the ole Maori boys — and some girls — were having a good time (as usual — hahaha!) partying up the large whilst the honks and the chinks had the old heads down an' white bums and yellow bums (with the sideways slits, so their shit must come out . . . — have to think about that one — like liquorice straps. HAHAHA! one thing I'll say, Jake Heke, you're still funny. Liquorice straps, hehehehe, smell like soya sauce.) And he started on down again, over this hard stony ground, and grey outcrops of larger boulders down there amongst the outcrops of busy whites and Chinese and their engines steady and constant, and a man knowing where he was headed and yet with doubts starting to get at him.

Or they did till he got down onto the flat and that closeness of other human physical presence brought out the MAN in him, so he lost a lot of his thinking and became almost a purely instinctive animal, and giving off the vibes of: Don't you touch me, muthafucka, not 'nless it's to pay homage, or show friendliness, or Jake'll waste you. Heading for where the partying action was and finding he had hurry in his footsteps, as if to get away from that now irritating fucken mmmmmm-uhhhhhh-ing, over to that party. Smiling, glad in himself at hearing his name — Jakey! It's Jake The Muss! Hey, bro! Come and join us — and then he was running. For them. To them. With this . . . this . . . (I dunno — Yes, I do know.) This sense of belonging.

Plunging himself into them, the welcoming group. Thinking to himself, now this's a tune I do know. And yet . . . yet . . . a man was hardly into the swing of it when his inner voice was telling him he didn't know this tune either. (But I knew all the words to the songs they were singing . . .) And next he was stumbling, cut, bleeding over the sharp rocks, and everytime he fell and was briefly and painfully down there on the hard ground, harder than his own muscles, he saw each flinty stone, their every tick and comma of layered grain, he saw brilliantly coloured red ones with the blue sea blended like long ago water caught in them when they musta been volcanic stuff connecting red hot with water till the temperature musta been cooled enough to marry with, not turn to vapoury steam, that water. Right by the groups of chinks and Pakeha white maggots to another group of brownskins like himself and the group he'd just left, 'cept they were droning the same working note as the others all over this valley of rocks, which he saw each group was building into constructions, houses and buildings, in shapes and beginning layouts of a complexity he for some reason understood. But he didn't understand why he understood, he was no carpenter, he hadn't even worked on a building site even though in his heart of hearts he'd long wanted to, walking past sites in town and seeing the miracle of a several-storey office building sprouting from the ground, from someone's mind and someone else's materials, and the mysterious glue of it: money, no not money but finance, money was the rub-together stuff that never lasted long, only from one payday to the next, or when he was on a government benefit it didn't even last that long, there was always a day, often two, short, of having nothing to eat or smoke or drink, just resentment and envy and a kind of hating confusion at it all, the process, of not being part proper of the *real* process. Putting together those office buildings wasn't cash, the folding stuff, it was finance. Nor did he understand why he kept falling over, let alone seeing the stones and rocks in such striking clarity and colour. But then he did.

It was cos his fucken eyes kept closing, a tiredness, a deepest sleepiness kept coming over him, so down he'd go. But up again. He was Jake The Muss, not Jake the Wuss. And look, he was making progress for that other group, of Maoris just like him, least the same colour and about the same features (I might be a bit more handsome, cuzzies!)

He reached the group. But they took no notice of him. Hey? he went, but no one looked up. They were doing what the other human outcrops were doing: mmmmmmm-uhhhhh and steadily a surround of arranged rocks was encircling them. One minute Jake on the inside. Next he was out looking in (like walking down the changing main street of Two Lakes, all them new restaurants and café places, the big windows, shutters, slatted openers of nicely stained wood even I 'ppreciate 'em) at something and someones he was never gonna be part of, but never. Like going past a new era (or even worse, a party) he wasn't invited to.

So he got up out of bed. Angry at the dream, because it'd promised such insight, a look at not just himself but the world he was living in that'd always confused him (I admit that. Now I do) and it turned out no one wanted him anyway, 'cept that groupa pissheads when a man did less of that now. Dunno why. (Could be I'm Jake The Muss Be Getting Older now.) He couldn't even smile, let alone burst out in his characteristic laughter at his own witty play on his once famous nickname. Yeah. I'm Once Was Jake. And he walked out into the kitchen to make some breakfast, got stopped at the sight of the fucken mess it was in, forgot about heating up the pot of pork bones and watercress and spuds, as he looked around for Cody. (Little cunt. I'll wring his fucken neck. I've told him about leaving this mess, him and his mates.) That was it: no more fucken parties in this house. Hold it: a man is at these parties more than he's not. Alright, they got to clean up after a party then, that'd be the rule. (And let one of them punks try and argue with me.)

Into the sitting room, the teevee in the corner there, the vase he'd bought with the cupla couches he'd picked up from Albie's Second-Hand Furniture, and lied to everyone ole Albie'd thrown it in when he bought the couches, a fucken flour-er vase, when it was him (me) secretly wanting (just the once) to put flowers in it to see what other people, more real people, saw in them, but he couldn't. For starters, just the picture of himself coming out of a shop, then getting the bus home carrying flowers was enough to put him off, and everytime he promised to do it when he was part drunk he just never got around to it and so the blue vase (come to think of it, it was one of the colours of the rocks in this morning's dream) just sat on the window-sill so the neighbours, if they were that interested which he doubted, or not in the permanently E for empty flower vase, could see the shape of it as part of their view of that corner of Jake and Cody's rented

State house in suburban Two Lakes where they swept the people who didn't count and sent out the cops to collect a few, like society's toll every week, all year every year, and trialled them, fined them, jailed some, weekend community-worked some, and generally let them, the scumbags, know that even their disorder, their own little sub-society structureless chaos was punishable. To let the town's nobodies know there was a greater order and, Jake suspected, one which didn't really want his sub-society to change, not for the better, since they made not just a living, but status (somehow — Jake couldn't figure how the process went, of a lawyer defending a gang member arsehole and the gangie getting jail like Jimmy Bad Horse did, that cunt, and the lawyer got paid twice, once in money and the second in status).

The vase which he still promised to fill, the teevee, the shiny material couches everyone called babyshit brown and had holes worn through the material, a coffee table that'd never seen a cup of coffee (who drank coffee around here?) and that was it: Jake Heke's total sitting-room furnishings.

In the old days a man and his flatmate Cody had extra — free — seats when the beer came in the dozen bottle crates but everyone drank the cans now, only old-fashion ones stuck with the big quart bottles or the flagons, but they were plastic now not glass you woke up to broken on the floor, or with lipstick marks from some bitch drinking straight from it, a half-gallon jar, or grease from someone's lips after he'd had a feed and carried on drinking. Things'd changed, so weren't no wooden beer-crate seats, so no splinters of wood if there'd been a fight, and even that was less these days, only if an old crew got together and lived the past, these people carried their grudges and old bitter memories like they carried their sideburns and sang old party songs even Jake'd got sick of, now this place a reminder from them days, a fucken mess, except say one thing for Cody and the crowd he got round with, they didn't fight much, though he remembered the time when one of Cody's mates pissed in the vase and Jake grabbed the cunt and marched him outside and tipped his piss over his head, treating his vase like that, and then he turned around to see the whole fucken lot of them standing there, 'cept Cody, and they toldim leave their friend alone, Jake you done enough, he's drunk he didn't know what he was doing so don't be hitting him. It wasn't their numbers so much'd frightened him, as the intensity of their loyalty to their buddy and proved by the fact they were ready to confront him (me. Jake The Muss). He was only gonna give the fulla one crack anyrate and, besides, a vase full of his own piss all over him wouldn'ta been so hot, so to keep his pride Jake told the group, Anyone so much as touches that vase he gets it.

But other than that and just now and again a bit of a scuffle, a couple of brawls, Cody and the boys just drank and danced and listened to that rap music of theirs, though a man did like some of it and he loved the souly stuff, could listen to it all night and often did, when he was in his bedroom not feeling like joining them, happy to leave the door open so their music sounds came down the hallway, one fulla they played a lot on the portable stereo on these modern CDs was Terence Trent-someone, Jake never remembered, cupla songs of his broke Jakey out in goose pimples and got things going in his — if it happened to be — sober head like that time he got stoned on grass: he understood. A similar understanding, funny thing, when he was sober and that nigger voice was howling down the passage throwing words together in great servings of emotion and nigger phrasing, oh how do they do it. But he took one look at this mess and the las' thing on his mind was Cody's music — fuckim.

Look at the state of this place. If that little cunt walked in right now he'd cop one. Out to the li'l bastard's room, he kicked the ajar door open, Oi! But it was to an empty bed, cunt musta fucked off to anutha party, a man didn't know what to do with this kid. Well, he wasn't a kid anymore, he was, what, twenty, twenty-one? Five years they'd been living together now — well, not living together like homos, but as buddies, mates. From the days when they were sleeping rough in the park in town, when a man was as low as he could get, his own daughter killed herself and everyone saying it was him when it wasn't. (It wasn't. I would swear before God, He who can read everyone's mind. He who has just seen me pull myself off, who knows it was Rita I imagined. I have told Him and told Him, God, I never did it. You know every person on this Earth, what our every thought is. So I'm asking You, have You got it on your records Jake Heke having any *thought*, nemine the act itself, even a thought like that? Have You, God? No. No, You haven't. Yet I got the blame. And was her, Grace, my Gracie, who I loved — in my own kinda rough way — who left that letter saying it was me.) Cupla weeks later the cops grabbed him as he was walking into McClutchy's pub and nex' thing he's down at the copshop being asked all these questions about sex and his own (my own) daughter. He near up and smacked the two detectives over. Then they asked a man for a sample. Of fucken what — the beer I drink! No, not his beer brand, his spunk. My what! To prove your innocence, Jake. (Well I would wanna prove that, wouldn't I?) But how was I sposed to do it? How did I think, the smart cop cunt asked. When the las' thing a man feels like is pulling himself — in a copshop? With them knowing? They ended up agreeing to do the bizniz at a doctor's (jus' to show these cunts they had the wrong man. An' when I was finished and they found it wasn't me, I'd give 'em anutha sample and rub it in their fucken white shit faces. Oh, I was wild.)

Took half an hour. The fucken nurse keeping on knocking on the door was I ready. Man, if she'd've come in herself naked I couldn't've got it up. But I knew I had to. And I did. I knew it was never gonna match with . . . couldn't even say it in my own mind what the cops were trying to prove or not prove — with my own daughter? — even if I wasn't the father of the year of any of her years. The kinder cop tole me a week later I was in the clear. But that didn't help things any in people's eyes. A innocent man was guilty for life. And though she was dead and never coming back, what about him, Jake the father, who was left living with the unjust curse she put on him when he hadn't done it? Thinking of curses, a man was puttin' one right now on fucken Cody's head for leaving this mess — again.

The vacuum was one of those roller ones that wasn't. Br-rimmm-brr-rimmm, over and over the thin carpet, with the machine that was in need of human power, over carpet Jake'd seen rope of better quality than. The ole State knew what'd soak up the piss stains, even the blood if that was what was being spilled here but wasn't, or not much, not like damn near every week when he'd lived all those years in Pine Block where he hardly went back to and not jus' cos of the reduced status, but the times he'd been back, once in a while, nothing'd changed; same ole parties lasting all weekend, same scraps, same bitches and bastards beating up on each other and when they weren't it was on their kids and one thing no one could say about Jake Heke, that he'd given his kids hidings. Though when he thought of it, there was no particular reason why not, he'd been thrashed by his old man and his ole lady (and my uncles and aunties and every second old fulla who I thought were all my grandfathers when both of the real ones'd died, one from a tree falling on him in the bush before I was born, the other from the booze Mum said, as if she could fucken talk). He just thought giving kids hidings wasn't right; what'd a kid do to a man that could get him so upset he'd want to thrash it? A woman, though, well that was different. And as for a man to man, he still couldn't understand why the whiteshit judges and magistrates had the power to punish two fullas for fighting each other when they were both agreed to fight. What'd it have to do with a fucken honky judge?

Oh well, he made the noise himself as if it was a real electric-powered vacuum cleaner, it took ages to pick things up, and even when he was through it didn't look all that clean. But what the hell, it'd do. Wasn't as if it was his mess. Fucken Cody, wait'll he got home.

Now that looked bedda. Next the kitchen. He lifted the lid to the big pot — sure enough: all gone. Last night he'd cooked up a full pot, took out his two plates, he loved pork bones and watercress and potatoes, but still plenty left for Cody when he got home from where else but the pub, even if he had some of the mates with him there would still be enough for a man to have a feed in the morning, it's how he starts his day, cos he don't have lunch. The only one at work who didn't. They'd stopped looking at him sideways for bein' a Maori who didn't love a big feed at lunchtime, after one time with a cold or something and not feeling hungry and finding he felt better without it, lunch, so it became a habit. Why a man's stomach was still pretty flat, considering he was forty-two now and still loved his piss, 'cept in less quantities, most of the time; so he could still stand front of the bathroom mirror, the only one in the house, a State house what else, on his tiptoes to see his stomach was pretty good for a fulla his age, it was. But going without breakfast? Fuckim! And the mess they'd left, plates of bones with flies crawling over them, not that there was any meat left for the flies, those jokers'd sucked 'em dry, splashes of tomato sauce like congealed blood, green strands of cress like infected snot, a . . . kitchenscape like from out of a dream — a bad dream — cans of beer all over the bench and on the formica table along with the ashtrays spilled over and someone'd stubbed out his smoke on the fucken table! Jake so angry he wanted to punch out someone. Instead, he sighed and found a cloth under the sink — man it stunk! — which he poured dishwash liquid over and rubbed it around the cloth and then under the hot water till it near burnt, and it smelt bedda, then he started on the table; pushing along the debris of food scraps, bones, sauce, salt, butter grease, chunks of potato, stirring up the flies, but they only hopped onto the next bit in front of his bulldozer-cloth, but it was a good feeling seeing behind him the clean path it made; and so he had a tiny little grin on as he made the third run down the length of table, pushing the stuff into his other hand waiting at the end like a dump truck, steering around the plates, he'd get them in a minute, making a sound like a truck reversing as he backed over to the sink cupboard and dumped his hand-load of food and cigarette debris into the rubbish bin, back over to the table, going through three quick gear changes to get there, smiling, and marvelling at what a simple wet cloth with soap liquid in it did to chaos. Indeed, to life, the life, the person doing it, itself.

Standing at the table at his good work, all clean now, yellow the surface, the punishment it'd stood up to, hard stuff this formica, he could make out his reflection, his shape down there in the swirly yellow depths, light coming in through the windows, have to go to work on an empty stomach but he still wasn't having lunch, lunch was over, like she was, Beth, his ex. When it's over it's over. He had time to do the bench before his bus to town. And that felt pretty good after it was done, too. Nice day it was gonna be, too. Long's he didn't start to thinking whilst standing at the bus-stop wishing they'd build a shelter so he could hide his shame of bein' one of those older fullas didn't have his own car. He just couldn't save the money, not even a deposit. Telling himself to think of the mess he'd cleaned and how it looked from the start, and fuck owning a car they only cost money, and anyway he got to drive one of the trucks at work if someone was sick, and plenty of Fridays cos the same driver usually got on the piss Thursday pay night, but the boss couldn't sack him, not these days when the country was scared of doing anything to Maoris, in certain things anyway, something to do with the Treaty of Waitangi, which Jake Heke didn't know nothing about and nor did anyone, not a single person he knew.

He always felt better once he was sat down in the bus, the first of the day, six-thirty, comfortable in the same process within, of telling himself this was only temporary. Even though he'd had the job for going on what . . . five years now? Gonna be a nice day alright. So he felt even better as he thought of having the excuse to work all day with his shirt off, so people driving past would see he was no ordinary dude like they usually saw working on these road gangs, with big fat gut and coughing their fucken smoker's lungs out when a man'd given them up five years ago, though only cos he had no money and got sick of hanging out for a smoke every three days after he got the dole, people'd — real people: whites and them fucken cruel-faced chinks'd — drive past his road gang and he could hear them, all day he could, in his mind saying to each other, Hey! Take a look at that dude's build will you? So his head lifted in sweet prideful anticipation of working all day shirtless and admired. It kinda felt like being loved.

TWO

'NUTHA SIX MONTHS t' go, six months (six years, six fucken lifetimes), Who cares, eh, bro? Jimmy Bad Horse nudged shoulder to shoulder with one of the Brown Fist bros on the top landing, Who-the-fuck-cares, right? And the brother gave back a high-5, like they'd seen Michael Jordan do to his Negro brothers in the Bulls basketball team (big muthafuckas, fucken huge) on the teevee down in the rec room; and they didn't have to give it words, words suck, who needs words, words're for other people, to express 'emselves, and what did they, Browns, have to express, to put in them smooth *words* or even adequately into words? Mulla Rota knew what Bad Horse was attituding about, that it was life he wasn't caring a fuck for, in here or out there where freedom supposedly was. But who said the boys weren't so free in here, what with having each other, The Family, in their minds and (broken) hearts like that, in capital letter starts and maybe like The Marfia, which they misspelt like that cos no one thought it'd be spelt any other way and they notioned, not read, about things outside of their gang membership life, only if they saw something on the teevee, a movie preferably, *Godfather II*, or one of the *Terminator* movies, yeah, but a documentary'd do if it was about The Marfia, or tough subjects like that, and only if the recreation time happened to afford the chance to see such a programme, which it usually didn't, and no one had time to watch much teevee on the outside, only in the mornings when everyone was sitting around waiting for a dope deal to go down and someone switched on a soap or sumpthin', at nights, well, nights're for being outiv it, nights're for gettin' wasted and, if the boys got lucky wasting someone with the boot, softball bats're bedda, anything, who cared, long as it was hurtin' some cunt — Mulla Rota knew exactly what his leader was saying without having to say it. Why he gave a crooked smile with the high-5, to show he was right on it, into it, with it, on what Bad was saying. Mulla was crooked smiling back that he was at and with his leader's very soul (well, most of it anyway. There were, uh, aspec's of the dude a man weren't sure of.) The . . . swathe they left behind was a wet glistening path the width of mops pushed in perfect unison, like most things close Brown Fist bruthas'd do.

Or it was till Bad's eyes fell over the rail and saw something which turned his tattooed Maori warrior features into near the monster he was reputed to be when he was upset, wild at something. And Mulla knew better than anyone in a kind of grudging admiration that Jimmy Shirkey had managed to hold the lie, keep the bluff, for all this time and all these circumstances, of bein' a prez of a gang chapter, the Brown Fists, with their avowed enemies: the Hawks. How Jimmy right now called back his cool, glazed over the fear in his eyes, said out the side of his mouth, Well I'll be, if they ain't sent us in a Hawk. They weren't allowed to say the word black, it was agreed at a council meeting right here in this prison several years ago that any Brown using that hated word of those hated cunts was out. The word itself was banned, which meant that Blackie Rogers had to change his name and so did Johny Black and they even had to call another meeting out in the exercise yard (so the utha prisoners can see how staunch we are) to discuss whether one of them's daughters named Ebony might have to have her name changed when one of the fullas told 'em the name meant black and about as black as you can get. That the fulla loved his kid — which was most unusual for one of 'em, they all knew that and laughed about their loving their Brown Family firs' — made it that much harder to make a decision, cos he was one of the toughest they'd ever had in the history (seventeen years, man, we been around) of the Browns, and he had his li'l girl in his mind, his less broken heart. If he, you know, axshurely loved this kid of his (which he seemed to at visits when his wife brought the kid every fortnight, he never let her go and photos everywhere of her in his cell and only one Penthouse one with the blonde sheila — She American, bro? Yeah, she is — with her twat open and exposed, it and she so beautiful it took Mulla's breath away every time he visited the bro's cell) she was a concept fixed — no, etched — in him, like the tattoo marks all over his arms and legs and face, what if he wouldn't accept the name change of his beloved child and went over to them, the Hawks, fought for them? That is what they secretly thought but not a one of the council of seventeen members, one for every year of existence of The Family, said. Was Bad Horse who turned it to a joke and aksed 'em who of 'em read anything to know Matt's girl's name meant what it did? So Ebony remained part of the permissible language, one of the acceptable mentionables, and it came in handy when they wanted to make a reference to mean black. Funny how even unejacated dudes adapted the only permissible word for black.

Mulla knew it wasn't cool to lean across Jimmy and see for himself, so he just went, Yeah? That right? They musta made a mistake? And then he looked at Bad Horse cos Bad'd stopped and was thinking; Jimmy Bad Horse was pondering. His great shaggy head of scalp-mop frizzle and sprayed-out beard came up after a few moments, in the waiting Mulla hearing the voices and opening and closing of grilles and cell doors below echo an ole familiar (tune?) but for some reason like out of a troubling dream this time, and his heart'd started hammering jus' a li'l bit more'n usual, cos he was hoping Bad wouldn't be aksing him to go down and take this bl — this Hawk cunt out. Mulla only had two weeks to go, and this was his third prison lag with only a cupla years of freedom in between, and the only women he'd ever had was ones on the block for all the boys to do and a cupla sheilas raped by the same boys after being lured, drunk, to a HQ party. When he wasn't thinking about violence and doing bigtime armed robberies, Mulla Rota was thinking about women, about having his own girlfriend who he could (secretly) love. And if Bad ordered him down there to whack out the Hawk with a battery in a sock or stick a blade up his bl — up his Hawk arse, then it'd be anutha five years of bein' here. And inside, a man knew he was getting to his breaking point, even if he never showed it not once.

Now Jimmy was looking at him with those ordering eyes as they stood on the top landing and the world at the bottom was far away and yet forever close if Jimmy was gonna make the decision to send a man down to do the bizniz, reminded in that moment of inner despair, got a picture of the kid, of that Nig Heke when Jimmy'd stuck the shottie in Nig's trembling hand and tole him he hadda lotta makin' up to do did Nig Heke, and poor Nig, such a nice kid and could motor jus' like his ole man who'd showed up Horse here in that pub he ruled, McClutchy's, ended up dead along with Fattyboy Peters, plus a Hawk, in that battle they done on the main street of Two Lakes. Come to think of it, if Nig was around now he'd a have to've changed his name, or would he? Mulla briefly distracted by that rather *serial* question of propriety and whether it could be said that Nig or nigger meant black or did it just denote a person's race in a slangy (and racist) way? Till he pretend-casually sauntered over to the railing and took a look for himself and then felt like diving off and sidewaying himself when he saw who the Hawk was.

But Mulla came back to his position, left of Jimmy Bad Horse, gave a sideways glance, took a deep breath and aksed (we never say ask. Ask is for them to say, real people, Utha People. We say aks) his leader, Want me to go down do it? Inside crying. Inside near to vomiting.

Bad Horse came right over to Mulla with suspiciously aksing eyes of, if the truth be known, a coward to anutha, how come you got so much courage when you never had it before, you know that and I know that, it's been anutha of our unspoken unnerstanin's, what we see mirrored of each utha, but now here you are volunteering your, let's face it, nightmare?

Mulla? you only got a li'l while to go, Jimmy Bad Horse was giving him an out, 'cept Mulla thought it might be a trap and he weren't walking into no trap, not one of Horse's, they tended to have a lot of hurt in 'em, he played cards like that, too: merciless and sly, and he cheated.

So Mulla gave anutha of his crooked smiles from all their repertoire of facial language, it was their ar*ticu*lation that childhood hadn't given them in word and emotional expression equivalent, repeating near to a word his leader's statements back there 'bout eight cell doors ago, Who the fuck cares, right? 'Cept without Jimmy's emphatic insistence, since Mulla did care. He cared very very much for his freedom soon to come after five and a few months long years and that was jus' this stretch, this third lag. He hadn't lost as much remission as Jimmy, who, bein' the bigtime prez, was obliged to do things that costim time off his remission, when they'd both got the same sentence for the rumble Nig and Fattyboy and the Hawk cunt got killed in, conspiring to cause grievous bodily harm. He was coming up thirty-six an' he'd hardly been free in sixteen years, just long enough each time to get into serious trouble cos each time out he found coping was his hardest thing. So, naturally he couldn't find it withinim, not now, to say those copied words and copied facial expression with conviction. Not with a tough cunt down there having to be taken out by serious means as no utha way'd work, that was the Hawk sergeant-at-arms down there and he was in here by prison authority mistake for sure, even they wouldn't do such a thing deliberately as to send the mortal enemy into the Brown's wing, just as they wouldn't deliberately do it to a Brown. They were arseholes, but they weren't cunts. But seein' he was here, Apeman

— blank, cos he was so mean and tough and with total consuming hatred for the Browns he'd changed his surname by deed poll to that word, starting with B you weren't even allowed to think it, though that of course was impossible cos the world, existence, was full of references to that word and so were a man's natural thoughts since he woke up middle of the celled nights seeing and thinking — blank, meaning black — thoughts, and the night was that colour and so was some of his own gang member mates, their skin colour, and so was Michael Jordan and mosta that basketball team and so was Mike Tyson himself (*and* he's just out of jail and all their singing heroes) and so . . . Mulla stepped over and looked down below again, but mainly to get out of Horse's too-knowing eye stare . . . so was Apeman with the changed surname that colour and tauntingly changed surname. And if Ape happened to glance up in this instant he'd be carving Mulla Rota's face into his bl — his dark dark heart and his even darker (ebony) mind. So Mulla didn't look down for long, just long enough to dig even deeper within himself so he could say to Jimmy when he stepped back alongside him, with mop in hand, If tha's what's, uh, required.

Why'd you say, uh? Jimmy accusing now. Huh? Why'd you say, uh? He knew why Mulla said uh and so did Mulla but fucked if Mulla was gonna own up to that, fucked if he was. (I volunteered didn't I? What does he want?) Jimmy, I gotta blade in my mattress, nice 'n' sharp for Ape's arse, that what you want, what you're aksing?

In the eternity of Jimmy looking at him with those burning, always bloodshot eyes from too much dope (making him permanently paranoid, or giggling at nothing, or thinking his dancing along the landing with his mop like a mike was anything like the Negroes — a word they agreed was alright since virtually all of their music, their sounds, was by Negro artists — he saw on the teevee, let alone sing like one of 'em) it seemed to Mulla his own life flashed before his mind's eye, jus' like he'd heard it did people who thought they were going to die. Not that there was much life to flash by, not with sixteen inside and that wasn't counting the borstal and the boys' home, add anutha three for that, it was childhood which he remembered only in seemingly unconnected glimpses and smells — stenches, more like it — of pain unbearable, of this deep missing, this deep aching inside, like a fucken dirty big hole inim, like a fucken big truck up and punched a hole through him, which he'd stuffed with stolen stuff from houses and properties he broke into from a young age, when the hurting registered, when he looked down at himself and saw the hole, and masturbated several times a day every day of his damn(ed) life, and laughed with sick irony at a hole trying to be filled with thoughts of filling a hole, oh how he laughed sickly inside at that. And when they threw him into a boys' home, a Children's Court did, he knew even then it was the start of his life as he would ever know it, he knew this more than anything he'd known in his entire life, that his would be one of slamming and locked doors. And uthas jus' like him. Jus' like him. (I'm in here, aren't I?)

Sharp, you said? Yeah, man, sharp. When Mulla really wanted to scream at the top of his voice that it wasn't sharp it was blunter than a boxer's broken nose, it wouldn't cut nothing, not even budda. But he just nodded, Sharp as. And even hope was dead then.

'Member that sheila, what was her name, used to be one of us, went out with Jake's boy, Nig? Jimmy for some reason was recalling when Mulla had expected him to give the final order. Aksing himself was this anutha of Jimmy's elaborate traps, that was why he had the spider webs tattooed around his throat, to show people he trapped somethin' good and terrible. Did he remember? Well, Mulla remembered everything, of his gang existence on the outside he did, it was all he had as far as memories went, the just short of two years in total of them. They were his photographs (in my mind) like utha prisoners — never Brown Fists — had in their cells to lie they had loved ones on the outside, when if they didn't love 'emselves, how would anyone love them? He referred to them like they happened yesterday; he found he had to change the musical references, update 'em, as time went by or he'd sound like the old codger boobheads, stuck in the past of when the big gate closed on 'em, specially the ones for murder. Old men who still thought Tom Jones was top of the charts when there weren't even charts no more, and nor Tom Jones, or not that Mulla'd heard of and he listened to the radio, to music, all the fucken time; up here in Auckland that Maori station Mai, played all the bl — the Negro music and didn't have no ads. Put a man secretly through a range of emotions (and, uh, maybe even like inta-lectu-al thoughts, yeah).

In the gang he was a ledge for legend, all that time he'd done and being staunch throughout it, not one falter in his (external) demeanour, his swagger, his walking the talk, which was effectively walking the landings, the stairs up and down to his cell, and the exercise yard out there in the days lovely or otherwise, and walking out to freedom, three times it'd been and every time like glory to God stuff, of being so good it felt the sentence'd been worth it jus' to experience this — this sense of 'ppreciating freedom so much, then hardly out than he was walking back in, driven through the big gate in the prison van the new sentence ringing — no, not ringing. Intoning, in whiteman, edjacated Judge's voice, not satisfied with putting a man away again have ta givim a fucken lecture, too — and walking into reception to the same old screw, Hoppy Hopwood, not a bad old fulla for a screw, that fatface smile of his: If it ain't our old mate, Mulla. Welcome back, Mulla! Feeling good to be greeted like an old friend, even if it was by a screw, even if it was anutha sentence. For that brief moment a man felt good bein' back on ole familiar.

Yeah, he remembered everything, so he gave anutha crooked smile, Tania was'er name. Used t' sleep iner shades. Yeah, Jimmy nodding, so she did. 'Member that time she put herself on the block for all us fullas to fucker, she never took 'em off then neither. Yeah, Mulla remembered that, was Jimmy took his right as prez to be first, yeah he remembered that; and, if truth be known which it would never be or not from his mouth (not 'nless

I meet me a nice woman I can talk to) how sad he'd felt for her but not so sad he didn't get a horn on and take his turn ater when it came. After all.

But he did remember feeling sad for Tania that she'd done this to show her disapproval of Nig Heke (such a fine-looking specimen he was, too. Jus' like his father, Jake. Jake The Muss, tha's what they called him. All our bruthas admired him even though we made it out as hatred. The way he fronted the whole lot of us, on his fucken own, in that pub he ruled. Wonder where he is now? Somewhere good, I bet.) That was when Nig didn't like the bruthas kicking the woman when they went around to the place to repossess the teevee for the Pakeha appliance shop owner in town.

Tania, tha's it. Tania from Mangakino, I remember now. Mulla wondering what was coming next and why this talk; as well thinking Jimmy wouldn't know something else about Tania, that story she tole him (and only me) of babysitting her kid brothers and sisters and going down to get them fish 'n' chips and coming back and, well, the house the kids were in, it was (holy shit) fucken burning. Mulla remembered that, he'd take it to his grave withim. A grave coming sooner rather than later now Apeman was accidentally put in their midst. (If only I could figure out a way of warning the screws what they've done. They won't be wanting a war. It's only Apeman, his stupid fucken pride, and Jimmy here, his lying to cover his own cowardice he makes out is pride, that'll make it war.) But then Mulla got a cunning idea. And so what trickled through with it was a kind of perverse courage. In a moment he was about to turn this on Jimmy Bad Horse.

What's Tania got to do with Apeman, bro? I'm hanging out for that fucka's blood. Jus' gimme the order, boss, and I'm there. Glad inside at Jimmy's confused frown, at the courage being, apparently, jus' that.

She goes with Apeman. Tha's his bitta twat. She changed sides. So? Mulla still couldn't figure Jimmy's angle, and anyway he was truly urgent with showing how he was gonna get this action down, he had it all figured out. If it could be called all, a simple screaming as he ran down the stairs brandishing the home-made knife from a stainless-steel fitting from the metal workshop machine room. To let the screws know there was gonna be some bad action and by the time he got down there, three floors, they'd have Apeman outta the way and maybe Mulla'd lose a few weeks remission for threatening behaviour, sumpthin' like that, but leas' it wouldn't be anutha six years for grievous bodily harm, or his own (not quite worthless) life of unrequited love out there in the free somewhere. So Mulla was chafing at the bit to act his part. Chafing. It solved everything.

So she's his weakness. Jimmy frowning all ovah, he hadn't 'spected this. Now listen, Jimmy summoned Mulla closer, about to change the fucken plan on a man which Mulla wasn't having. (Uh-uh. No you don't, Bad Horse.) Not when he had it all figured out.

So he threw down his mop. I'll givim weakness. And he walked off for his cell, knowing he was leaving Jimmy staring after him either incredulously or knowingly, or both, but unable to do a fucken thing about it. Not a fucken thing.

Then he came out of his cell charging. His scream the main . . . cacophonous (last year's crossword — I finished that one) echo in the prison wing. The high ceiling lights glinting off his smuggled precious bit of stainless steel. His facial tattoos jus' like his Maori warrior ancestors of old, and if he believed enough in the acted scream maybe that, too, from them ole warrior days of fightin', fightin', fightin', the necessary warrior madness. Screaming even louder when the screws looked up at him, hitting the second landing, and saw in their eyes the understanding he was coming for Apeman. By the first landing they'd formed a circle around Apeman though Ape was aping out trying to break out to meet this screaming challenge. Mulla Rota had to scream louder or he woulda laughed: for the firs' time in his life something had worked. For the first time he'd done something right. Oh, and even in the midst, the last melodramatic moments of this act, Mulla Rota heard a song distinctive in his mind. Funny thing, it was soft. And by a black (yeah, black. Blackblackblack! Who says we can't say or even think that word? Whadda stupid fucken rule that is.) The song was by a black singer, not actually black as in darkly brooding, unbearably sad. It jus' meant something.

THREE

THE GRASS'D BEEN cleared away yesterday by her mother when they visited on the sixth anniversary of her death, Beth and what remained of her family; so the nameplate was clear even if the painted indentation of name, date of birth and date of death was almost bled of its white by the sun, the elements that Polly never stopped wondering if her sister could still feel, specially the rain getting in through the lid that must now be, like, rotted in or why that slump in the earth? She always came the following day for a second visit on this yearly remembering; in fact, Polly Heke came several times a year and had done for the last two, from when she herself hit the same age as Grace'd been when she, uh, when she killed herself.

Yesterday, like all of Grace's anniversary days, they, which was Beth, Abe and Huata, had first stood over Nig's grave. And if a girl was long used to the fact that two of her siblings of six were tragically and long dead, it was Grace she felt for not the older brother she could not remember. That he'd been shot dead in a gang rival fight didn't help Polly's memories; she hated the gangs, they looked, acted, and were, disgusting. And those horrible tattoos all over them, on their faces, big kids posing as olden day

Maori warriors and thinking everyone was fooled. (Well, I'm not. Gangs suck.)

It seemed strange now that she should be older by two years than her older sister, her only sister (and that hurt the more). She remembered Grace more than anyone — anyone — on this whole funny, sometimes confusing, but sometimes glorious earth, and darkly and blackly sad when she thought of Grace, even though it'd been six years now. She remembered Grace's protectiveness, even though she hardly had memories at all of who and what Grace protected her and Huata from, which was their father. Fucken Jake. Who she saw from time to time but only by chance and from a distance. A couple of times sitting in a bus. Apparently he'd made all their lives a living hell with his drinking and violence, though Mum said, as if with pride in the bastard, never against them. And she and Abe argued that just being around it was against them, from what they'd learned at school, being told about domestic violence and effects on children growing up. How Beth could sort of stick up for the man after what he'd put her through, Polly just couldn't understand. As for what he did to Grace, and that it had been directly responsible for why she took her life — each time she took her thoughts too deep into it she heard in her mind a female cry, a distinct Oh!

Polly Heke only remembered Jake's voice, his singing voice, which she hated to admit to herself was rather a good one, or so she recalled, even if dimly, and good stick-up-for-the-ex Mum confirming he did have a good singing voice and he could dance. (But I still hate him.) And she always would. Specially on Grace's anniversary days; it built up like nervousness before an exam did Grace's remembered last day on earth. Nor did Polly buy that talk of her mother's that the letter Grace left said she *thought* it was Jake who was doing the bad things to her, since it was at night he, Jake The Rapist his own kids called him, did his awful business on his own daughter. He must've done it. Why would Grace lie?

She still plucked at the grass around the stone nameplate, as she ran her forefinger over the indented name, starting as she always did from the E and finishing at the G, for that's what her friend Toot used to call her: G. But he could never come to her grave, nor talk about his friendship with her. When he moved in with the family he used to talk about killing Jake, if he talked at all. But he was over that now and right into his rugby. People were saying he could go far in the game, but you know with their usual, If only, tacked on. If only the boy'd train more. If only he had a more consistent attitude. How would they like it living the life he did, of actually living in a car wreck right outside his parents' front door! Where would Toot learn discipline from having a life like that? They should leave him alone, or put him in the rep team regardless and then persuade him from there.

What bothered Polly, too, was how could she be older than someone who was born before her? In her mind Grace was always older. She wasn't the — the thing down there, height of Polly herself since she was tall like her father, beneath the weight of earth, the girl aged thirteen when she put herself to sleep, she was growing into a beautiful woman as her kid sister Polly hoped she in turn would grow into. Though in her heart of hearts, she knew she was now older than the suspended forever-in-time sister; Grace was thirteen. She'd stopped existing at that age. But then she hadn't: she existed in Polly's mind, dwelled in her (virgin) womb, floated in the liquid (tears) of her (loving, sisterly) existence. She was a girl who'd put a rope around her (gracefully long and slender) neck, tied to a branch on a tree at the Trambert property (why the Trambert place?) and jumped. That's what she was. Polly Heke, your big sister is a was.

No! You're *not* a was.

She was not a photograph that looked natural because no one in the Heke house at that time had a camera and the ones Mum had had done were from the class photograph when Grace was in form 3, which the photographer separated out from the classmates (as if Grace was born to be alone even when she'd been in a group photograph). She'd put aside her own suffering for as long as she could to give her younger siblings comfort, till that — Polly every time had to wipe at her eyes to stop the crying, six years this'd been burning and tearing at her, the more as she got older and began to contemplate the enormity of it — till that visit to Boogie in the rental car which she did remember, the car she did, the smell of newness and the luxury of the back seating, the visit that never happened. Poor Boogie waiting in a boys' home, poor Mum'd saved and saved to hire the rental car, slaved to make a big feast of a picnic to eat with Boogie at his court-imposed Riverton residence, and they never got there. (We never got there.) Which she couldn't remember. Only the terrible fuss next day of Grace being identified down at the hospital morgue. It was that night.

So she wiped at her eyes, she was sick of crying, it didn't change a thing, and she walked past the line of pine trees, avoiding Nig's grave (one is more than enough, sorry, Nig) and got a recall that that day had been quite cool, though this day was warm, and there was wonderful mass singing. But she dismissed that, too, as meaningless after the event, blaming most people in her mind for allowing a girl's life, her potential, to be self-extinguished like that. And she sat in the bus shelter and got thought of her father, a man in his forties without a car, and how life had not only left him behind but he probably also missed his share of buses, too, from being hungover. The black bastard. Dirty, raping, incestuous, drunken black bastard.

THIS IS WHERE she would have walked — or run. Polly Heke very much hoped her sister had run (swiftly) to her self-taken death. Though now it was three more streets wide with new urban development where in Grace's day it had been a paddock. Their State house had backed onto it, Polly remembered that place more than anything, the two-storey grimness of it, the neighbour through the wall next door, the streets she couldn't now imagine she had been born and raised in, not now they were in Charlie Bennett's house (wonder when she's gonna marry him?); it was scary coming back here like this, and confusing to start with because the new suburb stretched out hundreds of little boxes from their old place. Not that she was now living in ritzville, it was just a couple of steps up from this.

The looks she got; though there was one girl who in the middle of about to say something nasty had suddenly recognised her (I recognised you, too, Lena) so put a hand to her mouth, mumbled Polly's name and pulled her two girlfriends away. Polly thought she heard Lena say, leave her. She's cool. But not cool enough for Lena to linger and talk, say an old friend's name.

The strip of paddock she found was about half a width of a football field. Back on the rise of her old street she was able to see over the high brick wall (I don't remember it being that high) the Trambert house already with lights on when dusk was still coming down. And she could see the tree, a huge one it was, a towering spread losing to autumn coming on. Found her heart hammering. And her thoughts running parallel with the gathering dark. (Or my sister.) Trying to imagine what Grace must have been thinking. And why the Trambert place? Why there?

Sheep grazed in the paddock, taking no notice of her presence, though she knew there'd be plenty of eyes out those little box windows wondering at her. Stuff them. Let 'em wonder. (Why the Tramberts?) Her mother said the man himself had come to the funeral, a fine-looking man she said and with great dignity. He'd come to the house, too, just to pay his respects and ask if there was anything he could do. She said he'd got awkward all of a sudden and then she realised it was because he wanted to give her money. (But she didn't take it. Good for you, Mum!) Not that this Trambert man had meant anything except kindness. Though the neighbourhood was talking when Grace was hardly in her grave that there must've been something going on between them. Polly could hear the voices now — when she was too young to hear them at the time — So why'd he offer the mother money if he wasn't, you know? And why'd she pick his tree to do it off, there's plenty trees closer than his place. But the letter from Grace ended that: it was Jake, her own father. Grace'd given the letter to Toot and Toot gave it to Beth and that was it for Mister Jake The Rapist Muss. Oh, how she hated the man. Hated him.

It didn't take any figuring to know Trambert's missing land was money in the bank. Money. It was one thing Polly Heke couldn't get her mind around; she got emotional, she got angry, she got resentful and envious (when I'm not an envious person normally, not even at Kylie Leech getting a modelling contract up in Auckland). For it seemed to her that somehow white people — come to think of it, Asians, too, and probably even more so — had ensnared money with rules and mysteries only they knew so brown people, Maoris and Pacific Islanders, couldn't get their hands on it. And where she was right now, moving across a shortened stretch of land (I'm trespassing, hahaha!) behind her housing brownskins, it was like a one-way bulldozer carving out little pockets of area for a moneyless brown family to live in, whilst shunting the pay dirt over to the Tramberts. The fucken Tramberts, though she tried not to swear. Especially that Charlie had near fully converted his adopted Heke children to his way of thinking, which was about dignity and — shit, she used to think it was — stuff like that. Swearing, specially for a female, was on his hit list. (Well, I'm swearing now, Charlie Mr Welfare Officer middle-class Maori. Polly Heke's saying that Mr fucken Trambert gets to have all the money so fuck him.) Though she did put a somewhat guilty hand to her mouth at those thoughts, or those forbidden words, that is.

Grace'd never said anything about the Tramberts. Though she might've and Polly didn't remember; it was a long time ago. Now she was standing in the part shadow of the very tree Grace took her life on. Or from, as the Pine Block people put it. Part shadow because as she got closer the shadow came from the old brick wall and less the tree, which she thought must be oak for no other reason than oak would be these people. (These lucky white bastard people.) Why the Tramberts?

When she looked up at the wall several centimetres taller than her for the second time, she could see a clear line of it having been added to, though it was the same style brick. That got to her; it meant Grace must have been able to see into the house. She might have crouched right here at this spot and peered in. What would she have seen? Polly followed the wall, heedless of being seen, not as if anyone would think she was a burglar, she giggled at the thought and at her boldness.

She ran a hand lightly along the brick as she walked in its constructed shadow. Then it was sun rays at their last low angle as she came around the corner; and all was beautiful reds and pinks of backlit and underlighted cloud formation, and she had to shield her eyes until adjustment came. Sandpaper to the running fingers' touch she put end to that before her fingers bled. The wall stretched out for some considerable distance so it was some house in there. Or grounds at least. She moved out from the wall until she could see the roof of the house, grey it was, they looked like stone rectangles. Turning, she could see the tree, less what the wall cut off, and she tried to pick what branch it might have been, not the picture itself, of (my) her sis Grace hanging; that had been imagined and come forth in dreams, vomited out of her guts, her heart, a hundred times over. It remained a vivid, stark picture, but one with less meaning than what had brought it about. In her more sensible sixteenth year, Polly Heke thought of the death as the final miserable moments lasting however briefly long they did. But the life before it, leading up to it, as a never-ending — not nightmare, it was worse than that — as an endless lying out in this paddock, middle of bitterly cold, raining winter night with not even stars for comfort. That's what Grace Heke must have felt life was like. (And you — *youuu* —) Polly suddenly trembling in her anger (you didn't even think about what she was going through) as she thought of her father, all six foot three inches of him, of old measurement since he was from that era, of raping fatherhood.

At the next corner there was a long driveway, which took some working out and only from the line of trees and deduction and the break in the wall — when she got the courage to step out to get view of it — and open iron gates. Now she definitely was a trespasser, as well feeling suddenly like the girl Charlie Bennett's influence and her mother's good sense and love for the man had made her: sort of, well, a better class without being fancy-dancy about it, but not like what was behind that brick wall living in the grey-slated, white house she could see a slice of through the wrought-iron gate. Charlie Bennett's class was lower than that and Polly Heke was glad it was. (Happy as I am.) But I'm no Pine Block girl out here in a lost state, a wretched state, about to end her life for reasons unknown on the property of someone she neither knew nor was remotely like, no. I'm not here to commit suicide, I just want to understand, to put my mind at rest; and if they come out and ask me what I'm doing, I won't be no Pine Block bitch with attitude and thieving intentions casing the place, tell them I was just looking, that's all. Or just passing, even if on their land.

She was just Polly Heke of Western College with a mother and an adoptive father expecting, not hoping, more of her than what her mother in her earlier union had ever imagined; why, there had been talk of university. An otherwise impossible thought if it wasn't for the fact that Boogie was at one right now, as this sister baulked at several moments from the last of following up on their sister Grace's last, very last, moments. Old enough now to do this. But not quite ready to take it further.

She turned and walked off into the dusk, the colours all bled down into the horizon, the night just starting with that funny quiet, of the mothers cooking their kids' tea and (too) many of 'em wondering what the night was gonna bring; Jake Heke wasn't the only one of his type round these parts, the property behind her excepted. A sister wondering, wondering, what Grace's last thoughts had been and if she'd been cold that night her last. Which is what she figured she was crying for, that Grace'd been cold and shivering that last night.

FOUR

WHEN JAKE SAW the metal ball swinging on the end of the crane at McClutchy's pub, a clock pendulum against a fully clouded sky, he smiled inwardly and followed its progress like he would in admiration a punch, specially that it made a kinghit first blow and put a hole right in its side, a perfect body punch it'd been a man. Fuck the pub, is what he told himself, bitter at how everyone there'd treated him, same arseholes who'd sucked up to him all his years there (when I fucken ruled. I RULED) when he had the status in the place — the frequent of Two Lakes' lowlifes, specially the older sleaze and unknowing pissheads who'd made their lives the place and the drink the centre of their wretchedly tiny universe — of The man. (I was The Man.) Jake The Muss. Toughest in all of Two Lakes and, he never doubted, beyond its boundaries if it'd suited him to go out and show outsiders how tough he was. All those sweet years, of respect, only to come crashing down, for all of it to mean nothing, now like that building was about to when he just happened to be walking past to catch his after-work bus home and licking his lips at not being able to afford a beer not in any pub. It was the day before payday, he could never make his money last till then no madda how much extra overtime his paypacket might have he always spent up to it, and on piss what else, and being generous to Cody cos Cody didn't have a job and jobs were a bit tight, no denying, in Two Lakes, even with tourists everywhere here to see the thermal sights out the other side of town. Oh, to look at the Maoris, their culture which he'd not inherited and anyway was bothered by cos they seemed to have something he didn't. McClutchy's exposed guts now echoing with the booming of a ball, metal, pounding it out of existence; McClutchy's, where the sheer pressure of people not talking to you or, even worse, being hostilely uncomfortable in your company when ordinarily they'd've shook in their scuffed, dirty boots and outta date shoes and jandaled feet at jus' being in his presence; he'd stopped going and instead did his drinking at home or at another pub, Lakeside Tavern, where people didn't seem to know him and he could drink in his quiet corner with a cupla old codgers who did most of the talking, he anyway realised he never had much to say to the wider world, not really, that it'd been simply a physical existence with him in its centre on account of what he was and that they had done a lot of talking but none of it meant anything, not now he was six years down the track burdened with unjust shame for something he hadn't done. Pine Block inhabitants, Jake Heke had realised, were wordless people pouring out with words that didn't mean nothing. Whereas at least his corner pub companions at the Lakeside Tavern had a war they'd fought in to talk about, even if that was near all they talked and a man only had to give 'em half a ear he knew it so well, bombs and Italian names of towns and sheilas turned to easymeats (so they claimed), when he'd heard you ever touched a Eyetie woman her bros'd come get you — witha gun, or stab you to death, even someone like him — of fullas shot before these old codgers' eyes that never failed to tear a li'l bit in repeated recall, but that was alright, leas' it was company, and company he didn't have to be always on his guard ready to fight. And it was better'n talking drunken shit and mean-minded gossip. Though he did miss hearing the talk about who'd done pub battle with who, of the up and comers, the down and knocked outs, the fistic heroes and would-bes of his world even if he was no longer a member. He missed that.

But by the time the demolition ball had punched its way into the building and exposed it like the inner workings of a defeated person, exposed guts, innards, he could even imagine kidneys and liver (I hate offal) and the heart of the bar beating no more, just anutha target for the demo man prob'ly enjoying his fucken heart out taking this place apart, Jake The Muss Heke started to thinking it was his memories being destroyed there. He could see the timber framing where they must've removed the bar counter cladding and the solid timber bartop itself, wires hanging down, a tangle of shapes. He could see the linoleum floor and its multitude of liftings where it was cracked — and hear the NOISE used to make the place alive in there, on a Friday night especially. Oh, and Sat'days when a man could start 'bout lunchtime, get his horse bets on — not that a man'd ever been able to pick anything but his nose — drink all day, party at his place or someone else's when the closing bells claaaang-ed at ten o'clock. The music, the laughter, the howls that were meant to be laughter but could've been anything, ranging from emotional outrage to emotionally messed up to howling for someone's blood to howling for a husband too many days, and money, gone and the kids anutha day older of neglect. Was those memories crashing down, too.

As the hole got bigger he watched for the jukebox, the jukie, trying to recall the songs he got others to play for him (weren't that stupid I was gonna spend my own money on it). Sam Cooke, anything by him Jake loved. And he could sing a bit like him, too, when he was drunk and surging with that (false) confidence. He used to play 'Mean Old World', that started with a piano flipping out the rhythm and mood except Jake liked to play it, sometimes, with someone else's money a course, after he'd had a fight; with a smile on his face, not in keeping with the lyrics which he sorta heard as Sam sang about the world — for a nigger, Jake guessed — being mean, really mean. Jake only meant himself, when he was crossed. Beth, she liked 'Sad Mood' of Sam Cooke's, he remembered she sang along with it, the record, at home on the stereo; and, if he was honest, usually after he'd given her a biff. But that was her lookout. Anyrate, a man now was, well, kind of different, he thought. But wasn't exactly sure how or where. No one to show by example if he had changed. He couldn't see the jukebox so they must've taken it away to another pub, somewhere out in the wops prob'ly where people didn't mind it bein', you know, out of date.

One blow brought a section of ceiling and roof down with it. Made a great sound of collapse and looked a sight awful of sagging finish, like a man on his knees and still getting it. Dust and shit kicking up everywhere. That was it, Jake Heke started walking, he'd seen (and felt) enough. Now his eyes were smarting — only from the dust thrown up — though when he kept walking right past where he sometimes caught the bus he admitted to himself that his eyes were like they were for the memories being about all he had of these last many years, if he didn't count the last six. All he had. And he asked himself the question of damn near every man he knew: Wouldn't you?

Funny thing, when he heard the crash behind him of another blow struck against his life his past, he got a song Mavis used to play on the jukie, and everyone if they were drunk would sing along with it and depending on how drunk they could reach such heights, man, including himself lost in the song with closed eyes and a beer in his hand, surrounded by his own, his mates around him, as he was, taken on of the voice't was all throat, Dool did the voice best, pulled it from way deep inside him and let it gargle out his throat like the ole Negro dude they were all trying to copy; so it was a pub of fuck-ups and the lost temporarily found of 'emselves all singing like Satchmo Louis Armstrong, 'What A Wonderful World'. When it was. But it wasn't. That was what Jake, used to be The Muss, Heke walked away remembering, everybody (and myself) singing that song. And crying, damn near to. For the memories (I guess). And other things. Lotsa things.

FIVE

EVERYWHERE WERE FACES — stealing knowing glances at her, and then some. Little vases of flowers and a candle in a holder and a silver dazzle of cutlery on each stark white-clothed table. And before her, like everyone, this . . . this — she picked it up. What's this for? pretending a calm voice when inside she was anything but. And those faces (looking at me) and not a brown one except for him across the table. Who was now grinning. What you smiling at, mister? Which only made him chuckle, and her start to get mad.

    I dunno, might be a free hanky. She knowing he only had that smiling confidence because he had his back to most of the eyes and if he could only see them that'd wipe the smile from his face. They sposed to be for wiping our mouth? she guessed. No, your nose. And he burst out laughing, which fair jolted her with embarrassment as now the whole place was looking. Charlie! But he wasn't stopping now, not Charlie, he had a roll on, that's how he laughed, a kind of teasing process even when he wasn't teasing. Every (white) face seemed to be frowning disapproval. So Beth, who used to be a Ransfield before she married the nightmare (well, maybe not all the time) Jake Heke, joined her man in laughing, too. And exclaimed, Fuck it. Who cares? When really, she did. But damned if she was gonna show these people, damned if she was.

Why they got candles if they got the lights on? she wanted to know. Power cut, he was in a smartarse, joke at everything mood, even her sensitivity, her sense of profound unfamiliarity. In case they have a power cut. Bring your matches? Yeah, she snarled at him. To set fire to your black bum. Now, now, Bethy, leaning his big frame back. But at least he reached a hand for hers which she took with gratitude. And as if Charlie'd arranged it, along came a waiter and lit the candle, as was happening all over the little restaurant, and then the lights got dimmed right down. Magic had been cast. Her smile more relaxed. Tha's better. Squeezing his big hand, bigger than Jake's and they were big, yet not once used in anger. The difference.

You never told me this is your first time. You never asked. Well, don't be worried, it's only a restaurant. That's what *is* worrying me. Look at them they keep glancing at us. He smiled: Or you at them. What? You heard. Charlie, don't be laughing at me. I'm not, Beth. You are. What you ordering for starters? Now that put her back on the back foot. She grabbed up the menu again, where's it say starters? She peered at it, harder to read in the candlelight, It says soup and entrée. On-tray, he corrected her. Yeah, yeah, on-tray, whatever. Don't see no starters. She shot him a warning look: Char-lie? Don't tease. But he pointed over her shoulder, and she near jumped. Tell him what you want, at the waiter. She took a deep breath — Oysters. Please. Staring straight ahead, just to the side of Charlie. Who she could see was staring right at her, with that stupid grin. And the bloody waiter wouldn't move; she wanted to ask what the hell he was staring at, she'd just told him her order hadn't she? But still he waited.

You got a problem? she couldn't help herself. Stuff him. And that fixed him, see how he felt being on the back foot. Madam, I was waiting for your mains order. (Oh.) Oh. Well, I haven't decided yet. She gestured at Charlie. Take his. Mister Grinner's, she said it aloud. Though that didn't help, Charlie was still grinning.

But, you know, the wine — also her first taste ever — the candlelight, the realisation that oysters can taste like heaven just by being served on ice, with a bit of class, a wedge of lemon, a bit of bullshit waitering fuss, and a live three-piece band started up, a woman, well, she couldn't've been happier, or wanted to be anywhere else. And, funny thing, she gave him back the smile, They're not looking at me are they? No, he shook his large head, such a big man ('cept down there. But, he's average. And sure beats having a Jake and suffering his other side. Give me a small one, short performance, great company to be in anyday.) They're not looking, and even if they were, we can't put signs up saying they can't — Or walls around us, she added her own t'uppens' worth. And reached for his hand again and mouthed him, I love you. And he nodded in that dignified way of his, such a fine man, the irony of being grateful that son Boogie had had court dealings with this man as one of the town's child welfare officers but now the general manager of the department, and things'd just happened. Of a life in which so much had happened, none of it good (fucken tragic, in fact), not till the day she kicked Jake out. Though she was not convinced their daughter Grace's letter accusing her father of raping her was right. At the time she did. But she'd read it a hundred times since and so had Charlie; both were of the mind there was some doubt. Grace wrote she thought it was her father.

She and Charlie had re-enacted the possibilities of what might have happened in Grace's (and the other kids') bedroom. The way the bottom bunk would have been in darkness, even with the door briefly open, as poor Grace's rapist came in. Beth had played the horror part of her daughter — to the hilt — so she'd not only know if Jake had done it but how her poor child must have felt. It was almost as bad as burying her all over again. That it should not prove the case against Jake came as a kind of relief. Suspended judgement, the words Charlie in his profession's way used. Suspended, it would seem, forever. And anyway, even if Jake was innocent, she and Charlie were both agreed, now see how he felt being an innocent suffering unjustly. Though in her heart of hearts, Beth couldn't quite justify that kind of injustice against a man she had once loved, who had fathered her children even if mostly only biologically. Not that bad an injustice.

A few more wines on board, and they were on the floor dancing. Along with quite a few other couples. And everyone smiling at each other as they swept past in good old-fashioned waltz to the band assisted by modern gadgetry so they moved to a host of sounded instruments. The occasional figure passing by outside, vehicle headlights, none of it mattered, here life was: candlelight spears, the soft head fuzz of wine, food outta this world, conversation (oh, I hope he doesn't find me too uninteresting; I only got mostly sad and bad things to talk about), the music, the fact that all her first-time fears were unfounded. And love.

SHE CAUGHT IT just as they turned to sit down (from dancing? In a place like that?) not knowing her eyes had narrowed, slowing immediately her anyway slow waddling walk. Well I'll be. If it ain't . . . She didn't form the name in her mind, it was so familiar, so much used to be a part of her daily existence it — she, Beth — didn't have a name, she was a concept. Of a friend. A close, close friend. She thought it again: Well I'll be. If it ain't her. With him. Mister Welfare, who used to come round our area to round up our troublesome kids. Not that she had any herself, did Mavis. (Too fat. No man wanted to have sex with me. And even when I got me a desperate, he was always drunk with not much juice down there, or none at all.) And not that Mavis'd wanted to have a child; li'l thing squawking inner ear with its constant demands. No more li'the good times, not even the man who fathered it likely to be part of the deal in which case, in her more honest moments with herself, which were less and less these days and she knew that, she might've copped for it, being a mother, a de facto wife, a more meaningful citizen of this small city world or jus' Pine Block woulda done — just.

But life hadn't even given her a just. When it'd offered so much when poor Beth's world'd spun into tragedy of losing first Grace, then Nig in that gun battle on this very street at this very end, the lake end, of town, between those stupid Brown Fists and the jus' as stupid Black Hawks. How she and Beth'd been so inspired by the words of that Maori chief, Te Tupaea, telling everyone off at those Sat'day morning gatherings he used to have out on Beth's (the State's) front lawn, for their drinking, for not making something of their lives, for their children's sake he thundered at 'em like the pack of children they were; and how rapidly they'd built the hall, and the things this inherited title chief'd taught them, it'd seemed like he had brung 'em hope when otherwise there was none. It'd seemed that he, chief Te Tupaea, came along at the right time, when Beth's poor Gracie was dead, raped by her own father why she killed herself, and even Beth's famous fight-back ability was never more in need, and Mavis herself with a life purpose outside of boozing and playing cards and pleasuring the flesh teaching others how to sing, and as if she'd been born to teach (I remember how gooood I felt about myself) — all to end up like everything does in Pine Block, nothing. It jus' faded out. Their past'd claimed them. Their way of sordid, unthinking existence'd summoned 'em, damn near every bitch an' bastard, back. But not that bitch inside (astonishingly) that restaurant, oh no. Look where she was. When I, her best mate, poured so much of myself into helping pull her up from her tragedies and from that damn Jake fucken Heke. And she thought of that Shirley Bassey song, I (Who Have Nothing), did Mavis Tatana in her self-pity, and the line came with Shirley's and her own mighty-powered voice, as if Shirley was there or Mavis was herself singing it in the street, *must watch you, go dancing by*, which got her emotions roiling up for the line, *with my nose pressed up against the window pane! — I —* And there she stopped. Though not with nose against the window pane. And in her heart she'd sung the word with twinned meaning of pane and pain (oh, you can't know how much pain, Bethy-girl).

Mavis smiled bitterly. Not bothered if Beth happened to look out and see her — 'n fact I've a good mind to march in an' ask her who she thinks she is. And is she above all us now. Mavis felt like slapping Beth's face. But, lucky for everyone, Mavis got one of her less frequent moments of self-honesty, and knew the fault was (well, not all) she'd returned to the old way of life; only started off as one li'l drink, catch up with the people she'd known all them years of, let's face it, being one of the stars in McClutchy's, no bitch sang better'n her, big Mavis the Davis (from Sammy Davis) Tatana, so she was only catching up. 'Cept it ended up like Jake Heke and choiceless family's visit to Boogie waiting in the Riverton Boys' Home — it didn't. And nor did her resolve to have only one drink and go as every Thursday scheduled to the community hall where a bunch of kids were waiting for a singing lesson, raw though the lessons were (I knew that), it was that she was there, bringing — or trying to — out the confidence in them, seein' as their useless fucken parents weren't. She stayed on that night and ended up at a party. Then someone at the party said, Hey, there's a fortieth at my cousin's in Tokoroa, whyn't we put in for a keg and go over? With that beaming look, child-like and eagerly kinda innocent that it was, as if the welcome they'd get would be second to none (specially with the keg) Eh? Eh? Whyn't we go over in Tama's van? So they did. And stayed not jus' for the three days the party las'ed, but the lifetime it claimed back in doing so.

So Mavis took one last look at Beth in there sat down across from her Mister Welfare bigtime manager man, and she took her large (and gettin' larger) frame across the street, full of beer from the new pub she'd become a regular of jus' up the street, tonight bein' a Saturday having started, what, 'bout lunchtime, so she was pissed and hadn't any real idea of where she was walking to, 'cept somewhere in the direction of home, but now regretting it her decision to sneak off from everyone, not that they noticed in their oblivious state, singing that Bassey number aloud to herself now, but not loud-ly, *I. I who have nothing.* (Nothing, girl.) I. *I who have no one.* (No one. Not for myself.) *Must wa-atch you* — Voice coming out in more a simper. And someone watching her would've seen a picture of seventeen stone fallen womanhood moving slowly down the main street of Two Lakes, another Saturday night, like lumbering truck tail-lights disappearing into another somewhere.

SIX

THERE WERE WHITE ones, red, cream, black, and that was jus' the or'in'ry phones. And they were all different shapes, one even looked like a old-fashioned phone, on a cradle, 'cept it had shiny brass bits here and there, and a modern dialling face. (So where's the fucken cellies?) He looked around, trying to cover his burning self-consciousness, that funny buzzing feeling in his head a man always got when he first came outta jail, it took 'bout a week to go away, how he was dressed, what he stood for now, in the stark of Real People's territory, the opposite of what this place was these inhabitants these free to go every evening at five-thirty voluntary work prisoners, in this shop all lit up like the punishment cell in the block, where they never turned the lights off let alone down, day an' night, it reached right into your brain and picked out the part that said sleep, held it focused in its spotlight glare so the sleep signal couldn't escape to the rest of the body with its daily dose trickle of instruction, give respite to (any) body in its rightful entitlement to rest. A prisoner on punishment didn't have no entitlements, 'cept to breathe. Even having a shit when a man felt like one wasn't an entitlement, not 'nless he wanted to stink his (only) home out by having it in the pot, sitting in that corner like his only piece of furniture in the world, as each morning a man had to hand over his blankets, his foam rubber mattress (all sperm stained and with other man-stains) and empty out his pot. Then that was it, the day ahead like a desert.

He was glad he wore his shades. Real glad. Glad he had brown — very brown — skin, so they wouldn't notice the burning. This fulla coming up. A tie. White shirt (so you're fucken clean, mister. So?) His chest came up with his head posture — Yeah? He'd beat the cunt to it, 'fore he aksed a man in that tone they do: Can I help you? Which is exactly what the man aksed. Can I help you?

Mulla went, How mucha cellphone? Said it in one push of sullen air. Well, that depends, Mister Shirt-an'-tie came on the attitude on the spot. On what? Mulla shuffled his feet, feeling that embarrassment turning to its familiar anger, what all the boys did when they was embarrassed, confused, thought they'd been made fools of: they got wild. On how much you want to spend. (Wha'?) At first Mulla Rota confused; what'd this cunt mean, what the fuck was this, how much he wanted to spend? — but then he got it: fulla was just finding out which phones to show a man, what price range. But no way, he thought again, he wasn't being out-slyed by no straight white wanka. 'Pends on what I like. (Take that.)

The fulla looks at him, so Mulla knows he's one up. Felt like tellin' the fulla he'd come in here a different man ever since he called it right with Apeman — (blank) — that day. Only costim six months los' remission for threatening behaviour and illegal possession of a weapon, which meant he was here right now, out one day before his prez, Jimmy Bad Horse Shirkey. Why a man was here, to get Bad what he'd aksed for, a cellie. And he didn't mean a cell, neither! (Hahahaha!) Neither man needed one of those for a li'l while, Mulla in his heart of near-breaking (again) hearts, never. (I can't take anutha sentence. Next time I'll top myself.)

They went over to anutha section of the shop. Mulla the worst and most differently dressed here. Jeans, denim gang jacket laundered and held in plastic sealed bag storage, same brown shirt that smelled of mothballs they used to keep the moths outta the prisoners' civilian clothing, and his head-kicking steel-capper boots which at least were the same unpolished, scuffed dirty as the day they walked him in from the prison van. And this was the clean version, of fresh outta jail, he hadn't even got drunk yet, firs' things firs': the prez of Two Lakes Brown Fists chapter wanted to come home tomorrow to a cellphone. (To do The Family's drug deals. Yeah, drive around in his mean machine waitin' forim at the Quarters, selling a kaygee atta time, none a that foil bullet shit, not for the Browns.) Mulla even whispered it in his head so guarded was he on the matter of drugs and one, but usually more, of their number always getting busted. If Jimmy'd aksed a man to come in to this shop in a week's time, after he'd been a week outiv it, then they woulda looked atim like he was from outta space (hahaha) an' not like one a them nice planets, neither! (hahahaha! Ooo, you're funny sometimes, Mulla Rota who c'n still motor.) He knew even this clean version of him was so different to every person in this too-well-lit shop it was a wonder they were servin' a man, a wonder they hadn't called the cops, a wonder the girls here don't scream. But that was alright, who the fuck cared? (Well I do.) I don't. Here you are, sir. At that, Mulla leaned back, in total disbelief: no one'd ever called him sir before, let alone someone who a man'd admit (if none of the bros were listening) was his superior, like socially, like class-wise. (But not your fucken white colour, honky.) And his colour, if truth be known.

(Sir?) Hard to hide the smile. He felt good then. Real good. He flicked a woollen glove cut off at the fingers at the dude, how 'bout that one? No reason for selecting it, jus' a place to start the, uh, proceedings. On account of Jimmy arranging for Mulla to be picked up at the Intercity bus-stop by one of the boys who was waitin' outside in one of the gang's rumble machines, fucken 8 big ones unner the bonnet, Jimmy's instruction to aks for a discount seein' he was payin' cash, and if he got more'n eight percent Mulla could have the rest outta the three hundred. Not that he knew what that calculated to, typical Jimmy coming up with a figure like that when even Mulla could work out ten percent by just taking a nought off, and five percent by dividing that figure by two (long's it's not in odd numbas! hahaha) but he'd settle on some figure. Or look over the fulla's shoulder while he was working it out himself on his machine.

There were hundreds — no, not hundreds, but scores of cellphones to pick from. This's ninety-nine ninety-five, on special, the fulla toldim. You wha'? That pricked a man's ears up. Shit, he could give Jimmy a hundred change and look good and keep the utha hundred for himself. But he decided it wouldn't be a good move, not with Jimmy coming out tomorrow and expecting his instruction to be carried out and wanting a receipt. Nah, he shook his wraparound shaded head. Wanna good one.

So he settled on a cellie't cost two-eighty so at leas' he had a starting twenty for himself since he was goin' out to get drunk soon's this deal was over, soon's it was *gone down* — he liked the terminology, he even knew the word, terminology, liked that, too. He'd cashed up his social welfare cheque, two weeks of unemployment benefit at $147.50 per week, divided by going on six years made his life worth not even a buck a week, some earning life, man (some earning life); and then he aksed, How much the discount, man? Fucken near called 'im sir back. Oh, there isn't any, not on this phone, sir, it's on special. (No you don't.) Then I don't want it. Sir, I'd love to give you our normal discount of — he hesitated just a moment too long there so Mulla thought he had the fulla, though clearly not on this deal — five percent. Mulla dared to lift up his shades, prob'ly from being called sir twice. I was afta ten. Percent. His own hesitation for a different (diffident) reason, of nerve suddenly got to him without the hide-behind of shades. So back they went to get a phone that wasn't on special, even though the fulla tried the bullshit that the ones on special actually had twenty percent marked down on their recommended retail; seemed to Mulla Rota this fulla thought he was jus' anutha gang member there for the taking. And he left that shop with forty in his pocket for this arvo of pissing up so he wouldn't have to cut into his own money (man, I wan'it to las' at leas' a cupla days) plus the phone, plus the fulla calling him sir in parting. And he liked that.

Got into the waiting car with the pros who wasn't a brutha, not a proper one till he'd proved himself, feeling good, too, that the pros looked up to him, gave a man respect he deserved, man had he earned it, tole the fulla, honky fulla in the phone shop called me sir. Laughing. And the pros laughed, too, and aksed, Whatchu callim back — cunt? Yeah, I did, Mulla lied. Di'n't know why, lies fell out of a man like dropped lollies stolen in a lolly shop; lucky this young dumbarse wouldn't know.

THE CEREMONY WAS as solemn as it was deadly serious, of the welcome home for the prez himself, and the legend (he wasn't really a ledge, they only went along with it; the thought of Mulla bein' a legend was what they got off on, all those years inside and few of them in the gang itself on the outside. All those years of staying staunch to his Family, not the man himself. Weren't Mulla — the wankah — himself they were welcoming) Mulla Rota jus' part of that welcome home for the prez.

Fifty cut-off gloves of brown wool or brown leather (never that utha colour, ebony) and yet the shades each 'n' every lowlife unloved bastard and their handful of patched bitches were as black as the night would be tanight when their partying, amply assisted by the voluminous quantity of dope they'd smoke, would be at its maddest, happiest peak. The shades were, well, ebony, and so were some of the teeth rotting in the open roaring mouths to Jimmy Bad Horse near to, well, black, as he was aksing — aksing 'em! — WHO'S FIRS'? WHO'S FIRRZ! when he really meant what's first. And they were ROARING back: BROWN FIS' FIRRZ! BROWN FIS'S FIRST! that last quite distinctly properly said, by all of them. Like they all for that one-word moment, or the one just before it, understood that sumpthin', sumpthin' had to be done to a greater height so to do due and proper homage to their beloved leader — oh, and Mulla, too, seein's he was here, walking behind the prez witha glow on he thought was The Family roaring for him as well. He, Mulla, didn't unnerstan' that it is the man who manipulates, is cruel and loving and using of the members' emotions who gets to have his praises his qualities of (much flawed) human existence sung. There were dudes who'd had their fucken heads kicked in, their lights punched out, their li'l hearts broken but mended by the same man, Jimmy Bad Horse muthafucka Shirkey. There were bitches he'd fucked, raped, sodomised, slapped around, beaten up, humiliated, at the same time he'd picked 'em up, lifted their broken li'l bodies and hearts unto his and him, the body bursting in its gang regalia with not so much muscle as fat over muscle enough to fool people who didn't look too closely. Tha's what leadership was about: sticking it to people, specially your own. Long's you picked 'em up after and said there there, Jimmy's here, Jimmy had to do this to you, unnerstan'? Course they understood. And even when they didn't they sort of accepted that the fault was theirs. Same as they accepted their flaws as kinda and mos'ly their own fault, why they behaved like they did. Which is where Nig Heke'd goddit wrong but made amends (oh how he did that: jus', you know, with his life), whose handsome photographic portrait on the wall, by the gang insignia cut out of polystyrene and painted the necessary colours, had been somehow snapped by one a the members some time before he was killed, this is where Nig Heke had made himself immortal, cos he'd accepted he'd done wrong. He'd gone and done the RIGHT thing and shot that fucken Hawk dead — dead — 'fore they blasted back and got Nig and Fattyboy, whose ugly faced photo was also on the wall alongside Nig's for these (broken-hearted) people's belief in those two boys' immortality. Sumpthin' like that. Eh bro? Sumpthin' like that is how we see those two, uh, late bruthas.

THE SOUNDS THAT night: Barry White was back, Mulla and Jimmy noticed it more'n the uthas who hadn't been away as long as they had; deep, dragging along gravel voice, in driving rhythm, the bass reaching right into their (little) brains, their truly emotional hearts — if a li'l on the fucked side — in lyrics, Practise What You Preach, which had the whole house — two of 'em side by side, State-owned, the walls were knocked through — laughing, in stoned stitches at what they got from the song title, and big Barry White's voice, a star from anutha era come again, a rezz-erection! someone laughed. And they gestured with pointing fingers as they sang the lyrics — the men at either their girlfriends or the wife or the girl in their mildly scolding minds, with mildly scolding meaning, it was jus' bein' part of the act they was enjoying, and showing each in mirror form how they were with Big Barry White's impeccable timing (so'm I and we, man. So... are-we.) Tha's what the bein' stoned did and the, uh, potential it never failed to bring part out like a li'l shy nose poking from a dark hole, but never a black one.

When Barry White sang the cool aksing question to the woman he was tellin' to get off his case: *real-ly?* everyone raised a finger and sang with him: *REAL-LY?* At a female half-whispering chorus the sheilas took it over and so did a cupla the fullas with (beautifully) clear falsettoes. All ofem taken along on the clipclop horse ride on big bad Barry White's horse through a 'Merican ghetto fulla gangstas (like us).

Mulla in particular looking at the changes (of how much I keep missing out on, even in here, this place where nuthin' much changes only the music: they are right up with the music, man), of everyone drinking cans and not the quart bottles he used to like taking the top off with his teeth, and Sadie Palmer who could play a broken-off bottle top like a sax, now it was cans, an' cans don't play music, and when they were drunk the crush pop and crack of 'em bein' squashed in aggressive hands, violent hands, hands't craved their whole time and lives — for action, to do serious damage to other physical existences, it wrote the same story on near every member's face — but a man, Mulla Rota, was happy. Oh how he was happy.

What hadn't changed was the range of emotions the music, combined with the piss and especially the dope, took them through in near unison. Mulla aksed Loopy Davis who was that they had on the stereo — anutha change there, too, compact discs when it was LPs when he was las' out. Oh, an' he had an ever eye on Bad Horse, it was habit, and now with Jimmy pissed and stoned and already, he'd boasted earlier to Mulla, fucked, that one over there, in the smoky brown shades you c'n see her (lovely) eyes through, Mulla imagining Jimmy's sperm running out of her (lovely) twat, hurtin' at how come a woman wasn't arranged for him but refusing to think about it, the implications; jus' keepin' his distance from Jimmy case he brought up the Apeman incident: you know, of knowing he'd been outsmarted — and when he looked at Loopy's face answering, it was like a revelation was coming. So Mulla quickly gulped down half a can, first saying, holdit, holdit, tell me in a sec.

He burped. Wiped his smoothly shaven face, or his mouth, of the beer. Now, gimme a toke firs'. So he an' Loopy hadda toke together. Mm-uh! As if they weren't already stoned. Now, he looked at Loopy, his eyes not quite aligned but his mind as sharp as it would ever be, so he truly believed. Who's that you got on? Hearing his own voice speaking so crystal clear, with the li'l whisper at the end of each word like a back echo, of the smoke reminding it was doin' good things to a man. But Loopy lifted a finger, waita minute. Went over to the CD player, mus' be a stolen job, pushed a button, came back, swaying as the music started up on a new number behind him. Volume right up. RIGHT up. Same as everyone's — but everyone's — heads came up. So did fingers in instant clicking, and bodies bobbing and swaying, eyes closing. And mouths started to move, to sing. Not loudly. Not yet. Mulla saw Jimmy's gesture to Sadie who'd taken his years of spunk, not counting the arses he fucked in jail, to turn the volume up even louder. She did so, gave him a slow, sexy smile while she was at it, iner tight, navy-blue leggings hugging and stating her body specially her box bulge to Jimmy in a certain promise he c'd have more of it and her, twat and whatever kinda woman she was with it — if Jimmy was bothered to try and know — lader. (Lader, baby.)

Out Jimmy came, all bad rhythm thinking it was sumpthin' else. But it did the trick. Everyone stepped out, which was the centre of the floor anyway cleared to act as a dance floor or a meeting room or somewhere to kick someone around the room, whatever. They were arms going and eye-closed postures of a kind of released ecstasy that had nothing to do with their two members' prison release; this was something else altogether. And they took their harmonies like they had rehearsed and rehearsed it, this number, a Negro blasting ask (aks) of Where Do U Want Me To Put It? Hips going, arms like swaying stems of brown leather and brown tattooed arm in an easy breeze, staying with it all the way to the faded las'. 'Bout thirty-five of the total company, the males, having every man's secret question aksed on CD for him. The females, not all members, mainly associates, not minding in the least bein' part of the same harmonised question. Fullas like Mulla knew the question was bigger than that, of simple crudity, of basic sexual anatomy. Mulla knew it was in the arms, how they were raised and swaying and flowing in perfect time, it was in the voices, not knowing how far they could go, even in their stoned, drunk state, even as they understood jus' what this musical expression was about: the question wasn't what it stated to be — Oh, this's Solo, bro, Loopy finally answered the question. Groupa bl — ebony fullas name a Solo, bro. Ya like 'em? (Do I like 'em?) Mulla ran a hand down Loopy's tattooed face, Do I *loooove* 'em, ya mean. Loving Loopy while he was at it, for the song, for picking it jus' right, and for love itself. Yet total though the song felt and with it Mulla knowing who the group singing it was — Solo — the question wasn't answered. Cos it wasn't aksed.

The question was about place. These people's place. That they didn't have and'd never have. Not even a traditional flow, a musical river full of tragedy and freshwater equivalent of sharks, beaten (nigger) bodies floating down it, of desperate ebony dudes clutching to objects to float to (fucken straws more like it), to the last of air they were gulping — some of 'em survived — a Mississippi, a mighty muddy flow bobbing with heads enough to form something, sumpthin' good; BIG things, better things, musical creations from all the suffering, the drowning, gasping, gurgling cries. Something to grab onto. Like those they were listening to and getting off on: something good'd come of it when here, in this place, it hadn't, not even potential. That was the question. The (fucken) answer, too.

Mulla gave Loopy one of his crooked, most meaningful smiles: To have or not to have. Right, Loop? Yeah, righ', man. Righ', Loopy outiv it now, not knowing what he was agreeing to, it coulda been someone's death sentence. Someone put on something else; the range moved on. Mulla saw it.

SEVEN

FUCKIT, JAKE'D HEARD enough about Monte Cassino and Germans and Kiwi soldiers dyin' in a war — he couldn't understand why they were involved when even he knew the closest country to New Zealand was Aussie and that was what, 'bout a thousand miles or more away, and far as he knew there'd never been any trouble with them so why'd this whole country go to war against Germany? And yet they fought in Italy and one of the old codger fullas had been a prisoner of war in Austria, and they spoke of fighting in Egypt, too, and another place Ethiopia, he was gonna go to another pub. Didn't know where, though when he stepped out onto the street and saw it was with stars this Friday evening, and nice 'n' warm to justify his tight-fitting teeshirt, he thought he'd try somewhere that wouldn't be so, you know, rough.

Wasn't in the place long, at this table that only had one fulla at it, though the place was quite full and looked just about what he (the doctor)'d ordered, when the fulla spoke. Name's Kohi, bud. Stuck out his hand. Jake didn't like being called bud; and been a long time since a man'd looked atim with such smartarse confidence and got away with it. But then again he was grateful for someone, maybe — he hoped — to talk to (long as he don't 'spect me to do all the work). They shook hands; each with but a glance at each other, though this Kohi's glance had that ole familiar glistening linger in it; both then with eyes out at the human landscape, drinking, pretty happy-looking spread of mostly men from their corner, elbow-lean table view. Jake liked a corner table when in the ole days he'd liked his own table smack middle line of the bar, and his place at it side-on so no one could come at him from behind without having to go past his vision, and he would've spotted a likely fool or the chance fighter trying that, would Jake The Muss; the middle line at now no more McClutchy's, but up nearer the toilets (so I didn't have so far to walk to have a fight). Now, he was a corner man, which was a shame because the teeshirt he had was the best fluke-fitting buy he'd ever had; his chest muscles stuck out, from being on the shovel and a man did try and keep up his daily dose of a hundred-and-fifty press-ups, missing just the odd day, and he'd always had good arms and what with the gut hardly having any fat on it, a man felt he might've been bedda off closer to the centre so people could see him. Ah, but then again, what if they knew? Or, rather, thought they knew.

It did occur to him that he'd not been to many pubs, not when he stood here thinking about it seein' as this Kohi fulla wasn't following up on introducing himself, just a big arm leaned there on the table — he mus' weigh seventeen stone — it occurred to him that he'd kept his pub life simple. He didn't think of it even remotely like a fear of anything new or unfamiliar; just that a man'd stuck to who and what he knew.

Then this Kohi's saying to him, Spose you think I'm gonna buy you a beer — what'd you say your name was again? Jake. Oh yeah. Jake. Tha's right. And who said I was wanting you to buy me a beer? Jake taking offence. But Kohi grinned and said, You got that look, Jake. The water in your eyes like the alkies get, brother, an' how they lick their lips. The reference to the alkies stunned him, he'd had a time right after Grace left that damn(ing) letter when the only company he could find who'd havim was the corner of alcoholics. He'd even moved in with them, the house they shared, till he found out he hated the sherry they started each day off with (man, I liked my booze, but not that early in the day and not sherry), and besides, he was used to the company of men, fighter men, men who'd stood their ground in their lives even if they weren't such, you know, achieving lives, there's such a thing as a minimum of manhood a man's gotta have and these alkies didn't, so he moved out, ended up in the park, sleeping rough (but I made me a little house with my own two hands, first thing I ever made like that. Felt like a tree hut, 'cept it was on the ground), and there he'd met Cody and made friends (I never worked so hard to make someone my friend as that kid), so what the fuck was this Kohi saying? It's hope, Jake. I call it hope, is what he added.

Hope for what, man? Kohi came up, stood himself up straight, looked at Jake: don't call me man, bruth-ah. Not in that tone a voice. But immediately followed with, Now, where were we? Oh, that's right: hope. It's hope for a free beer seein's all other hopes've gone, how's that for an answer, Jake? When Jake never knew this man from shit that he could be so familiar — dismissive — with him.

But I gotta rule, Jake, I don't buy no one a beer who's not gonna buy me two back! Then he laughed. Jake copped the spit from it exploding on his nose. So. So Jake Heke thought about hauling one off on this Kohi's nose — a punch, not smartarse laughing spit drops. And he straightened up his posture. And he sees Kohi glance somewhere else. Next this utha fulla comes over and he's not fucken small neither. Jake, meet Gary. My brother. I'm the good lookin' one in the family, of thirteen. Laughing again. Jake noticing the cunt hadda thick neck, too, so he'd be able to take a punch. Have to be square on his chin to takim out one hit, if a man was gonna throw it, which he wasn't so sure he was. Not now there were two of them, when normally he'd've thrown it if there wassa fucken hundred of 'em, how he got when he was ready to fight: blind with wanting to cut loose. Blind with hurt that someone should want his blood, his reputation, or whatever it was they wanted of him.

Kohi laughing and pointing out into the crowd, An' there's another brother, Jake. Tha's . . . ? He frowned a look at his brother Gary. Which one's that, Ga? Hepa or Haki? Turned to Jake, We got so many we can't 'member who's who. This Gary was half turned to Jake (like he don't give two fucks about me. But he will if I get any wilder) and, without so much as a glance at Jake, drawled, It's Hep. There's Hak over there, chatting up the one in the shades. Asking his brother, Why she wear shades inside, man? Jake picking up on the word man, and how it was alright for Gary to use it yet when Jake'd said it this Kohi fulla threatened.

Who cares, Kohi shrugged as he kept looking around. She mighta escaped from the Blind Institute. (Or covering a black eye) Jake thinking with just a tadge of guilt. Oh, there's another brother, tha's Jason. And Jake could see he was big, too. The whole fucken lot of 'em were. The two fullas with Jayse're our cousins. And they weren't small neither. Kohi turned full on to Jake Heke: You gotta big family, too, Jake? The question not unexpected. Yet it was: seemed to Jake this Kohi guy was telling a man he was all alone in the world even though Jake had yet to answer the question. That Two Lakes was a bigger place than Jake'd always thought and it was even lonelier if you didn't have family like these fullas, no madda how tough you were as, like, an individual man. That jus' didn't matter, not against five brothers and the two cousins just to start with, all about your own size and, funny thing, just as confident. In fact, more so.

So Jake shifted his weight from one running-shoe foot to the other. Not that he went running in them. Yeah, I gotta big family, Jake said not quite truthfully. Not here, like, living in Two Lakes, no. No, Gary piped up, with meaning. Which they both knew, he and Jake. Where then? Gary wanted to know — Auckland? Chuckling. And Jake didn't know why. Nah, Murupara, Jake more or less told the truth; they were from east of Murupara actually, a li'l rathole of a place. If they still existed since he'd not set eyes on a one ofem for over twenty years. Half ofem'd be dead at leas'.

For some reason that made Gary lean back and look funny at his brother, who was really the ugly one in the family as Jake could see of the five brothers represented. They exchanged eye signals and tiny little facial muscle signals that Jake in his heightened state picked up on, from being family he figured, in his mind (family I never had family. Not close like this and with the supporting numbers and, yeah, the, uh, love. Sure, love. Why not love? What families do isn't it, is love each other?) Murupara, eh? Kohi chewing on nothing Jake'd seen him put into his mouth. Looked at his brother again, We done a bitta hunting in that area, Murupara. Haven't we, Gary?

Gary finally shows he's got a whole face and not half a one as he's showing since he came up. Don't think Jake here's done much hunting, Ko'i. Hey? Jake had to stop himself from bunching a fist, just who'd this Gary think he was making a — he didn't know the word — well, thinking Jake'd never hunted? He had. A long time ago, when he was about twelve, thirteen, but leas' he'd been. And got pig — you gotta stab it in the throat, right where I was told to by my uncle: Inis throat, boy, and wiggle it till you feel the heart — as well shot a deer, jus' the one. Who says I haven't — you? Jake'd just about had enough. But this Gary don't bat an eyelid, not one blink. I'm guessing, Jake. I'm guessing, not much.

Yeah, well, never said it was much. But I been. Yeah, Gary nodded like one a them wise old men too smart for his own fucken good, I thought it wouldn't a been much. Then he let out a sigh. Trouble is, Jake, hunting's the sorta thing you lie about you get found out. Jake went right back at him: Same's a lotta things you lie about. (Take that.) Yeah, yeah, Gary rubbing his chin, none a this hunter with the bristles stuff either, smooth as a baby's bum. And quite smartly dressed. Come to think of it, the shirt he was wearing bein' white suggested he might've been wearing a tie. (Must be in his pocket.) You'd be right on that one, Jake. Then the brother Kohi comes back in.

Jake The Muss they used to callim, Ga'. So inside, Jake's heart flooded with a kind of relief that at last they knew who he was and what, it didn't take much figuring, what he was (and still am — I think). That right? Even Gary looked impressed by that; so from a little inner flood of pride it became a bigger flow, sweet — come to think of it, like shooting, like when a man spunked his balls off into a woman, that's how good it felt to be acknowledged like this. So he got a brief thought of Beth (oh Bethy) but quickly threw it out in thinking of her with another man, even though he'd had years to get used to the fact. Anyrate, he was right now in a good state. All any man wants is to be acknowledged, a word he did know, though from whence or where he'd got it he didn't remember.

Used to. Gary said it like a statement of cold hard fact; took a moment before Jake picked up on it though. But he did when Gary repeated it and then asked, They used to callim that? So Jake with another internal flooding, the opposite of the first; he wondered how it could be that a big moment of just seconds ago could so suddenly feel like it was long past and maybe hadn't happened at all?

He wanted to yell in this Gary's sneering face that it was still Jake The Muss, not in the past (tense) but right now — still. Except one of the things't happened to a man was he couldn't hold onto his best, his stronger moments, long enough to believe them like he used to. Used to. Gary was right then. Used to. (Used to be called Jake The Muss.) So, if the truth be known, and it was in this moment for Jake Heke, he felt like crying. For what was. (For what used to be but wasn't.) But not in a pub, and not one he'd never been in before. Why, he hadn't even cried at his daughter hanging herself. Nearly. But he'd got put off by the McClutchy crowd all bawling their drunk eyes out and falling over 'emselves with cheap sentimental shit which he knew was false in expressing their, uh, condolences. Hidden at son Nig's funeral service, though, crouched down in the pines and behind a low hedge with Cody, a man'd cried for his son killed in the gang gun battle. 'Nless the tears were for himself, what his life had come down to, or 'nless those hundreds of people singing that sad hymn in Maori at the grave'd got him crying. Anyrate, Cody was crying, too, and he didn't even know Nig.

Up came Gary's eyebrows — Now what? Jake expecting the worst now. Of smartarse comment, something sarcastic. What's Muss stand for? (What?!) Jake astonished at the question. He'd never been asked that. It was just understood; and no madda how many times a man'd heard the term said crawlingly, suckingly, homagingly, fearfully, to or in hearing reference, he got the picture in his mind of himself, of the man of slabbed muscles, the weight of his chest muscles and the feel to his hand, the reassuring weight of them, the awesome always-ready power in both his punching arms. That's what he saw and understood of The Muss when he heard it.

Was the brother Kohi who stuck his own bicep bulging arm out to show his brother, and Jake, what Muss stood for. Here. Tha's what it means, Gary. This. Smiling all over he was. And his brother back at him. Like a secret exchange of laughter at a man used to be called Jake The Muss.

OUT IN THE NIGHT, it was still going in there, the new pub, pubs didn't close anymore like in the old days, they could stay open till as late as they liked. He didn't know, hadn't realised, the town'd changed so much; new buildings, restaurants, them café type places, bars that weren't big barnhouses like he grew up with and loved, he thought he knew this main street, Ruataniwha, from the lonely days of being toppled from his status by Grace's cursing letter, of criss-crossing the street so he could see his reflection in the shop windows, take sustenance from it. He'd seen tourists around when before he hadn't noticed them or maybe they weren't so many a few years back, them Asians, but not Chinese like where he got his takeaway favourite, spare ribs, they had flatter faces (and crueller eyes) different bone structure in their face. Now the chinks had a bigger place, too, built a big fucken restaurant nex' door to their takeaway place but closed that earlier now, he figuring it was cos they didn't need the drunk Maori cussimas no more, not with the restaurant, and anyway the drunk Maoris from pubs like McClutchy's were scattered now, and as he wasn't one ofem he didn't know what they got up to, where they got 'emselves a feed at the end of a drinking session. Come to think of it, walking up the main street pretty quiet now at two in the morning, he didn't know nothin' about anything of this world. Not nothin'. But one thing he did know, he was gonna take those brothers up on their invite to come hunting one of these weekends, wipe the fucken sneers off their faces, specially that Gary's. Anutha thing: he wasn't so drunk he was staggering all over, all ovah, the road. Drunk, yeah, but not blind.

He headed for the taxi place, his shoes padding along the footpath jus' like a stealthy fucken cat, a big, muscly black one. Yeah. And the stars out. And a — suddenly he brought to a halt. The fuck was that I jus' thought? Trying to recall the flash of, it seemed like insight. No, a memory of some sort. But no, it wouldn't come. He walked on, a little bothered by losing it, started humming to himself, Armstrong's 'What A Wonderful World', when he got it. And he stopped again. And lowered his head so he wouldn't lose it. It was the humming, not by himself just then but from the dream.

The humming of that dream of the chinks and the whites and the snobby group of Maoris was the same humming he picked up from the Douglas family back there in Marty's Bar, still humming right now to maybe the tune of music but still a family hum, still the engine of togetherness. Whilst he, Jake Heke, had and heard no such thing. Any wonder he gave out a long, resigned sigh. Nothing to hum about. Though he did manage a grin at that thought, nothing to hum about . . . Jakey, you ole fool, you. Yet he was humming that Satchmo song.

EIGHT

HE'D HAD THE wall built onto the existing so they couldn't see the encroaching (and quite architecturally hideous) subdivisions of cheap tacky housing of, one must face it, the masses. (On land he'd sold to the developers he should have realised would have the social responsibility of cockroaches.) But he hadn't even got that right — or the bricklayer contractor hadn't; Gordon Trambert had simply let the man get on with it, he anyway had far more important (and pressing) matters on his mind, simply assuming that the chap would match his bricks to the existing wall, given old bricks were long a middle-class demand for walls and paving (and their unoriginal sense of the aesthetic) and were freely available. Nor had he noticed in anymore than a peripheral sense the difference of matching, buried that he was in his financial affairs. The height he'd ordered meant supportive columns, again he assuming the contractor's taste, but the extra thickness of brick columns every six or seven paces were out of proportion and with poured concrete centres, and that distinct line that showed where it had been built onto — all in all a bloody disaster aesthetically. But he could hardly demand the fellow tear it down, although he did have an angry session of re-negotiation of the contract and damned if he was backing down on it. Though he did settle at a what-the-hell five percent off the price. That was when he thought he had more money than he did.

He'd had it built, he came to realise (rather late), so he'd not see the truth of not just the approaching spread of imitation-woodgrain-cladded box houses (that poor families could get into on little or no deposit and not often get out of for reasons Gordon Trambert had stopped trying to fathom of the poor, their low-ceilinged attitudes and aspirations) but the other truth of his folly — foll-ies. Failures. They were a plural.

More and more he saw the truth in the adage, that the first generation builds it, the next consolidates, and the next spends (blows) it. One managed less and less a laugh of irony when ordinarily he tried to find the humour in even the worst situations. Not that one was the life and soul of parties. But he could enjoy a laugh, including at himself.

Each morning he woke at exactly three, no matter what time he put himself to bed, which was usually late as he pored over his papers, his undeniable evidence of mounting debt, his files of land sales so the family farm was no longer viable in size, and anyway farming had always been a roller coaster, with more downs than ups; farming was a way of life not a business, or certainly not run on business lines, a simple equation of return on asset value showed that. And he hadn't accepted it should be just a way of life; so he'd looked at various businesses and was especially attracted to the idea of having a capital partnership in a restaurant, given Two Lakes' steadily rising tourist numbers attracted by the thermal spectacular sights out at Waiwera, and the lakes themselves, as well — oh irony — the professionally run farm that entry-paying tourists poured into daily by the tens of coachloads to see sheep being shorn, dogs rounding up sheep, and other stereotypical farm activities that were a novelty to Asians, Americans, Europeans from crowded cities, and had made its innovative farm-owners rich. He thought he could clip the ticket by feeding some of the tourists.

It started off in a rush. And ended in a long extended hiss of escaping cash, virtually all of it Gordon's, which he'd acquired by selling land and then a parcel of Glaxo shares left by his father's estate, after a successive run of poorly chosen chefs and that business dream — or nightmare — word of mouth with the tourist operators who wouldn't touch the place, meaning it was off their recommended list. So morale went down and down; he and his working partner blamed each other, they tried desperately for local trade instead, but word of mouth was waiting for them there, too, they'd signed a long lease, it took over a year to find another tenant, and even that cost a cash incentive plus the first six months' rent paid on the new leasee's behalf. When Gordon Trambert's accountant told him his venture had cost $320,000 in just two and a bit years, he'd put on the big act of bravado and told the long-serving family accountant whose firm had looked after his father's affairs, nothing ventured nothing gained, in that somewhat pompous voice he'd acquired from, he figured in his honest moments, private schooling and, back then being young and vulnerable, wanting to be regarded as truly one of the chaps. As in traditional farming family meaning landed gentry, which he was but wasn't: something about Two Lakes, probably the Maori influence, made a mockery of that snobbish outlook. It wasn't New Zealand anyway, though there were enough anachronistic pockets of the type, especially in Canterbury, where inordinate pride in one's background was *de rigueur*.

It might also have been the town's particular love of rugby, a game which brought people together and had nothing to do with their racial, social or financial backgrounds. Solicitors played in the same team as meat workers. A Maori carpenter might captain a team containing a doctor, an accountant and successful businessmen. A Pakeha labourer might be the best player in the team. Gordon Trambert thought it the country's great equaliser. So why the acquired accent in times of stress, Trams? he did ask himself from time to time, and applying that nickname he'd got at the very school the accent came from. There was just something about Two Lakes that precluded any form of extreme social separation and he hated himself when he lapsed into snobbery. Or took refuge in it. Though God knows his home in comparison to his encroaching neighbours, let alone the two-storey State houses still visible from their upstairs windows, was a palace. And so, they all had reason to know, was the way of life utterly foreign to what they, the Tramberts, and the Heatheringtons of Isobel's clan, knew.

Before the girl hung herself on the oak of Gordon's maternal grandmother's planting at the turn of the century, he and family had occasionally looked at that line of ugly State two-storey houses and yet assumed the residents to be happy-go-lucky, and content. Indeed, Isobel had gone further to say how glad she was that this country, almost alone in the Western world, had a social conscience that housed those whom she called less well off, less fortunate, less educated and how she didn't mind paying extra taxes if it was essentially achieving the egalitarian New Zealand dream, when what she did know was her family under her husband's financial management hadn't paid taxes in years and used every avenue there was to avoid them as an honour-bound duty. Besides, one was entitled not to pay taxes on losing business ventures. (If, that is, a man wouldn't face up to what the losses reflected.)

On still nights the singing, partying State-house voices had carried across the paddocks as they were in those days (only six years ago) and on occasion, when he and wife and children had been having a summer evening drink at the outside table, he and Isobel had sung a few grinning lines to snatches of song carrying across to their own pleasantly, slightly fuzzy heads of a few gin and tonics. They had particular memory of a Patti Page song they used to sing, if in raucous and somewhat tuneless voice, when he and Isobel had met, at Lincoln University doing agricultural degrees, no comparison to that song that drifted regularly to their evenings' outside hearing: 'Tennessee Waltz'. One night the air conditions must have been perfect for they'd heard a woman singing it with such astonishing voice at first they thought it must be a recording, though brief pause of laughter and then continuation of the song by the same voice told them it was real. A voice resident there, in that light glowing outline built along a low ridge that sloped gently down to their farm and had in fact belonged to the family, sold by Gordon's father at a price he couldn't refuse. A voice that, with proper training, could be gracing the nation's ears.

Then that poor, wretched girl, her self-taken death, had changed their outlook entirely. All was not well with that visible world from their own. All was not well with the Trambert's smug assumptions of it. And most certainly the child's world was about as bad as it could get. Both still had dreams of it.

He'd spotted her — in disbelief to say the least — from their bedroom when he happened to glance out at the day to come. She hung like a portrait from his father's war encyclopedias of hanged captured soldiers, political figures, of anyone hanged: a quite quite gruesome sight. Except this was clearly suicide. He'd near collapsed with the shock; called out to Isobel who happened to be sitting on the lavatory, that she'd better come quick. Before she arrived at the window he had thoughts — fears — of his children seeing this, his eyes riveted to the sight unbelievable, of the corpse of a stranger hanging from their tree.

Isobel proved calm in a crisis, calmer than he; she went straight to the children, a sharp rap on each door, telling them something terrible had happened and to come immediately. Out on the landing she'd told them straight, that outside a tragedy had happened, she didn't know why or anything else about it, only that on their property was a girl who had hung herself. Then she called the police. Nor had she ordered the children not to look for themselves. After the call to the police she'd hugged each in turn, Alistair first because he was the more sensitive one, then Charlotte who was hardly without frightened and confused tears herself, but still made (born) of sterner stuff than her younger brother. But it was Alistair who'd be likely to dream about this from hereon, Alistair who'd near to wilfully embrace it as a tragedy which he'd churn over in his always turmoiled mind and somehow include himself in the process. His father thought this even as he stood awaiting his wife's decision on what to do next.

They went outside, but with firm words from Isobel to Alistair alone that if he felt the sight would upset his delicate nature then he'd best stay inside. But if he thought not seeing it would cause him self-doubts on himself, then he should ready himself (*Girl, prepare yourself, get ready your spirit . . . for the journey to the Spiritworld, it is yours, girl . . . yours alone*). Gordon had taken the trouble to ask a Maori friend who had once worked on the farm, knowledgeable in the cultural ways of his people, what the different chants at that last day of funeral at the traditional meeting house he'd attended would have meant. Harry Pukapuka had told Gordon that particular farewell would have been said at a suicide; Gordon Trambert had memorised it from Harry writing it down. Harry had gone to pains to explain that the words of the girl going alone should not be taken in the European literal sense, but be seen as a journey which she had, for reasons of her own which her people respected, chosen to take. Her arrival in the Spiritworld, Harry explained, would be met by all the ancestors welcoming her. Welcoming, Harry had emphasised in that quiet but firm way of his.

Alistair had chosen not to come out. Either way Gordon knew his strange son was going to make something of this in his mind. Charlotte walked behind her mother. A bird was trilling from the same tree. The sky overcast grey, and chilly. The child's face a deep red, her legs splotchy, tongue between her teeth. Oh, it was a terrible terrible sight. The more poignant that she was barefooted, and her clothes had that poor look. (Gordon Trambert thankful there was no breeze putting sway to the awful sight.) Just a teenager, Charlotte's age.

AT THE FUNERAL Gordon Trambert had not seen sight of the father, or anyone likely to be, in the Maori meeting house, itself a large building built along traditional lines and big enough to sleep a couple of hundred mourners. Magnificently carved outside and in, he'd never seen one before, yet Two Lakes, he later took the trouble to find out from Harry Pukapuka, had dozens of such buildings. But then Gordon had only dared stand at the doorway, or just to one side of it, in the last hour before burial proceedings and try not to be seen as staring in. He caught the last of male elders making speeches in their flowing Maori tongue, punctuated by explosions of emotion, but Gordon Trambert with musical, discerning enough ear to hear the lilting quarter-toning in the chants, that the enunciation of even a foreign tongue to him was perfect. Going from the meeting house to the cemetery had worried him for the Range Rover he drove (even though it was five years old). But no one seemed to notice it, perhaps they didn't care for such things either way. The whole funeral process had moved him; the way the emotions were out in the open, grief getting to grieve instead of the restrained manner with which his English/Scottish ancestory people saw off their dead.

He had a call to make not so far away which he did after the funeral. Found himself driving back past the cemetery, out of a morbid curiosity he supposed and of course that the girl — Grace her name, such a lovely name for a child he had got better glimpse of in her open-state coffin, amazed at the undertaker's skill in transforming that face that had been so grotesque when he first set horrified eyes on it — that she, uh, had killed herself on his (our) property. Then he saw that rather bizzare-looking figure whom he now knew as Toot Nahona, this wild-haired apparition lurching as though drunk, or on that glue these kids sniff, and the two sextons staring at the same figure as he sank to his knees one end of the grave. Gordon Trambert's first thought was of a dramatic Shakespearian-like posture. Especially when the kid picked up the flower and held it to his chest, his head fallen on his shoulder. Except the stage this kid had walked tormented onto was his alone, or so he clearly believed. Gordon Trambert felt then that in a way he was privileged — if that was the word — at seeing a fellow human being in a moment of spontaneous purity expressing grief, love, friendship, possibly guilt.

Why, one had actually found himself weeping as he sat in his engine-idling Range Rover, again as though a window had suddenly been opened on part of his township; his parents and their parents, and the Trambert before even them, great-grandfather Arthur who'd started the process of breaking in the land bought from the Maoris last century in the 1870s. Yet of the Maori they knew nothing. The compounding ironies there, of the land returning to them, even if in tiny pockets of individually owned land with those dreadful working-class houses put on them. But the circumstances of money being a leveller were not lost to him. The Trambert generational money was dwindling.

Six years ago Gordon Trambert had observed this wretched Maori kid expressing his grief like a dog howling to the moon. Or, in this case, the sun just peeped out from cloud and putting a shaft down on the cemetery but not on the youth. (Now that would have been just too much.) The sextons, one of them with sandwich still halfway to his mouth, suspended in this boy's time, what he'd made of this moment at this freshly dug grave ready to be filled. Same kid who now dominated the rugby fields he played on.

His love of rugby and the fact he regretted son Alistair hated the game (he hates everything, including himself) had him going most Saturday mornings to watch a younger grade game then a senior match in the afternoon. He supported no particular club, a fact he prided himself on (he just loved the game), and nor thus socialised at any clubroom after a game; though there was the odd time he would have liked to, just to talk rugby with like minds, and yes, to enjoy a beer in the company of men with less social constraint than the company he kept tended to be.

A couple of years ago at a morning match of young men in their late teens at the main rugby park he happened to recognise a face but couldn't figure from where until well into the match, so dazzled was he by the youth's play and anyway with shaven head and not that wild mop of warlock's hair when Gordon Trambert had first observed him. He was big and fast, a devastating tackler, a tearaway flanker in the true New Zealand tradition. He'd drive into a tackle and as often as not emerge with the ball ripped from the opposition player's hands. More than anything, he played as if with some inner flow.

Rather than trust his own not very illustrious schoolboy player judgement, Gordon Trambert made comment to some of the more knowing looking rugby heads on the sideline and they confirmed that this boy was an exceptional player. Every Saturday from thereon he watched T. Nahona, as he was listed in his St Johns Under 21s teamsheet, heard the comments that the young man was ready for senior rugby and the wiser heads suggesting it should begin with lower grade senior, not straight in at the deep end. Whatever, Gordon was just another convinced this could be an All Black in the making, that this Two Lakes boy now with shaved head, who had already imprinted himself on Gordon Trambert's mind from that graveside scene, might one day join the country's rugby élite. If only he'd turn up for every game, which he didn't. If only he'd get himself fitter instead of relying on raw talent. If only Gordon Trambert had more rugby mana so he could approach the young man and perhaps help him find his potential.

BACK IN '89 he'd been (easily) persuaded to become a Lloyds Insurance Name. Like some of his better-off farming friends. Amongst them it had a certain prestige, one didn't deny that, it was part of the attraction. For three hundred years the venerable Lloyds of London had made its investors money, some would say its own printing press making the stuff. And all that was required was a small deposit of $50,000 — which was a bank borrowing against another housing development parcel of land on which

Lloyds paid interest — and the signing over of an unencumbered asset with a realisable worth of $600,000, which was a couple of hundred less than what the debt-free farm was worth; and once had been close to double that (if one hadn't sold off chunks here and there). It was the gearing that was so attractive: it gave, historically — and there were few businesses in the world with a longer history than the venerated Lloyds Insurance Company — very high returns and few instances of loss years, all against an asset one could continue, in theory, to earn off as well — that is, if farming was profitable which it wasn't, hence Gordon Trambert's decision to find something that jolly-well was. But imagine if farming hit an upturn, too, is what he dreamed about.

Backing natural disasters not to happen and health litigation on a mass scale against international chemical companies and the like took time to come through on the Lloyds books. In 1992 Gordon Trambert was just another Name informed that the 1990 year had been the worst in Lloyds' underwriting history and so instead of a healthy cheque in the post he received a bill. For cash he didn't have. So off was carved another twenty-acre part of the farm to housing developers. And soon another ugly hundred little box dwellings one had to look at getting nearer and nearer to his stately old place. 1991 was an even worse year. Furthermore, the local market for housing land was depressed so he had to sell double the acreage for the same price as the year before. And what with the restaurant gone sour, too.

Hope being another name for desperation, Gordon Trambert hung in one more year, knowing he'd have to wait for at least a year before he knew if he'd called it right. He hadn't. '92 was another disaster. And then he found out his undertaking was unlimited when he had assumed it to be to the value of the asset he'd pledged. Murphy's Law now.

Disgruntled Names hit as hard as himself and worse began making noises about the underwriting process making them, the faraway from London Names, sitting ducks for such things as mass employee asbestosis claims which large conglomerates had hastily insured against in those bad years. By some miracle of picking up a conversation between two friends to dinner — indeed it was at the very dinner of Grace Heke outside hanging herself — both of them Names, Gordon had heeded this private exchange of advice (bugger them, as a friend they should have warned me, too) and written express instructions to his Lloyds agent in London not to underwrite anything that included any form of health claim by employees against their companies. And as the noises about serious mishandling by underwriters became a loud outcry, Gordon Trambert joined those who were refusing to pay out on these Lloyds letters of demand for huge amounts. Or he'd have to sell the farm, the house, everything. The letter was his only hope, as representatives of Lloyds were in the country going to each and every Name demanding they honour their contracts.

He started seeing ironies everywhere, of his parents, their parents, modelling themselves, more or less but usually more, on the upper middle-class English societal model, adopting the style of well-enunciated speech, the private schooling, the pieces of imported English antiques, and the English reserve, and now this member of this generation losing most of the family fortune to one of the Mother Country's most venerated business houses. And there was the Saturday rugby sideline irony of whispers about him being rich. And there was that troubling incident of one Grace Heke ending her life on his inherited property, it just wouldn't go away.

Losing himself in his sombre Russian choral music became more and more Gordon Trambert's nightly habit — helped along by the gin bottle. Hardly noticing a wife losing respect for him.

NINE

SHE SEARCHED HER purse, a seven dollar and seventy cent start, the house beginning upstairs in her room, found a few coins there including (glory be!) a two-dollar coin, so she was getting close, forget the kids' room they wouldn't have any and she didn't wanna wake them, not yet; downstairs to the sitting room, the ole plunge the hand down the couch-back trick even though she'd exhausted this one a few weeks ago, since there'd been a party las' week so there was a chance, a small one, which is what her groping fingers found down there in the second-hand twenty-year-old couch, a twenty-cent piece and a lousy five. But it was adding up. She went through every pocket of clothing she owned, which wasn't many things, thirty-seven cents when there hadn't been two-cent coins for a few years, so mus' be she'd not worn that dress in a while, nor bought anything new since, either. She pulled out every kitchen drawer, looked in every cupboard before facing the inevitable of having to count the total she had. (Long's it's over ten — no, I need eleven and some change, I should know that by now. Please, God, let't be that much.) Though she'd settle for less if she had to, even though she knew come the day's end she'd be in this situation again except with all her finding places exhausted. And even she had learned to be more long term than that.

The coins and five-dollar note no sooner spread out on the kitchen table than she had to scoop them up at sound of one of them coming down the stairs. Turi. Morning, Turi. Morning, Mum. (God, why do my kids give me the blues, their faces like they wake every day to a fucken fun'ral?) Watched him go to the cupboard and just before he pulled the food one open told him, No good lookin' in there. Only fresh air in there, boy. Look at his face how it fell even closer to the floor. Made her angry. Hey! The hell you lookin' at me like that for? What you 'spec' me to do — make fucken magic and nex' thing you look there's a fucken feast in there? Eh? Watching her son back (cower) away. But he knew bedda than to say something.

And now the other one walks in. Gloria was sharp with her from the off (cos she bothers me) Yes? Yes? You got something to say 'bout no food in the house, too — madam? (Kid getting too big for her boots — well, her school shoes, which were coming apart at the seams: smilers) — only eleven and like she was getting ready to leave home.

Mum, I never said anything. No, no, Narissa hadn't. But it was her look. No, but you are gonna say something aren't you? Mum . . . ? Go on then, open the bloody cubbid, check for yourself we're out again. (Again. Story of our lives: always out of things.) Including love. Love's the first thing out the door when the groceries run out. (And the smokes even worse.)

Narissa did check. And in that moment her mother got all sentimental for her daughter's name, remembering how she and the baby-to-be's father'd gone over the names they liked. Narissa won easily. But, come the day she was born, he was nowhere to be seen, the fucken father. Harry Hippie Martin he called himself, from his favourite song by Bobby Womack (kinda liked it myself, till what he did) had just up and gone, no kiss my arse nothing. Then along came — named what else — Bobby Taita, a woman's introduction being jus' that: You heard of a singer called Bobby

Womack? Nah, he hadn't. But he smiled back, But I heard a this Bobby, and I ain't got such a bad voice myself. Wanna hear it? Yeah, well, she did hear it, and he could sing, and he sang his (easy) way into her bed and Turi was the result. 'Cept he never hung around much longer than pas' Turi's firs' birthday; jus' started a big row one night an' up an' left, the cunt. Now, eleven years later and a woman her share of lovers, a few who'd moved in for a few months, one for two-and-a-half years but he'd abused the kids, hit them, so she finally got the courage up to tellim to leave, which he did, but not before giving her a farewell hiding (men, they're jus' arseholes) 'cept a woman needed a man, and the ones she was attracted to turned out, every one, bad. Dunno why. They always seemed so, you know, ideal, Mr Dreamboats, when she first set eyes on them.

Eleven years down the track and a woman couldn't even feed her kids breakfast. Not and smoke as well, and was (me) her who had the long day spread out before her to get through, and tomorrow, too; she was entitled to have something for herself. And not as if she wasn't hungry herself, as if she was gonna be eating while her kids weren't. She'd rather die than that. She was, well, not the worst mother around here in Pine Block. (Not the best, neither, Glor) she did inwardly concede that. But being on a single-parent benefit like more'n half them around here, she just couldn't make ends meet. (An' not as if I take one of them holidays in Fiji you see in the papers on the Hindu shop counter.) A woman, and her kids, survives.

Fuckit. She stood up, but carefully so they wouldn't hear the coins jangle in her dress pocket. Go up to Nicky Hodge's, she'll give you something to eat. But Narissa was shaking her head, telling a mother they'd done that too often and they felt stink keeping on doing it. Which made Gloria feel instant hatred for Nicky Hodge even though Nicky was one of the best people in Pine Block, a heart of gold, didn't drink, had given up smoking, and carried on where Beth Heke'd left off when she started that community-spirit thing here (before she met up with the flash

Maori with that good job working for welfare and left us to rot here) trying-her-best Nicky, when everyone knew they had all returned to what they were, which was bitches and bastards, hahaha, gotta laugh about it from time to time or they'd cry — or, even worse, wake up having to face up — they even had turned it into a laugh, a joke at 'emselves, their slack ways, their partying up the large — Then you tell that fucken Nicky Hodge I'm gonna pot her to the welfare for taking money from them to feed kids when now you're telling me she won't! It just exploded out of her, Gloria's unplanned hatred for Nicky Hodge, the only woman who'd stood up to Jake Heke when he had the cheek to be having a party when his own daughter was buried that day, Nicky'd tole that fucken Jake to his face what he was doing was not right. (Yet here I am speaking like this of her.) Now get! Gloria Jones turned her defeated — and guilty — state to the window, that used to look out over the Trambert paddocks but now the rich white bastard was even richer with selling his land for all those new houses out there as the view now.

She remembered Beth Heke had had a thing about him, white-man Trambert she used to call him, all the time asking her friends what it must feel like to be him, his side of the fence, when really none of the girls Gloria knew gave Trambert one thought, 'cept in contempt if they happened to be down in the dumps and looked out and saw how big his house was compared to their side-by-side, two-storey State boxes. The daughter who killed herself, Grace, she'd been like her mother, never satisfied with their lot in life (and look where it got her, the kid) used to walk around talking about ambition and things like that — around here! For gawd's sake, where did that kid live in her head? — Thinking of kids, she winced at the front door closing, the faces of her children looming in her mind. But she was also glad because she was that much closer to relieving the aching need in her — aching.

Down the street trying to keep the hurry out of her legs (a woman's gotta have a bitta dignity, eh Glor?) inside feeling happy, on balance, on balance against the kids whom she'd already in her mind turned into faded figures, a trick she came to know of years of denial and struggle, pas' that damn gang house, barbed-wire along the top of the high, corrugated-iron walls (oo, I hope no one comes out while I'm walking pas', they give me the creeps). Yet she'd had her times of going past and hearing the noise of what sounded like a really raging party going on there and half hoping someone she knew'd give her a invite. (I'd go, I think. Jus' to see what they're really like.) Though she did have the thought of being gang-raped, which not even a slut would want. Smiling to herself (not even I'd want that).

At the dairy she first looked around for her kids, case they were lurking to shoplift a packet a biscuits or something, from these thieving fucken Hindus who owned it and parked their every year flash brand-new car out the back in the locked compound guarded by two dogs now, used to be one till some Browns Fist prospect kids threw a meaner dog over the fence, sikked it onto the Hindu's alsatian and they were yelling at it to scratch the car, too, but shit it was only a dog not a trained ape like some of those bastards looked like. Not that Gloria knew anything about dogs, she only heard that the new dogs guarding the Hindu niggers' car were pitbulls and even the Brown Fists didn't mess with them.

She looked around the dairy, funny how it seemed like that story she remembered from school (the only one) of the house Hansel and Gretel found that was made of biscuits and cakes and lollies, that this little place should seem like that whenever she had no money, which was routine.

She bought a 30 gram packet of Park Drive tobacco, $9.85, 55 cents for a packet of papers, Ziz Zag, to roll them in, 65 cents for a packet of filters and finally 25 cents for a box of matches which she could dimly remember cost five cents once. Eleven dollars fifty cents please, fucken Hindu at it again as Gloria wagged a finger at him. Add it up again, Mista. Comes to eleven thirty. Oh, I am sorrrry, with the r's how they do these black thiefs, make mistake Mrs — I mean Miss — Jones. (What'd he mean by that?)

She came out of the dairy looking around carefully even though she was dying — dying — to stop and roll up and light up, she mustn't. (I mustn't.) Not till she got home. She saw the backs of her children disappearing into a house 'cross the street and up from the Brown Fist place, glad the school didn't require a uniform which she couldn't have afforded (even if I gave up my smokes), feeling better at seeing that, meant they'd found someone else to call in on and get a breakfast. She changed the packets of smoking items from her outside pocket just in case one of her kids came out and saw the shapes in that pocket.

At home, in the kitchen her hands trembled in tearing open the packet of filters; she slipped a paper out, opened it and put a filter one end, opened the plastic pouch of Park Drive meaning to pull a minimum of shreds of finely cut leaf from the wad (so lovely and damp and soft) but first she brought the whole 30 (precious) grams to her nostrils and took a deep drink of the aroma: Ahhhh, better than sex, at this very moment — Nah, fuckit, make it a big one this first. And so she added another paper to the end of the first, like rolling a joint, not that she'd had one of those for a few months (makes me too sexy anyrate) and rolled herself the longest, fattest cigarette in her life. Then got up, grabbed a rubbish bag and took it outside as an excuse to check her kids weren't coming back for any reason. All clear. Back inside with the bag as it had some room left in it and bags cost fifty cents each, eighty down at the thieving dairy, taking the match and striking it, flame first time, smoke in her mouth, and she took that first drag. Heaven. Not Pine Block but Heaven.

OI! BOY? WHATCHU crying about? Someone hitchu? Whyn't you hittim back? Cantchu fight? You a crybaby? Mulla aksed the boy. He happened to come out of the side door to the big (locked) gates of the HQ, on his way to buy some smokes, clear his head from anutha good pardy las' night.

Then he noticed the girl jus' in front and when she saw him her lack of fear surprised Mulla. And the firs' thing he thought was, she old enuff to fuck? 'Cept she wasn't. Not even to him. Maybe to some of the boys but not him. He was no child molester. An', tell the truth, he felt sorry for the kid to jus' come out on him like that, crying. Then he remembered how he mus' look to the kid, even though the Browns were part of this street and had been for years, the closeness of a fulla tattooed up with spirals and fern-curls in ole Maori warrior design would prob'ly be frightening. So he smiled one of his bedda missing-tooth smiles, Or someone ya know die or sumpthin'? he toned the question down.

The boy looked at the girl, Mulla saw her nod jus' the once, and seein' the boy didn't up and run it meant she'd tole him, prob'ly her brutha, he was alright. And he liked that, bein' trusted by a kid, a girl at that. (And a pretty bitch, too. Real pretty.) Hungry, the words came out of the kid's mouth. Took Mulla Rota back in the instant to his own (fucken) chilehood. So he went Yeah? Are ya? That right, ya mother don't feed yas, she's what, out on the booze sumwhere? Playin' cards down the road at your aunties, when he meant it aren't-ies, as in not being real aunties jus' what the ole lady tole her kids to make it seem alright to be playing cards all night with aunties rather than jus' mates. Up an' gone to the Housie, plays six cards atta time and leaves the cubbids empty, that whatcha crying for, boy? Or what? It jus' poured outta him, did these words from Mulla Rota, aged thirty-six and over half of that time spent behind bars, of the mind and heart, too, and much of it locked back there in the chilehood that't jus' burst from 'im.

No. She's broke. Broke, the sister echoed, so they were sticking up for her. Like everyone 'round here, the sister added. Which brought a li'l smile to Mulla's tattooed features, Oh, tha's alright then. Was thinking you mighta had a ole lady like mine (a bitch). And he reached into his jeans pocket now filthy like they were sposed to, came out with a handful of notes, tens and twenties, they'd las' night done a good kaygee deal to a honky gang who were neutral, one of the few who were, and so everyone in The Family was loaded. Here. He handed the boy ten bucks. Go buy you ten pies, cuzzy. Feeling all soft as he offered it. All soft. But trying not to show his Santa Claus grin.

But the boy looks at his sis firs' — Mulla saw the subtle nod; he liked that, respected it, specially from jussa girl what, 'bout twelve. So he peeled off anutha ten. Here. For you, too. Go on, take it. Pointed a cut-off mittened finger at each in turn: An' don't be telling no one. Ya hear?

Yeah, they heard. An' don't be thinking I'll give you it every time 'cause I won't. (I ain't no easy mug can be taken for a ride, used.) The las' thing the girl tole him was, Can't buy ten pies with ten bucks. They're a dollar eighty each. Which was double what Mulla las' remembered paying for one, mighta been less. The changes a man inside missed. Oh, well, such is life, hahaha! Walking down that Pine Block street feeling, you know, pretty good. Laughing at the thought of smokes — tailor-mades, not roll-your-owns — the price they must've gone up to. Shet, if a man couldn't afford to smoke then he may as well not live. And laughing cos he felt good. Come to think of it: real good.

TEN

THEY'D GOT IN so close to her they had her walking backwards, to keep them off, pawing at her, mild slaps (so far). Bunch of homie girls who'd changed after school and caught her coming home from a late study period; mean and thinking they were so cool in baggie dark trousers, sports jackets, a couple of them with baseball caps turned backwards. Living in a world of false assumptions, thinking they were like the real thing from America. (Can't even be themselves.)

Two with shades, even when the day was overcast. They with the most mouth, teasing, taunting her with names, spat poison, and not as if she'd done them any wrong (it's for existing as I do) got themselves into a lather at her being, it didn't take much guessing, a try-hard.

No reason in their ugly forming of crowding (crowd) faces, Polly Heke could see it missing like a hole in them, a truck driven through their centres (of life, girl. Of the life) her own inner hurt worse that they were Maori girls like her, doing this because she was going well at school. She remembered her brother Boogie (now look where he is) had experienced the same, teased, taunted, in his case beat up, by his Maori peers for being the same thing: a try-hard. The same kids who walked around with sullen lips and permanent scowls at this world not being fair to Maoris, and increasingly so Polly Heke had noticed in the last few years. The same who blamed their lack of progress on everyone and thing but themselves. Ask any Maori kid doing, or trying to, well at school where their pressure came from.

She didn't try and talk, she knew the faces well enough, the pack they moved around the school in and that she was one of many (or any) they did this to, it was just her turn (it's just my turn, my unlucky number's come up); the eyes bereft of reason, faces of girls twisted into expressions of boys, of violence therefore, aggression, blind belief in what they were and what they were doing — words weren't gonna work with them. She knew that. More than anything on a late afternoon in this better part of Two Lakes (so I thought) Polly Heke knew this was her turn for the gauntlet.

One of them, a fat girl hiding herself behind shades (as if that reduces your size you idiot) shifted the mood on: What are you, bitch, a fucken HONK now? The question raced through their faces like a stone in a pond. To be so accused. You been working late, have ya bitch? It was the shades gave the extra edge to their nastiness. Another shaded one announced, Well she ain't one of us now is she? As if a girl had to be. And all their heads starting going from side to funny side. Far's we're concerned she's a reej. Meaning reject. She wanted to tell them surely you have to be a member before you can be a reject. But someone slapped her face — hard. And she knew it was all changed then; for a moment, it was so very fleeting, Polly Heke felt like the daughter of her father, ready to lash back, to — (go to work) the words flashed through her mind like some genetic memory. But only for a few seconds, maybe not even that long. Then she braced herself. And the blows started coming.

AT HOME, BEFORE the mirror of her dressing table, bought by her mother but at Charlie Bennett's suggestion since Beth — who everyone still called Beth Heke that's how much the bastard's name stuck, his reputation — didn't know about bedroom furniture items, just like she didn't know much about life being other than a basic issue of day-to-day survival. A chest of drawers was just drawers to Beth, and she got shitty at Charlie teasing that he'd have to educate her on the wider ways of the world, like the restaurant he'd taken her to, a first, their humorous recounting of it.

Before the mirror as she remembered her mother before the cracked bathroom mirror back in Rimu Street, Pine Block, looking at her beating wounds about once every month, maybe more or it could have been less, Polly wasn't counting the times, just the hours, the days, the years, for when she'd be old enough to leave all this behind her. (Oh, but not life itself, like my darling sister, please no.) Except it had happened that her mother, and Grace's circumstances, did it for all of them. And now they had a stable father-figure in their lives who was going to be horrified at seeing his step-daughter like this, with a black eye and bruises on her face, shoulders and back from the punches that pack of girls had rained down once the fat bitch'd started it. All for working hard at school. Not for being Maori suffering at the hands of whites (as some did, no denying) but for being Maori suffering at the hands of Maori to whom the whole notion of success, having goals, being ambitious, was as if a threat to them, the collective. (They beat me up because I want a better life?)

It did occur that in her anger of wanting her attackers to have the same violence inflicted on them, Charlie wouldn't consider that as one of their — their: he called all matters affecting them *our* problems, which always lessened the load — options. Yet right now, looking at her marked reflection, especially the black eye where the punch had felt like a bus had hit her, Polly Heke had aching only for revenge of the same type as she had suffered. Thinking of the punch that it was the first time in her life she'd been punched like that, with full force; as Mum liked to boast, Jake hadn't hit his kids. And having a stern mother meant the siblings grew up not hitting each other either. No, it had to happen from members of her own race, the same who claimed they were so staunch to each other. The fucken liars who claimed they knew and understood more as a people about love than the whites they, yes, hated. (Fuck them! I hate them!) Why don't they leave me alone?

The tears ran again, she knew her mother would urge her to be strong, to shed her tears quickly and get on with attacking the problem causing them, that's how she talked, guess she would after sixteen years living with him, the bastard. Polly'd shut the door on Hu, didn't want him seeing her like this. (Same thing my mother used to do, shut the door, go away kids, I don't want you seeing me like this.) Thank God it was girls who'd done this, not a boyfriend, or a man. Otherwise a girl's life might be mirroring her mother's. Astonished at what it felt like inside at being physically assaulted; as if she had been raped, violated. So she wept again in thinking of Grace's sexual violation; hating so much of the world.

AT HER DOOR he heard her, wanted to rush in ask why she was sobbing. He hated the sound of pain, of emotional hurt. And he had caught a glimpse of her eye, so he knew she'd been hit. He wanted to go and hit back. He wanted to sort out whoever had done this to her. Already he was the tallest in his intermediate class, the strongest, the best all-round athlete, but not a fighter. (But I could be if I had reason.) He could feel the strength in him. But refused to consider from what genetic source. (I hate him.)

He didn't remember his father like Polly did. Nor Grace and nor his oldest brother Nig (man, they shot him, the Black Hawks did. They shot my big brother and he shot one of them.) Charlie the only adult male figure in his life who counted; every day he looked forward to Charlie coming home from work. It was Charlie's (Dad's) reassuring and calm presence, his attention to whoever was speaking; his surprises of food treat for the house, especially shellfish from the fishmonger's. Hu liked to have surprise of his own, a chore done around the house, hiding behind the door and springing out on Charlie (jus' an excuse for a hug, Hu!) Hu's sporting achievements were part of the evening routine as they sat around sharing each's day with one another. There was no other man Huata Heke — he wished his mother would change that damn name to Bennett, even if she wasn't married to him — wanted to be like than Charlie Bennett. Every night he went to sleep with that wanting.

One of Charlie's strictest house rules was no violence nor even talk of it. A rule Huata embraced, in perfect accordance with his nature, despite his physical prowess. (Like my big brother Boogie.) Though right now, hearing his sister in that state, had his young (Jake Heke) muscles flexed and surging with desire to get the person or persons. Stuff it, he could stand it no longer. He grabbed the door handle, walked in.

Who did it? he demanded of her mirror reflection. Go away. No. Who did it, Poll? She turned then, her eye . . . He closed his eyes. But the eye was still swollen when he opened both his. Don't be forming fists, Hu. Which he didn't know he had done. He forced his fingers rigidly straight. Poll, who did it? Girls did it. (Oh.) No boys with them? No. And if there was, you know the rule. He knew the rule; so he shifted his weight from one foot to the other. Now what?

Now what? She looked like their mother in that moment; from memories he thought he didn't have, in asking the question not of why she had been hit, but why the life handed out her, that's what Huata Heke's sister was asking. But their mother again as Polly turned the expression into a slow, managed smile with her arms outstretched, How about a hug?

HE WAS SO hyped up and anyway in instant disapproval (at a time like this?) he whacked away Mookie's offer of a joint he'd jus' lit up, Nah man. Makes you too easy. Las' thing we fucken want. Throw it away, man. Later. Later we c'n get stoned off our fucken faces. I said: throw it away. And to show he meant business he took over hefting the block of steel-reinforced concrete they were lifting onto the back of the ute and finished the lift by himself. The rear end of the Holden ute sagged with this third weight added.

Le's go, it came out like his final words on this planet. Which they would be if the job, the bizniz, didn't get done.

The journey into town was one of forced self-discipline, of telling Mookie to shut the fuck up from telling him to go faster; he wasn't breaking no speeding laws, no nothin'. He jus' wanted to get there, and get it done. Mookie cracked a cupla cans, which he didn't mind, beer was alright, a can or two, settle a man a bit, though he did tell Mookie, don't be sticking that can up in the air and advertising us, man. Alright? Yeah-yeah, alright, man, you fucken worry too much. And he swung on Mookie in the confines of their single-cab transport: Mook, you'll be the one worrying if this fucks up. Unnerstan'? Mookie's silence told him he understood alright. This night equally important to the two young men.

They drove past their back-up vehicle parked, of all the places, in a firm of solicitors' carpark on the street adjacent to the one he next sat parked up, watching Mookie walk casually down the street, Mookie's hand flicking out as he scattered the z-shaped nails onto the road. Then he moved forward and picked Mookie up and, with pounding heart, it was all on.

Engine screaming, but not as loud as his mind was, as though this act of this night meant more than even the utterly important event it was; as if it meant his lifetime (and others' shortened ones) as if the entire meaning of his existence on this earth hinged on this, which is why, for once, he was wearing a seatbelt and so was Mookie but only on his orders — *Oooooffff*! Jeezuzfuckenchrise! that was why the seatbelts, the shattering behind them, the force of the jolt like ten-thousand punches in one as they reversed into the very building. Looking at each utha in that milli-sec mo of hearing the short shriek of metal being assaulted, how the ear picked out the descending order of sounds, the last tinkle of glass pane, the last sag of window-frame falling, a man's senses so sharp that mighta been the last of dust and light debris he could hear falling, too.

Out they jumped from the reversed vehicle — (holy mack'ral!) brought up short for a moment at the damage they'd done in just a few seconds: one moment it'd been a bank front and an automatic cashcard machine, the next it was one of those sites after the demolition ball's been at it. Mookie broke the silence: Man, it fucken worked... Which it had, close to. Wait a sec. He jumped back in, drove the ute forward, slammed it back in reverse, hit the pedal, dropped the wheel left, and put that ute in under the ATM machine like a (good) daddy scooping up his child.

Just a few rivets with last cling as they rocked it hard a few times till it fell the short distance onto the back of their rear-weighted vehicle, back in they leapt. LE'S GO! he roared it this time. Had their departure path exactly picked out, between nails (to flatten the tyres of any John Citizen cunts, or the cops) everything — every-thing — so clear he could have been stoned on good head, or it could've been one of those dreams like he'd read somewhere of diving visibility in the South Pole being three kilometres, that's the kind of dream he meant. 'Cept this was fucken real — he punched Mookie's arm, We did it! Laughed when Mookie pulled away holding his arm going, Yeah, alright, man. No need to knock me out. But then he laughed, too. How they both laughed. The more when Mookie pointed out the windscreen, Jus' watch where ya drive, bru-tha, might be nails lyin' around! Oh how they laughed.

THEY, THE PREZ, the newly released from jail sergeant-at-arms (with the most disturbing eyes a man's ever seen) several of the bros, counted out the last (sweet) stack of notes, new, crisp, (man, almost glowing) then the prez got up from the (dirty) floor on his filthy (cool) black jeans, for a moment his smile caught between showing leadership and jus' plain poor boy grown up not 'specting much, or not dough, from this life and yet here it was, thousands and thousands of the sweet stuff — they heard him take breath, as well saw the look he shot at the sarge, still with the eyes of green ice (for me, I know that an' I know why. But I'm here, aren't I?) told them, Eighty, boys . . . A long pause.

There's eighty of the big ones you brung us here. And the room was silent; the mouths were slightly agape even when they were trying not to, of everyone fighting to regain the reality they were comfortable in, which wasn't this (it wasn't this they were comfortable in, this was cell talk, pass the time away of anutha sentence brag, of the BIG job they were gonna do when they got out, but no one, or not many, ever did, and even those few got caught). But THIS, this'd happened; and to make it worse, by two pros's not them, the fullas sposed to be the bigtimer hoods, the gangstas, the patched-up with ferociously proud gang-insignia tough cunts.

The tension as if the pair'd done the opposite of this incredible achievement, of eight fucken losers arseholes, an' that was jus' those who happened to be present when these two hero hunters arrived — Yeah, we know it, too — fighting to come to grips with their only dream right in front of 'em (Money! Jus' gimme the money, honey, and shut the fuck up). Eighty fucken thousand in cash, and taken of everyone's voice it seemed.

Finally the prez turned and nodded to the sarge't-arms and he came forward, all long arms from the leanest, meanest body clad in filthy gang regalia, even his fucken fingers had muscle, tattooed arms hanging out bare from the waistjacket, that funny thing had a gold chain of a fob watch, not that the pair knew what that was, nor cared, and the light in here with blue cellophane as crude tone shades around the bulbs so it was though death was always present, an' it looked Death himself was coming toward them in the form of the sergeant-at-arms. They were just prospects about to lose that lower status, they were about to be crowned princes, they were the young hunters returned unexpected with the big kill slung bloodied over their shoulders. This big handsome bastard was about to knight them. (Or was he?)

No music going, no nothin'. Just those stacks of money on the dirt and beer and blood and cigarette ash and dropped food and tomato sauce ('nless it was more blood) stained floor. And then the voice saying, Welcome, bruth-ahs. Welcome to our Family. And it sounded as though from above them, from heaven, that it was an invite to heaven for the two strapping young warrior prospects no longer. Which brought both chests up, specially the more powerful one, his head to his six four, though Mookie weren't exactly liddle, jus' a cupla inches in it. First Sarge shook Mookie's hand in the handshake, then he hesitated, as if fighting some private principle, some past matter unresolved, before he stepped up, gave the special handshake, then hesitated again before giving what he gave Mookie, an embrace. And powerfully strong it was, too (he mussa been doing some helluva working out while he was inside) he was the sergeant-at-arms, a ledge in his own right let alone what respect, awe even fear, the position commanded.

He said, Wha's your name, new brutha? to Mookie. Mookie Hawea, uh — Mookie lost his voice at not knowing how to address the sarge. Call me Sarge, bruth-ah. Sarge, it's Mookie Hawea an' I'm — an' I'm — Ya don't have to be Mutha's Day 'bout it, Mook. We all know you're glad to be in. He turned to his bruthas, the prez firs, Aren't we, bruthas? And every eye but one set went down to the money. Yeah. Yeah, guess they were. Sure they were, both newbloods saw the final decision register in weight shifts and grave-faced nods.

And wha's your name, new brutha? The eyes gone even colder they had murder in them. Abe. Name's Abe, Sarge. But Sarge stepped forward, Abe Heke could smell his beer-drinking breath, see his half-carse Maori green eyes, the red in them, see the little tremblings of muscle quiver all ovah his rather handsome face. Abe who? came forward anutha half shuffle. Abe who, man?

Abe Blackie, Sarge. Name's Abe Blackie. So even he, Apeman Black, of himself the changed name, gave smile. Hard though it was. Then put an open-fingered hand up, a black leather glove without the fingers, entwined it with Abe's, 'cept Abe wasn't yet with the cut-off gloves, but he was gonna be. And the bruthas nodded with much grave-faced propriety of most serious ceremony now concluded and the prez himself spoke the words: *Black Hawks firs'!* Let me *hear* it . . . Cocking an ear, a stubbled face to his men, Wanna hear it. *Black Hawks firs'!* Abe who used to be a Heke spoke those words as though a commandment — they *were* a commandment. The First, too.

SHE WENT UP to him in the street, the main street of town as it happens. Just one word to him, her son: Why?

And he gave one word, just one word in reply: Nig. Before he moved on with that walk they get, of attitude. Of so much missing from their life.

ELEVEN

A MAN'D FALL down, tripped by a tree root, a rock, a growth obstruction of some fucken sort, cut himself, put bruises on bruises, scratched on face, neck, hands, exposed arms from rolled-up sleeves but fucked if he was gonna roll 'em down, that's how he'd started off this hunting trip — expedition that cackling Kohi'd called it — with his sleeves rolled up, borrowed pack on his back to which he'd transferred his bringings, his borrowed hunting boots from Gary a size too big but better'n a size too small, or so he'd thought when they started out but now the ends of his toes were rubbed raw and felt wet with blood. This was exactly like that dream he had a while back, of falling over on a harsh landscape 'cept this real one had bush and sharp branches and big ole slippery, fallen logs to clamber (and slip) over, to a ground always waiting with sumpthin' hard to hurt a man. And the humming from that dream was what came every so often from Kohi, up front in the lead there and not panting, not even breathing hard, and when it wasn't his humming it was Gary breaking out in a whistle, and boy could he whistle, reminded a man of Dooley (who used to be my closest mate) as if inspired by the birds going in the scrubby trees, the real ones to come when they got glimpse through clearing or another (dozens more to come?) rise reached, a breather, roll a smoke, the only pleasure he could take of saying that first stop nah, he didn't smoke, with his own smug glance at Gary. 'Cept when the brothers lit up and the smoke drifted right to him, Jake Heke felt like starting up again so good did it smell, so apt to this setting of just three men, the birds, insects, and a nice day looking down on them, what it did to a man's sense of smell, his every sense. But then that would be showing these fullas weakness and that's what they were looking for, why they'd brungim, why they'd reminded everytime they saw him at the bar he'd now made his regular, they were going to take him out hunting.

Cupla nights ago, paynight Thursday, they said their rugby team had a bye so Sat'day was it, Jake The . . . Gary'd held the word back for a sarcastic eternity . . . Muss. Pick him up his place this morning at 5 o'clock — on a Sat'day? Shit, a man was only a hour or so asleep on a Friday night meaning Sat'day morning, his head swimming with beer and thoughts and often troubled wonderings and bothering dreams. About lots of things really, even at that hour. Though this morning he was up before his alarm. Packed some food for tonight, cupla blankets since he didn't own a sleeping bag and they were going to be overnighting in a hut, and he sat at his early morning kitchen table drinking tea and thinking about holding a rifle they were gonna lend him. Thinking: Bang! Bang! Gotcha! And not all the targets were pig or deer, neither.

About a two-hour drive in the dark to a forest block utha side of Taupo, Jake not telling the brothers it was further 'n he'd travelled in his forty-two years, to however many miles it was past Taupo, when that trip years ago to go and see Boogie in the Riverton Boys' Home (in that nice rental car) woulda been further but a man'd made a fucken mistake of going in for one beer with his mates and that was it, he never came out and nor, he did see the message therein, did Grace ever come out again, like as a living person — fuck thinking about that. (How many years I been living my own death over that, over her, over everything?)

This was the longest journey in his life and he was quite excited, the thrill wouldn't leave his stomach, and the rifle beside him was dying to be picked up and cradled (and fucken fired!) but he'd have to wait or they'd know. They parked the jeep up at the hut they'd return to, hid the packs in the scrub — Even out here, Jake, there's thieves. A reality that kind of troubled Jake. (Out here?)

Half an hour walking in the dark under torchlight over scrubby, tussocky country to start with and, once the sun came up and showed what a beautiful part of the country this was, once that'd subsided, Jake thinking he could do this at double the speed these bigmouths were, but he'd bedda not push it or they might get pissed off, tellim, Well *you* lead the way then, Jake The . . . Muss. Oh, he didn't like the way Gary held back on the word, it used to be a word people spoke with — with reverence. Respect. (But then what if I don't measure up today, what about respect then?) He was thinking about that.

Then it started getting steeper, and the manuka got taller, and he found if he so much as lost a few seconds of concentration imagining what a hero he was gonna showem he was when he shot a fucken deer from quarter mile away (or run it down from behind, hehehehe), he'd look up and could only (shit!) hear 'em. How quickly a stranger here could get lost. So he kept close and kept his thoughts on their one blood-red and one bush-green Swanndri (broad) backs, the rifles slapping against the same broad expanses. The dogs somewhere up front, maybe way in front, chasing pig scent.

Four fucken hours and they were still walking and still climbing and not a cheep from the fucken dogs sposed to be pig dogs, smell one from ten miles away, and a man hungry as well. When he never ate lunch. Hadn't even brung any as he was gonna show off he didn't need lunch and that was why he was slimmer than them, he just had a leg of lamb half-eaten, some buttered bread and three boiled eggs. Oh, and a bottle of rum, a big 1.5-litre job for tonight, show these fullas how to drink the hard stuff, two big 2-litre plastic bottles of Coke to go with it. All he needed was some ice and it'd be like finishing off a (successful) day at the pub! Hungry, but laughing to himself at that thought.

They kept crossing this same creek, slippery with smooth stones or underwater green stuff, so by the third crossing a man was soaked and, if the truth be known, fucken miserable. Yet everytime they got to a rise and it afforded a view out over a landscape of forest he'd never seen the like of, or not that he remembered, Jake more or less forgot his discomfort, found a little more reason to go on. Not that he had a choice even if he packed a sad and turned for home, a man'd be lost in about three minutes flat — and then what? Help! Help! that whatta man'd be saying? Fuck that.

He started noticing the smells, the scents; the manuka was the constant one, but they kept walking into others, from sweet flower aroma to strong scent of rotting vegetation but kind of nice to the nose. Same as he'd spot little bits of fern a brilliant pale green, or a sudden portrait of plant so perfect in formation even he noticed and appreciated it. Wasn't for going up and down and having to keep crossing a fucken stream, or a creek, they called it differently without any reason he could see, this was starting to feel, you know, not the end of the world.

He must've lost his concentration, cos next minute he near ran into the back of them. And Gary turned and snarled at a man to watch himself, back to his brother, the two of 'em standing there with cocked ears for nothing Jake Heke could hear. But then he did: a distant barking, like echoing in a canyon somewhere; the brothers looking at each other. Le's go. Kohi with a covered-up urgency Jake still got. And they broke into a steady trot despite the thickness of bush.

Every so often they stopped as one, did the brothers, and Jake the follower's stop having to be more abrupt, and listened for a bit to that barking getting nearer and changed direction slightly as they ran on. Well it was crashing, not running, and Jake just couldn't find the pace to set himself to. A foot would hit something sticking up, send him off balance and it was all he could do to stay standing and moving at the same time, what witha fucken pack on his back even if it was only small; and the rifle keeping on slipping round the front of him. All of which was throwing off his breathing, he even thought he might be panicking, though only at not being able to keep up if he hit the deck since they wouldn't be stopping for him.

But he got that closing barking fever, too, so he forgot about his lost dignity (my stupid fucken pride all the time worrying about it steada jus' goin' with this flow, we're out hunting pigs not standing in a public bar worrying how good we look here, Jakey) and ran with them.

Funny thing, he started to find his balance a little better, of feeling the ground the instant the (bleeding in the boots) toes struck and knowing what shape was down there, the adjustment to make. (The way the flow went.) The dog sound they ran towards was like some deeper instinctive calling, it came to him the more he found his rhythm, the flow, of partnership from caveman days between dog and man; and then the flow itself, now he had it, as though another instinctive thing but this one a place, yeah, a place. As if now he was run into a tunnel that the dogs were summoning them (me) to. And all was with excited hunter's instincts, so it was wholly instincts with a man and men.

Three dogs barking, going off their dog faces, not that they could see them yet, as they got nearer. And damn if it wasn't rock walls the noise was bouncing off in this kind of valley, or a canyon divide, Jake didn't know what they'd call it, only that he was right: the barks did have echo in them. A canyon of sheer rock and in parts thickly lush, moss-like growth on the forest floor a most beautiful green, the more with the sun on it; the trees not so high so it could be secondary growth from a fire, or maybe now its time in about noon sunlight was the only hour it got sun due to the height of the rock flanking walls. Whatever, it was beautiful even with the dogs going and now the grunting, snorting of their prey which set alight something more in an anyway *surging* man, Jake (The Muss) Heke.

Now they slowed to a cautious and charged walk, rifles off; never had Jake felt so glad at the feel of weapon, such power, in his hands. Till Gary turned and glanced at Jake's rifle and stepped back and did something to it and said, safety catch, Jake. No good having a cock if ya don't know how to use it. (Fuckim.) Then they saw the thing. Meaning the pig, before Jake at least saw the dogs even though they were making all the noise. He never realised a pig was so fucken big, so powerfully squat and hairy. He raised his rifle. Got a helluva fright when the barrel got slapped down — No! Ya miss and hit one of Ko'i's dogs, he'll hit you! (Oh yeah? Would he jus'?) Jake had to shake his head to rid himself of old habits of reaction. Had to look at the closeness of dogs and that damn scary this-way'n-that pig with its huge head and tell himself Gary was just showing his greater experience.

Next a knife was in his hand, thrust at him by Kohi. You're the sticker, Jake. A blade that he tested too hard with a thumb and made it run with blood. And he was confused. And thinking this was one of the same of six confidence-sapped years, of every good moment melting on a man, of his strong moments being just that, when in days before they'd lasted a man his whole (magnificent) fighting life. When he looked up Gary was looking at him. Felt like using the knife on him. *Come on!* Kohi snapped him out of it. (But now what?) As he moved forward in a state of such uncertainty it was all he could do not to stop and beg for some advice.

His advance was too slow and he knew it and so did they, the brothers, themselves moving up quicker on the animal which itself suddenly saw them, or it saw Jake Heke. (Jesus chrise!) And inside he felt closer to the most humiliating collapse of his whole meaning of existence in front of these fullas. He made a burst of footsteps forward, as much in desperation than anything. The pig swung its huge, long-snouted head his way! (Oh!) He wanted to tell these fullas he'd take 'em both on in a scrap if they were doubting him, if they wanted (real) proof of his manhood. But Gary only stabbed a finger at the pig, gave Jake the wildest eyes, Well? You gonna do it or're you — But Jake wasn't letting him finish. This was it. All or fucken nothing. He couldn't just let his manhood disintegrate here even if it was in the middle of nowhere — there were two witnesses who'd have it all over town by tomorrow; he just couldn't. (I had my taste of that six long fucken years.)

And then he remembered. Jake Heke's childhood, or the start of his teenage year came back; he had a reference point, something to go by. Now Gary was yelling at him, *Stick* the fucken thing, man! Stick it! He looked at Gary: alright then, mister. It's a sticking job. And he came forward at a crouch for the moment by moment changing scene in front, to the side, other side, back to the middle of them as the pig took its three animal pursuers, and this man, this way and that in a frenzy of flashing tusks and terrible noise.

One dog kept losing its hold on the pig's tail. Another kept darting in under to bite at its balls — if it had balls, none that Jake could see. The biggest one hung onto an ear and the pig was trying desperately to throw it, flicking its hairy, thick-neck head, tusks catching in the sun like flashing ivory knives. Then it suddenly dropped its head, did a full about-turn and charged into one of the dogs. Yelping echoed in this canyon. Sunlight bathed it and participants in this ancient practice (ceremony, initiation rite) man had made of hunting. The bailer dog that had been gored still managed to scramble out of the charging pig's way trying to finish it off. Helped by the holder dog on its ear pulling hard backwards bringing the pig up short, and when the other rushed in and took a mouthful of back leg and twisted furiously, the pig sank onto its hind quarters, squealing — more like screaming — to the heavens and sound-bouncing rock walls.

No one told Jake to act, he just did; charging in like making a rugby tackle — no, a rugby league tackle, they hit harder — when he'd only played the game till he was, what, fifteen — and he drove his shoulder into that hairy body, knocked it off balance onto its side, feet pawing at air, scratching the side of his face; and he saw it as clearly as a fight (in a fight I can see everything), so he snatched a handful of ear in a grip that registered like a vice, and he plunged the knife hand exactly where he was sposed to, at its throat, and he saw his two companions right there, one grabbing a back leg and yanking it outward so it was belly up, and the other, Gary, standing with rifle ready in case (you're hoping) Jake was going to fuck up.

He had his weight (and strength) straddling it, the knife thrusting down, his fighting weight driving his stabbing arm — *uhh!-uhh!-uhhh!* — stabbing it downward, *down*ward, find the fucken heart, his fist around the knife handle sinking into the creature's body, dogs going mad, the holder still on its ear, Jake probed and probed and the animal struggled and gave off great struggling strength, so he thrust even harder downwards, reached into the core of this creature's being (die! die ya fucker!), and felt the thing come alive in sudden but, he knew, last flexing of its power, the failing of even its great(er) strength, to men and as many dogs, if they no longer counted the dog ripped by the ivory knife the animal was born with, lying whining on its side. He held the knife down there till the very last, blood vomited up over his sticking hand, last violent convulsions went its hairy length and muscular breadth, he punched his sticking arm even further as red liquid gushed up around it. Held it there till there was no more and his ears could register the birds in (oblivious) titter.

Then he stood up, wiped the blood on his track pants, as Kohi called his dogs off but had to haul the holder from its ear-grip, Jake looking first for his rifle for no other reason to get fully on top of this setting, this stage he'd launched himself onto; a life lay there on its side staining the lush green ground a red made brilliant by the overhead sun; birds, insects were going, and a man was feeling inside like he'd never in his life. Not even in defeating several men in a brawl on his own.

He looked at Gary. Gary winked. Jake nodded. Gary looked down at the defeated beast as he shouldered his rifle but not without first flicking the safety catch on, told Jake, Good one, Jake. But then that pause, like he did with the word Muss . . . Your kill, your carry, eh ‚Jakey? But with a li'l more respect in his eyes as Jake Heke could see it. And he'd called him Jakey. He liked being called that.

CARRY IT HE did. But first he used his head, ran a one-cut slit down the carcass middle, thinking of the pig as an honourably vanquished foe, and pulled out its guts, knifing away organs and bits that stuck to the inner gourd of once-living body. Then Kohi told him, Cut the balls out, too, Jake. Sours the meat. Jake with a li'l smile before he put his knife to work on that, too. Never thought he'd be cutting a creature's balls out.

Then he hefted the carcass onto his shoulders — shit, it was heavy — and Gary came over and tied the legs together with twine to free Jake's arms, giving him a pat on the face while he was at it. Made him sigh inside, it was like having his hair ruffled in affection and/or respect, made him feel so good about himself. Then they walked, heading for the hut. Could be walking back to Two Lakes for all Jake Heke cared. Funny thing, not calling himself that nickname as he always did in his mind whenever in physical triumph or in just trying to lift himself. Who needed it with a pig carcass on his back out in the wilderness where the only other humans were his partners and now respectful of him?

Later, outside in the lovely, round a fire, billy on the boil, hungry stomachs full from reheated fried lamb chops and Jake's half leg of lamb sliced and between chunks of buttered bread, the stars up there as clear as ever a man'd seen 'em, the pig plus the deer, a small hind Gary'd shot just on dusk, both hung between cut manuka sticks, silhouette testimonies in the firelight throw, the embers on the ground, warmth outside but even more inside — Oh, and sheetless woollen blanket bunk bed in the hut behind them Jake was looking forward to, the rum and the Coke he'd produced from his borrowed pack, telling the brothers, Thought you might be thirsty, with that smile of his he hoped they got in the firelight, and they were surprised; and it'd loosened them, if loosening is what was needed, and Kohi was telling a story, of being out illegal spotlighting for deer — They stop dead in the spotlight, Jake, so you just shoot 'em. We picked places where we could see down for the ranger's headlights and when we did we'd just slip down a bank, lights out, and watch 'em go past. But one night they got us; set up a road block and they did our trick, sitting there parked, no lights, in the dark. We came round a bend and whoa! they had one of their jeeps parked across the road. But this Maori boy's got eyes in the dark, haven't I, Ga'? And Gary went, Yeah yeah, get on with the story, Ko'i.

I spotted a gap between their jeep and the road and a steep bank. But down I went, nearly lost it but we got back up on the other fucken side! Jake joining his laughter with theirs, and not wanting to be anywhere else in this world but here, under the stars at one with nature and tale-telling man and men.

But fuck me, if one of the rangers hasn't jumped on the back, on the bullbar, and thumping on our roof: I order you stop! You're under arrest! And I look at Gary here an' he groans, he knows what I'm like, I'm asking myself, who's the stupid cunt here if I'm driving and he's riding on the back? I lean out and askim, Hey bud? — a term Jake was laughing at when normally he hated it. Ya wanna go for a ride or are you getting off? You're under arrest! he yells again. I yell back, I can't see no handcuffs — ranger! Then I hit the fucken pedal. And we never stopped till we got to the top of that mountain there — Jake could see a prominent high outline, a thin glowy line in the sky — Kohi pointing, his face more smiling shadows under his eyes, his smiling teeth.

Cunt was frozen stiff! But, oh well, had to lettim inside the ride down. Though if we'd known his mates'd called the cops out to wait for us we'd a left the bastard up there.

Jake laughing, telling Kohi he shoulda charged the ranger a taxi fare. An' oh how (lovely) good those stars looked is another thing he'd liked to've said and nearly did in his sense of, well, complete contentment.

'Nother funny thing: a man was so worn out from all that walking and lugging the pig he was the first to bed. Left the brothers to the rest of the rum. In under his woollen blankets caressing his naked skin, who needs a sleeping bag, talkin' to his blankets how he did: There, there, I know it's cold and lonely out here in the bush, li'l sheeps. But Jakey's here. Jake Heke's here. Asleep before he knew it.

TWELVE

SHE MARRIED HER worst and a few best qualities to Mulla Rota's, whatever his qualities were and publicly and lawfully had been deemed as weren't, her envy of money, her meanness and selfishness (and partly justified from her own miserable upbringing) with money, serving her own needs first, which Mulla wouldn't've seen, not when she was serving his sexual and very quickly love needs, from his kindness to her children which she was told about but only after she said she'd wring their bloody necks if they didn't tell her where they were getting this food from — after all, the food cubbid hadn't been its usual empty three or four days before the fortnightly domestic purposes benefit was paid out into her Post Office bank account for some several weeks — and when they told it wassa Brown Fist, she at first became alarmed. But then thought whoever it was he couldn't be that bad, not if he was giving them twenty bucks every week, a cupla times forty when he thought he mightn't have it the next week, not if he'd given it only on the condition they buy food for the house, which twenty didn't buy a lot of but it was several loaves of sliced bread, it was Weet-bix and it was a cupla cartons of milk, and it was the difference between life turning sour and mean and miserable every two weeks at the same time, give or take a day, and meant she could buy her smokes as her first priority, have some toast or Weet-bix, oh it made a difference alright. Thing is, she couldn't unnerstan' why she couldn't make savings every fortnight of that amount to bridge those last, run-out days, it was only a lousy twenny after all. (But I can't.)

So she'd dressed herself to the nines — or the threes as she gloomily said to herself in looking at the selection of clothes she didn't have, so oozing sex'd have to bring it up to the nines — and took herself down the street, not far behind her children, and sure enough, the side door opens and out pops this (hideously) face-tattooed gangster, with tight curly hair, crushed features like he'd been beaten from birth, and greets her two kids like a visiting father when the real ones — different ones — had never come and seen their kids not once, and Narissa indicated with her eyes that she, Gloria her mother, had brung herself along (well, of course I would, I'd be mad not to. I wasn't to know he was gonna be this ugly) and she went, Thanks for what you been doing. Ignoring the lean-back look her smartarse daughter gave her of never having heard her mother talk in this tone. (I've never had a chance to.)

Stepping up to her one big moment in quite some time, maybe some many many years, of money opportunity it was and money is all't counted around here never mine what they say in denial, that it ain't a Maori thing, it bloodywell is a Maori thing, it's the biggest factor in their indulging, arguing-over-the-stuff lives is money, or it is the ones she knows; it's the juice life runs on and if you ain't got it you don't run, simple, whatever race you are. And Gloria Jones was sick of running out of juice every few days to go before the gov'mint paid her the solo mum's benefit.

She offered him sex wither eyes, her crooked smile (which accidentally slotted into his repertoire of the same, of differently crooked smiles to mean a host of things) and she told him thank you again, from here, touching her breasts ever so meaningfully and he lifted his shades and gave her one of his crooked smiles so she knew it was on. Her body for his dough. Where else could she get a chance like this? In Pine Block it was the solo mums who gave their toyboys, their few-times-a-week lovers, money out of their benefit, not the utha way round, the boys' drinking and smoke money. All the gals sat around over cups of tea or afternoon beers if someone'd won big at the Housie somewhere, laughing at having to pay for their bitta cock. Laughing some more that really, it was the gov'mint paying for their sexual (what about emotional) needs. After all, they were permanently kind of employed by the gov'mint but to do nothing but look after their growing families of babies had out of wedlock that'd never happen, they knew that, too, why that got laughs as well.

And when the kids were gone on to school — but not before that damn Narissa gave me a knowing eye when I woulda thought even a forward girl like her wouldn't know about sex yet — and Mulla was lost at what to say, Gloria Jones wasn't so lost for words: Whyn't you come over home, see what your money's been buying our house? Even she swallowed the nervous lump in her throat and not for sex either, it was fear of blowing this one big chance, tha's what folded like a page turning in a tight space downer throat.

And Mulla nodded, he thought that wasn't a bad idea, but she'd have to go first, he'd come a bit later, with an awkward grin and explanation 'bout it being to do with his bruthas what they would think — But, like, jus' to start with. So he was not so blind he himself hadn't seen this for what it was, an invitation to not just her home and likely bed but quite possibly her life.

It was only ten minutes or so wait, time enough to check her pussy that it smelt nice for him, she had to get it right firs' time, gave down there a jazz-up wash, wishing she had bedda-smelling soap. Brushed her teeth again. Reassure herself she still had it, what men want, even if with some of the sags an' slumps't come with being over thirty. And he did knock. And she said, Come *i-in*, in the nicest voice she'd heard herself in awhile.

And she showed him the cubbid his money had put the kaygee pack't a Weet-bix in, the loaves of bread in the otherwise empty freezer, a big jar of peanut budda las' week, the budda on a saucer (dammit, I shoulda put it on a nicer-looking plate) no need to show him the milk in the noisy ole fridge, she anyway couldn't remember cleaning it for, oh, ages. But she did show him the bedroom, her bedroom, and what she had to offer that money couldn't buy, not someone as ugly and kinda lonely and strange from the off, like him. He didn't las' long (how many men do?) — but he wasn't rough, say that, as she might've expected — so not a long time to put up with, just that strange event't took place in a man, this man no different to any utha man, like a balloon suddenly released of air from the tight, expanding, this c'n go anywhere tension and want, to his or any utha man's urgent furious humping, faster an' faster (Hey! take it easy, fulla, women need ta breathe, too) and whoosh, all the air, the meaning, the urgency, the gotta have it or I'll die, gone. Gone. In its place something quiet, a calmed beast laying beside a woman. But still, not such a bad exchange if it would take her to his money supply.

Which she turned the conversation to even though he wasn't actually talking about anything, he was jus' lying there after the deed and playing with one of her tits, not hard, very gentle 'n fact, making her hornier forim than the firs' time which she'd only done to gettim. So she thought if she gave it toim again and with the feeling he'd aroused iner she could talk money all she liked after it. But firs' she got to the heart of the only thing't matters round here in this routinely, just-surviving Pine Block house.

Found out they, the Browns, made a lotta money from selling drugs, dope, and they shared it depending on how long a man'd been in the gang, and as he was the second-longest serving he got the second-bes' cut. He tole her, sometimes if they shifted kaygees in a week they split 6, 7 grand up between 'em, and his share was 5, 6 hundred, and they had weeks in the season when they moved maybe 5 kaygees, so a man had so much he didn't know what to do withit — Gloria listening having to stop herself from crying out, in joy and despair that she might not be able to make herself part of this, she might not be able to end her life of struggle — 'cept he was never out of jail long enuff, and you didn't get a share if you was in there, only plenty of hash smuggled in to you at visits from the bruthas and the handful of sistas posing as the de facto missus. Gloria Jones had to stop herself from exclaiming her very real fear that she'd miss out on this one opportunity even though she could see, it was obvious as anything, this was one lonely, kinda cutely troubled man and it should be him wanting to exclaim not her.

So she fucked him again, used her aroused tit as her own starting basis, pushing the nipple into his mouth, Oh baby! atim so he'd be flattered and anyway it did feel good. Then she got on top this time, showing him what nature had been pretty kind in gifting her with, a pretty good body considering she didn't do no exercising (exercising sucks. Too hard) if he didn't mine the stretchmarks (from having those fucken kids) which he didn't seem to, he jus' humped up from beneath and called her baby back, and she turned his tentative touching of her other hole to giving him what he wanted, it was one of her favourites, a finger up there, or it was with the main opening taken care of. Oh baby! she tole him again, this time not having to force it this was gooood. Li'l bit longer and she was gonna come — Oh-ummmmmmmm! Maybe why she thought she heard the word love escape from his tattooed throat, get loose from his tattoo-surrounded mouth but couldn't be quite sure, cos she was coming.

What she was sure of, he'd be back for more. Specially when he dumped a fifty-dollar note on the tallboy on his way out of her bedroom (with jus' the biggest of smiles pretending it wasn't a smile). Specially then.

And she sat down on her bed edge with the fifty iner hand, wither clothes still off, his ejection matter running from her body, sweat from her forehead, tears from her eyes — she cried. She cried and cried — and it was with joy, mostly, and relief that only the permanently poor woman with children can know. Looking at the beautiful money portrait iner hand, not the portrait itself of some famous person (hey! but he's a — a Maori?) she almost looked at the name on the fifty-dollar bill to who the Maori famous enough to be on a big note like this could be, but fuckit who cares about fame round here, it's the portrait of money sweet money, whoever's face is on it, that counts. As for the sex, the las' thing she'd planned or expected was to come. She only went to hit herself onto a nice li'l jackpot for, you know, as long as things las' round here. Having a orgasm was a bonus. But, while it lasted, she was gonna make the most of this. And fuck what her (solo mum) mates say of her going out witha Brown Fist. This wassa hard life, you gotta look after numba one, sis. The tears long stopped. Thinking of what she'd spend the fifty on.

THIRTEEN

SHE KEPT GIVINIM glances which even behind her shades bothered him, cos he sure as hell wasn't givin' 'em back. The music from the stereo was being pumped out, peeled back, near overwhelming the emotions whenever it surged to a peak in the club-house hall, which original members had built 'emselves and not a bad effort for a buncha untrained rough dudes if, sure, some of the inside painting was pretty rough, it was still sound and whoever'd dream'd the carpet had got it started with about a quarter of the floor done, who was complaining. But that sheila member's glances were bothering Abe Blackie standing there in the Hawk clubroom bar where virtually all of their gang life took place, he and Mookie knew this already from jussa few months in the gang, and didn't mind in the leas'.

He wasn't wearin' his shades, felt they kinda had to be earned if a man, a new member, wanted to wear 'em inside like the older bruthas; he'd tole Mookie earlier, Man, I wouldn't be wearing the shades, not yet, bro. Might be a rule of, you know, seniority with shades. So Mookie'd taken 'em off and slipped 'em into his jeans pocket. Yeah, man, you're right. Thanks, Abe. Love ya, man. I mighta got in trouble.

All night he'd tried to steer the conversations — if they c'd be called that, which even he knew they couldn't, more like bursts of yeahs and nahs and swear words between periods of silence and clicking fingers to the music, singing along with it, not yet time of being freed up enough to dance to it, talking fights, social grade rugby league games cos some a the bruthas played league (and made out they were playing this Aussie Winfield Cup stuff when all Abe saw las' Sat'day was fat, outta condition dudes with the dreadlocks, with their tats, running puffing around a field trying to take a opposition player out with a big hit or a coathanger — ooops, man was jus' waving out to his mutha, hahaha, on the sideline — round the fucken throat and who cared if the ref sent a man off, might even stick one on him he wasn't too tough which this ref was, he musta been cos he sent two of the bruthas off — You! And you — you're both off! jus' like that when the two bruthas started punching up a fulla and the members on the sideline were off their faces yelling and that got their dogs goin', but no one exactly ran onto the paddock and smacked the ref; Abe heard uthas on the sideline saying the ref was one of the Douglas brothers and you hit one of them you hit the whole family, meaning about nine brothers and the fifty-five cuzzies, too, which made the Douglas family, even the dumbest Black Hawks could figure that one out, bigger than their own gang. And with the law on their side, seein' as they were straight, it meant the bruthas, if they were gonna take it further which they usually did (cos they hold grudges sumpthin' terrible and they're jus' kids't heart, made wild, turned rotten, so they'd go so far as kill a man on jus' the way they think he's lookin' at them) they'd have to use guns on this referee and his reputed staunch-as family, which jus' wasn't worth it, not killing straight fullas who weren't the avowed enemy, it was them the Blacks wanted to waste, maim and kill, the Brown Shits, so they had to cop their sending off with jus' some bluff and bullshit noise and hollering, and (secretly) hope the rugby league board officials didn't ban them for too many games) — well, everywhere Abe Blackie moved to in the community-like hall of about small-town dimensions, so they, the players sent off, wouldn't have to go too long suffering — HAHA! — at having no one to hit, dirty tackle, stare gangster's stares at and, you know, show off to the boys, he jus' couldn't get anyone off the game, which they'd taken their bull terriers and rotties along to, to scare everyone, specially the straights who were whites, specially them cunts — Abe wanting to get onto the avowed enemy, them, the fucken Brown Fists. Brown Shits they called 'em round here, and then some. Abe wanted to get the talk to the Shits' prez, Jimmy Bad Horse, an' what he'd done to Abe's (Heke) real brutha, Nig. Why Abe'd joined and changed his name to show the ultimate staunchness, on account of his late bro. Who Jimmy set up to be killed by this gang, 'cept Abe forgave them that, they couldn't help it, jus' doing their job their life-chosen code of duty, the opposite of the duty Bad Horse was sposed to owe Nig (ya don't set up one of your own members). Abe wanted to find out who of his bruthas here was ready and willing to take the Shits' prez's scalp. Tha's what he was trying to find out: who'd go do the bizniz with him.

But that patched-up sheila kept looking atim. And he knew who she was with; and if he walked in and saw this going on Abe'd have to take what came, which'd be something terrible done against his person 'nless he wanted to fight for her; and her man'd fight to the death, Abe knew that, the whole fucken world did. So he wasn't returning her looks, no fucken way. Even if inside he felt he could give her man a run for his money. Maybe he could. But not why he was here. And anyrate, she wasn't his type. Truth was, he preferred white sheilas. (Gonna get me one, too.) Dunno why. Maybe I like a woman to be more like one and not like the ones around here, specially the patched-up bitches.

Then fuck me, if she don't drag her pretty arse over to a man. Givim the handshake. Hey, man. Hey, sis. Howz it? I'm cool, bro. I'm cool. You too? Yeah, sis, I'm cool. I'm cool. But not so cool he still wasn't hoping she'd jus' fuck off leavim alone. Pretty thing, too. But wrong colour. No class. Wrong vibes coming off 'er. I know someone you know, her voice a million cigarettes and joints croaky, as well this definite sadness about 'er. Oh yeah — who'd that be, sis?

She sucked in breath for no reason, 'nless she was stoned, which she could be, yet she didn't seem in that space. Di'n't ya know? Know what? Who I am, who I knew? An' she glanced over her shoulder, he thought nervously. Nah, I don't know anything. Then she started up chewing and he definitely hadn't seen her put nothing iner mouth. He waited. Then she toldim, I used to go with your brutha. Nig. And it was like an electric charge'd gone through 'im.

That right? He kept his cool. Yeah, she nodded. He was starting to shake all ovah. What, like his . . . ? Yeah, we was close as. Abe fought to gather himself. What, when was this you an' him were . . . ? She sighed again. When he, you know — Abe's turn to suck in breath. Died? Yeah, it was then. Her voice'd gone down to this whisper. And she was ready to move back to where she was leaning, on a elbow-height table jus' like at a real pub, waiting, he sposed, for her man, Apeman.

He went, Listen. Can we, uh, like talk sometime? She wasn't even looking at him when she asked, Why? What's there to talk about? He's gone. I'm outta that shit gang and here with the best one. An' so're you.

Abe downed a fresh can to calm himself. Sis, he was my bro. I, you know, I never loved someone like I did him. (Why I'm here. Why I joined up with this outfit.) That right? Looking atim turned side on. You know what happened? Yeah, I do: fucken Bad Horse? thought he'd turn it into a question case she had more to add. His anger welling up something terrible: (I loved my brother.) She nodded — witha scowl — No, it ran deeper than that, this was sumphin' else again. Not even jus' hatred, though hatred was the bedda part of it. He set my bro up? Yeah, she nodded again. Set me up, too. Why I went and, you know, hugged your mother at the, uh, the fun'ral. You see me there? No, he shook his head using the gesture to hide his swallowing. She gave a sad smile: You mussa been too busy crying, eh? He gave it back, a kind of stress-relieving chuckle: Yeah, I musta been. Fucken near choked on the words.

She turned three-quarters from him tole him ovah her leather jacketed shoulder, Talk to you 'bout it. One day, eh? Yeah, you do that. He felt like crying. But of course didn't.

HE DIDN'T UNDERSTAND it, standing here drinking with them and fucken five of 'em at that, the Douglas brothers, and Gary's got that tease in his tone, after the number of times he'd been out hunting with 'em. (And I showed 'em didn't I?)

What position? Gary was asking Shaneyboy one of his other brothers, you say prop? Jake a prop? Nahhh. Looking at a man like he was a small pig not worth all the trouble, like he'd let a man go rather'n waste his time considering him. Ko'i, can you see a prop in Jake? Kohi shaking his (ugly fucken) head. Nope. Prop's gotta be what they call immovable. And he's too tall to be that. I'm a prop. What, a lock then? Yeah, maybe a lock — nahh. Kohi shaking his head again, tall enough, an' we know he's got the strength, but too fucken old, Ga'. What, you'd be forty-five now Jake?

Two, Jake straightened up in a huff. Forty-two. Same age as you, Ko'i, he'd taken to dropping the h in Kohi's name as much as a sign of their friendship (or so I thought till now) as how the name naturally came out. Yeah, yeah, you're right on that one, Jakey. But, you know, I'm playing. Been playing my whole life, or since I was about five when the football was's big as my li'l body then. Not that it is now, hahahaha! Jus' remembering back, Jake, at how long I been playing that game. Still get excited before a game, too. Then he looks at Hepa. That how you feel before a game, Hep, like you do before, uh, making love? Or having a fuck, Hep drawled back, laughing: shet, it's better'n that — lasts longer! HAHAHAHA! the table erupted. How about you, Shaneyboy? Same, bro. And Haki and Gary nodding yeah, they felt the same way about playing the game: excited. See, Jake? Ko'i lookin' a man right in the fucken eye. Tha's how much we enjoy it. Then running his eyes all ovah a man, clicking his tongue, then tapping his chin as though really giving this some thought. Oh I dunno, Jake, I can't see where you'd fit, fulla your size . . . not quite tall enough to match those big Pakeha locks in the lineout, 'nless you know how to do the business on them which you wouldn't, not if you haven't played the game in — How long you say it was since you'd played, Jake? Fifteen, Jake said. And immediately Kohi shook his head, You see? You see? (Does he have to say it twice?) What I'm saying, they'd eat you alive on the field I'd say, Jake. All, you know, due respec'.

Jake pulled himself up to full (fighting) height. I don't remember bein' eaten by no one, Ko'i. At anything to do with — he stopped. Fuckit, may as well say it: to do with body, Kohi. Formalising his name to keep the record straight.

SO THEY HAD him at practice, an' a cold, wet Tuesday night it was too; running these impossible-to-unnerstan' grid lines, scooping up a ball here, gotta put it down there, run around a fulla here, catch a ball there, run up the line of team-mates, pick up another fucken ball, now drop down and do twenty press-ups, now spring! and run to the halfway — *le's go! le's go!* Man never knew such a short distance to feel so long. Back though an' not the last. Take a breather. Okay, that's enough now, twenty sit-ups — Oh, all night long, or two hours feeling like all night, this shit went on.

A man dragging himself into the huge (nice) thermal bath with the team-mates, too tired to hardly smile. You right for Thursday practice then, Jake? Who else but Gary. A whole lot of smiling heads in a steaming bath as though they were laughing at a man. But he'd showem. (I'll showem.) Looking back at 'em with big asking eyes, Wha' no practice t'morrow night?

FOURTEEN

MULLA THINKING IT muss be the cellphone'd made Bad Horse so fucken sure of himself, when normally Mulla could see that flaw inim, that secret lacking of manhood — he firs' saw it that night in the bar when Jake The Muss confronted Jimmy and Jimmy blew his arse — he could see it in Jimmy Shirkey like a crack going throughim. But, lately, the crack seemed to have closed.

Engine roared out front of 'em, shuddered their smelly-socked feet sitting sticky in steel-capped head-kicking boots, Mulla an' Horse in the back, Chocky driving and Chylo (where'd he get a name like that?) with his tensed, murderous (wanting to) existence 'side Chock as they sped through anutha suburb doin' the roundabout way case there was cops to shake off and drama denied. Brrr-brrr Jimmy took it firs' ring. Yeow? Mulla able to observe his leader because he was sitting in a pretend-relax slump against the door (hoping it don't fucken open on a man!) not wanting to be seen to push down the lock cos that'd mean he was a fucken wimp being sensible, that familiar profile of hair explosion like that Negro fulla the 'Merican boxing promoter — King, tha's right, Don King — hair like his. 'Cept Jimmy hadda beard and Mulla swore it had its own colony of insects in there cos it moved, Mulla'd seen it, and that was inside the Quarters, no fucken wind in there an' only breeze coming was from dudes' mouths shooting off at sumpthin' the same or other of (admit it, man) their fucked-up condition; Jimmy Bad Horse is colonised! was the thought Mulla got when first he saw the beard moving, inside pissing himself at the thought.

Bruth-*ahhh*, I godd it, Jimmy sneering in a fast passing streetlight casting on him. Sound of him pushing a button on that contraption; he toted it and used it like a gun. Cunt tryin' ta gimme di-rections, as if I don't know my own fucken town. Chocky, it's Matai Street, up by that church they light up't night. Church? Chocky laughing. Yeow, bro, ch-hurch. You know the one, down by where Rubie used t' live — Till she died, Chylo couldn't wait to cut in with. Have to be Chylo on the subject of death. Yeah, till she up an' died, Chy. On smack, Jimmy as if he had to remind 'em that smack, even for them, Brown Fists, was out. Ya know why we don't do smack, boys? Cos it makes our sweet life short, Chocky knowing what to answer (refrain) now. Yeah, bro, you goddit: cos it makes our sweet life short. Now *dope* — HAHAHAHAHA! the car exploded spontaneously, affected by the same stuff smoked back at the Headquarters. Though Mulla'd kept his intake low, on account of where they were going tonight, the smoke made him too mellowed out; Jimmy might order 'em to do some bizniz when a man was feeling like smelling a flower, or sumpthin' (nice) stupid like that. Or smelling Gloria's sweet twat, or jus' her toothpas'e breath'd do as she tole a man sweet things. Man, had she grown on a man.

Brrr-brrr Jimmy got the cellie call firs' time; like when a man was waiting around for Gloria t' ringim at the Quarters, hanging around the phone, starting to have jus' a few vague doubts about the company he was keeping, and talking of keeping, he was keeping those thoughts to 'imself, not even'd tell Gloria of such, what-they-call-it, heresy thoughts, Mulla 'membered the word and its meaning fitting here from a crossword even dumb jailbirds learn to do cos they're such an effective way of passing away the time — Br-rruhh-br-rruhh a orn'ry phone rang different (please let it be Gloria) he'd got her call jus' before they left tonight, 'nough time to hear her say take care and stuff like that, grabbing it firs' ring (oh Glor) Gloria? Yeah, it's me. Let her do the talking, a man'd done his bit jus' by being there to answer. Jimmy across from him on his cellphone giving instructions to the utha carload a bruthas where to be positioned and so the excitement in the car air, maybe danger, to go with the cigarettes, sock odour and someone's week-old armpits't hadn't seen water 'n' soap, mean to say, even a Brown has a shower a few times a week, even a Brown. It was that murder-wanting Chylo, he and water was like him and people he took a dislike to — didn't go.

Mulla thought the kid, Gloria's young fulla, looked like Chylo would've when he was the same age: kinda handsome, in that Maori way of if only they'd clean up their act a bit. But the comparison ended there. Chylo's growin' up years musta been worse than even Turi Jones (till I came along and rescued it. I got plans for that boy) or so Mulla hoped in his internal window-demisting changing view of this world, that Gloria's kid didn't end up like this (or me, come ta think of it): wanting to be a murderer.

Chylo was tall and lean an' not jus' mean but bad; Chylo hated the world, everyone and thing in it, he only liked his bruthas and even some a them he hated and for no other reason than he took a dislike to certain members the way Mulla'd seen some deaf mutes do, of taking one look at even a stranger and hatinim on the spot. Cunt carried knives strapped to each leg, a Stanley knife for cutting faces not lino in his jean jacket pocket, and he was the firs' if they were going out on a serious madda to haul out the sawn-off shottie and whatever gun was going down. He'd come from anutha Brown Fist gang, up pas' Auckland somewhere, where he said they had white women for breakfas' an' lunch an' tea and fucken supper, too, if they could lure a slut into their pad. He'd moved down to Two Lakes cos, so he said, he wanted a change of action. No more fullas left t' rumble with up there, boys! I beat 'em all! ('Cept you didn't beat yourself, Chy) Mulla did get that thought. He did now he was experiencing, uh, love.

He called out from the front seat — cos he never turned around and faced people when he was sitting in the front, case it was the moment the Hawks were hitting on the bruthas with a driveby how they do in Ameri-ca, our ebony bruthas, bet they'd love us — Man, I hope these cunts're gonna try and rip us! *Hahaghhahagh!* Cunt had his own laugh, too, always with that menace married to hope that the menace could cut loose. Weren't a day went by when Chylo didn't tell everyone, Man, I wanna *waste* someone. Lately he'd changed that to smoke cos tha's how the niggers in the 'Merican ghettoes talked, he'd seen it on video and once on a late night movie, all the boys'd happened to be up drinking when it came on and at the end — well, during it — they had tears in their eyes when the fulla's mate who was gonna be someone in the better straight world got wasted. Was Chylo jumped up when the fulla in the movie was dying with his chest blasted out by a shottie, screaming he'd be smokin' any man who did that to one a his bruthas. When, if he'd looked, he'd a seen the bruthas having a quiet li'l weep, seen the point of the movie. Oh, but then plenty of people don't see even when it's right in front ofem.

Yeah, man, hope they do, man I hope they do. Chocky. Jus' showing a face, how staunch he was. Man couldn't fight for shit. But he could drive like a racing-car driver, why Jimmy keptim on. Jimmy aksed: Chylo, you put some artillery in the boot? For the firs' time ever Mulla saw Chylo turn his face. This head and shoulders outline saying in a hollow voice, No one said . . . Man, no one tole me . . . With a back echo of, what else, murder therein.

He swung Chocky's way in not panic so much as it was his shame (and the smoke) in maybe not getting an order right. Chock, you sposed to tell me, man? Were ya? No fucken way, Chyl. Jimmy, did you tell us to bring artillery? And Jimmy taking his sweet fucken time in answering: I might've. When he coulda eased their fretting an' tole the truth he hadn't given the order. Instead, Jimmy was dialling anutha number.

I got my Stanley, Jimmy, you want some cunt's face opened up. You tell me, I'll give you a gap in any face you c'n put a truck through, Chylo trying to make up for what'd already passed. And Mulla in the back, right behind Chylo, thinking: Well no one can drive a truck through my existence no more. When it used to be a fucken highway for all of life's woes to come through, or the hole I tried to stop up with my lifetime's acts of stealing stuff and hurtin' people. Not now I got Gloria. Which is why he was shaking a bit, case the bizniz really cut up rough with these honky dealers from outta the bush, tough as, and a man was gonna lose his firs' love in a — till her — rotten life an' go back to fucken jail. (Can't do no more time, God. Jus' can't.)

Don't worry about it, Chy. Utha car'll have sumpthin'. Get one of their guns when we get there. But stick it your side, on your seat, seen's you're the one wanting to use it. (And the one who'll cop the biggest sentence if this goes wrong, as it does more often than not, Jimmy Cunning Horse.) But you use it when I say, unnerstan'? Town lights going by outside, it could be the inhabited moon.

HE WAS DIALLING one after the utha. To move this big deal of stuff bought from the Bushies, ten fucken kaygees. And they grew good stuff and they weren't too greedy about it neither, their leader'd tole Jimmy, We got a saying in our organisation — he said that word crystal clear and very firmly — when you do business, leave room for the next bloke to make his profit. And never rip anyone, Jimmy, that's one of our laws we live by, too. This Trev'd given Jimmy what Mulla knew was a knowing eye when he tole him that. But Jimmy, how he is, rocked his shoulders, scratched his (colonised) beard and went, Yeah, yeah, I always tell my boys, don't be ripping no one, man. When he toldem no such thing. Fact, he tole his boys rip anyone who can be ripped even if it's your ole lady. But this deal'd gone smooth as. And Jimmy knew it.

Chocky chuckling. As for Mulla (man, inside I'm in *exstasy!*) he was happy at the deal going down jus' fine. No hassles. (Means a man's love is saved to fight — I mean love — anutha day.) The tough white cunts from the bush in their thick, checkered bush shirts, a few with them hunting Swanndris, belts with hunting knives sheathed to 'em, and no doubt rifles close't hand in this place they used when they came to town in their jeeps and Toyota hi-luxes like that Barry Crump fulla on the teevee ads does, Mulla knew all ofem with beards and Mulla — at one stage once he knew the deal was not gonna turn ugly even though Chylo was doing his best to eyeball every manjack of 'em to make a fight of it, the shottie out at where his stinking feet'd been ready to run to an' come back blasting, aks no questions, not of the dead — finding himself looking for insect life in any of the beards; it mus' be his relief and the residue of the dope effect turning his mind like that, and of thinking of it as them, whiteman the same as Maoris, being colonised and how fucken funny it all was.

The Bushies even brung out a cupla cases of beer, the right brand, too, Waikato stubbies, so the fullas waiting outside in the back-up car ready and hoping for their call had to sit out there while the prez's carload got to enjoy some, uh, social-ising, hehehe, with white men from Mars if on Mars they all got big fat beards and bush-green woollen hats and stand staunch and unmoving with hairy, whiteman arms quite unafraid of Maoris when Maoris are tough cunts. And if Marsmen've got wild eyes that don't flinch, don't blink firs' even witha madman like Chylo trying to stare 'em down, but having to move onto the nex' set of eyes and he'd kept going like that, the whole time, then the Bushies — what they called 'emselves — were Martians.

But not bad ones as one of their bitches — pretty as, too; Chylo's eyes lost some a their murder and got lusty instead — came out iner tight-fitting jeans, big tits like them country 'n' western singers and (stink) fucken music they listen to, brung out some strips of meat she said was venison and wild pork marinated in something, steaming-hot grilled, with stripes where they'd been seared, and Horse said, Hey! This's good meat, man. Got any for, uh, sale? The uh was him hoping they'd offer it for free. But Mulla knew they wouldn't; these were tough cunts and tough cunts don't fall for that shet.

Not even for sale, mate, their leader tole Jimmy in the way they talk, the mouth more open than a Maori's (and how unbelievably cold their eyes look, being blues and greens and greys and hardly any browns, and the whites of 'em so clear even when they're stoned which these were, they'd started proceedings by bringing out some joints, just thin ones so everyone wasn't wasted off their faces — even stoned they had clear cold eyes). It's our secret recipe.

Chocky, his stoned state doubled by the Bushie's joints, broke out giggling; and when he got it out he had everyone smiling and laughing 'cept for Chylo who never laughed at nothin' in front of enemies. Chocky aksed the whitemen from Mars out in the bush, How bout swapping some pork bones and watercress for some of that meat! Since that's what the boys lived on, mostly, big huge pots of it on the permanent simmer out in the kitchen no one remembered whose turn it was on the roster to clean. But the laughing leader — they never introed him as prez — tole 'em, Whyn't you blokes come out and try hunting 'em for yourselves? You'll enjoy it, tell ya. But the boys took one look at each utha saying the same thing: Fuck that, man. Might tas'e good but nothing's that good have to go out walking through the fucken bush. Might be lions an' tigers out there, too! It was funny how that same thought seemed to be in each Brown's face, three of the four anyway, that there might actually be wild beasts out there even if New Zealand didn't actually have lions and tigers. And how Mulla confirmed this in telling 'em in the car on the (victorious) way home: Man, firs' thing I was thinking when they said go out to the bush — oh yeah? What about the fucken lions and tigers? HAHAHAHAHA! The laughter explosion even joined by Chylo, specially when Chocky said toim, Chylo, you're laughing cos you got your share of meat tanight, right? Right.

HAHAHAHA! Another laugh bomb going off, started by Chocky for no reason than he felt part of this success, this ten in the boot fast being sold by Jimmy there on the cellphone to the bullet and bag dealers round town — holdit a sec, fucken batt'ry's goin' down. Gimme a batt'ry, someone. Mulla dug one out from a plastic shopping bag that had several spares in it. Jimmy dialled the number again, Now, where was we? One kaygee? For you, bro, only cos it's you an' I like you — well WE like you — here, lizzen for yourself, my boys tell you how much they like you. Tellim, boys. BRO, WE LIKE YOU! Three ofem, in chorus. Di'n't even know who it was on the utha end — who the fuck cares? Jus' buy a kaygee and piss off till we need you nex' time, Chylo whispering to Chock. You wanna hear it again, cuz? No? Aww, you're spoiling my boys, you know, ex-press-ing 'emselves. So, you a buyer or what? . . . One of those moments of silence and circumstances in which all the factors come together and each man, even Chylo, thinking — no, realising — where and what he was and what'd gone down and what a bigger slice of meat they had that they'd never let on they hit onto in moments like this — broken by Jimmy Bad Horse informing 'em in his tone gettin' more and more riddled with arrogance: He's a buyer. YEOWWWW! the chorus in unison once more. Jimmy showing he was cooler in his muttered, yeah-yeahs. But the utha three, even Chylo, maybe especially Chy, they were bruthas. Soul mates. Straightsville, boring fucken Straightsville going by in all them li'l glows and floods and spears of houselights (homelights) catches of utha people, Real People, in their kitchens, sitting rooms, cars with the interior lights and open doors of people come back from wherever they'd been, wherever Real People from Outer Space go to on a Sunday that has 'em coming back after nine. Cunts don't know what they're missing, eh boys? Chocky to the company of the pardy coming up, and in denial, as they heard Jimmy move anutha half a kaygee, then his dit-dit-dit-dit-dit dialling of anutha number, informing 'em: Only three an' a half t' go, boys. Any wonder he was their leader — the influence, the *bizniz* contacts the man had!

BACK AT THE Quarters, crack some beers, 'nutha twen'y dozen to add to the million pile of sweet bubblin' foamin' (releasing) history behind 'em, and ten thousand same repeated stories only thing't changed was the names — but hunters returned with the kill, Jimmy'd moved one more kaygee before their mean machine pulled up at the big gates — To heaven, eh boys! Hahahaha, they'd laughed quite seriously at Jimmy saying of arrival at the headquarters, each man to his private thoughts on that, if but briefly. But all one in going HEA-VAN! Bruthas! (If this's all you know) one ofem thinking. And pas' the unpearly gates of welded sheet-iron and razorwire-topped swinging frame they went, opened by Jimmy's remote control, *bzzzzzzz*, he laughing at the power he held in his hands of being able to open that fucken big gate with just a touch of a button. Mulla thinking: Anyone'd think you invented it.

Jimmy in the middle of the room, music going, Chocky knowing to keep it cooler, low and toned till the beer trickled on down to their dirty li'l toes in stinking socks and went back up the utha side of veins and blooded pathways to the brain where it would mingle with the smoke, tanight's success (even though they weren't sure how they'd contributed to it, but claiming it jus' the same — 'fore some utha cunt does, eh bro!) Permanent feelings, a strange swirl, like clear water clouding, to that beat-perfect voice and instrument-backed output of that bl — Negro group, Solo. Lookit the shoulders moving, tha's the sign of what's to come: shoulders and eyes keeping down a blink for jus' a few secs, maybe a minute or two, when a man's got his eyes closed he's in a moment of a kind of honesty, with self or God or the God dwelling in even the murderous hearts like Chylo's . . .

Though the man observing this, Mulla Rota, spent half of his life behind bars, thought of all the people in that room, of — he'd never counted. No one had. It never occurred to 'em to count their numbers and weigh then analyse what they had and maybe were or could be or weren't — it was thirty tonight, 'bout that, more'd be arriving, this deal going like it had'd bring 'em from fucken everywhere, their li'l ratholes and gloomy residences, those who didn't live here permanently; Mulla thinking: of all the people in the room Jimmy Bad Horse would have no God or man or idea (I mean principle) inim. For years he'd thought this. Of seeing Jimmy Shirkey as a man whose very core had turned to a slag, and it was utha people's fire he pulled in as his own, utha people Jimmy built his existence with the crack running through it on, ovah there on the cellphone, centre of the room, and how he'd made 'em, this lot (me included) reliable on him again, that was one of his secrets, it weren't hard to do with this lot, who of us can cope with the world and the money it runs on? None, tha's how many. Fuck none.

Mulla watched the sheila with the smoky shades come ovah to Jimmy, stroke his beard (catch you some cockroaches, sis!) jus' when the nex' Solo song starts, 'In Bed'. Yeah, it would be. But this time Mulla not aching, not hurting at his own status never once attracting a sheila to come toim, not now he had one, his own woman, that was her walking in right now, so her (our) timing was right, too, with this song it was. Mulla gave her a li'l smile, more for the fullas lookin' atim than for her, she'd know he meant sumpthin' else which he'd prove to her lader, sooner rather than lader, hehehe, upstairs in his room an' bedda not be anyone else using it.

The song just cruising in wither walk she'd developed since he knew her, more sure of herself, touching fullas on the face as she passed, coming for (me) Mulla. How you doing, baby? She knew not to kiss him with too much, you know. But she was allowed to givim a hug, bring her tight-hugging blood-red dress to his shape, his man outline, like a 6 an' 9 fittin' together. You look good, Glor. Which made her snap her fingers — blit — like she was tossing something utha than jus' her fingers, her hip at the same time (it was love she threw) and went, Really? Ohh, Mulls. I like it when I'm, you know, 'ppreciated. And he went, with all the burning of his previously troubled being now sustantially less so, the emphasis had shifted: I never 'ppreciated no one more'n my life . . . Had ta swallow. And his arms went out, You know . . . ? Yeah, she knew. And his smile coulda been the sun, even though he said it in half a whispa case one of the bruthas heard. Her smile wasn't so bad either. Not after he tole her that come t'morrow they were gonna have one huge fucken payday. Not after he tole her it might be in the thousands — cash.

SOME TIME THAT night *Glori*us, Mulla remembered Jimmy Bad Horse'd gotta group of prospec's together, summoned 'em to his mighty (reputed) presence and tole 'em the Browns were on their way and what they were gonna do was, like, extend their activities; Mulla and Gloria stoned off their faces but of course something in the being stoned having the opposite effect, like the water was cleared again, so he had recall that Jimmy's edict to these young fullas was, they should pick places that were good places to burgle, they should look around for good hold-up jobs, like banks an' that when Mulla Rota couldn't figure what else was a that. Which'd get 'em in the gang, patched up, like in their dreams that Mulla Rota in his heretic mind was beginning to think was a stupid dream, why didn't they come to him and aks what it was like spending mosta that dream life behind bars. Why di'n't they come to Mulla Rota so he could tellem (in private), Man, this ain't what you think it is, bein' a patched-up member. Whassa use of a gang patch if you gotta do five, six, maybe more years inside for it? An' tha's jus' each stretch. An' what if you kill (smoke, waste) someone? What then, kid, of your life?

But he c'd hardly tell 'em that, and anyrate he was stoned and so was Gloria. They danced to a Solo number, Heaven, what they'd laughed and thought about as they drove in the big gates tanight, a cruisy number, soul baby, it was soul they flowwwwed to, 6 with 9 dancing 8's on the (dirty) floor. Who loves ya, babe? Oh, Glor. Oh, Mulls. Then it was XXTRA the nex' Solo number and utha couples, and lone dudes, out on the floor, this world (of sounds) belongin' to them and they were both saving up their horniness till they couldn't stand it no longer; so Mulla and her went upstairs to fuck and make love, Jimmy's words to the pros's even less than half a echo as they walked down the passageway above and the sound below farther and farther away from, well, love. It mus' be love.

She said it herself and so did he. (I did. I said it.) He tole her: Glor, oh shit, Glor, I — Well, I, uh — Hon, I love you, too. It was like a starburst above the blanket-stink bed, no sheets, a score times his sperm stains and her wet juice stains'd added to the bed's history, on the wall a name scratched where uthas'd lain here, one was Nig H. Beside it a T. Mulla knew the H stood for Heke. And he knew who it was Nig'd shared this bed with, the T for Tania. As he knew who it was sent poor Nig — man, he was shaking so hard he rattled — to his death. Oh look! the stars are all out tanight, hon, she snuggled up to chest, his arms feeling so protective, so with wanting that went beyond this room these walls this converted two houses, beyond even those stars out there if it is man who gives the stars their meaning an' not the utha way round. For the firs' time in his dreadful life Mulla Rota wanted to give his entire soul to someone, and it weren't jus' her, Gloria Jones (Mrs Rota) beside him looking out the curtainless window at the stars, it was her kids, Turi an' Narissa (whadda nice name that is): Mulla Rota wanted to give himself to the whole unit of 'em. Why he was smarting with tears inis eyes, trying to keep them from rolling down his tattooed face, his endured electric-needle marks meant to signify he wassa tough cunt.

FIFTEEN

OH, JAKEY, SHE'D said. But you still the man, honey. You still love the best. 'Cept he'd thought if tha's the case then how come she don't, you know. Not that I love her or want her to love me. But shit, a man — a man needs a boost now and then (even me).

He went, Tha' right? I'm still a good lover? Her round-faced smile up atim, he'd only jus' rolled off her (done it good, even if I say so myself), her moaning still in his ear, twice she'd come. Still, Jake Heke, she said it again. But he finding himself sorta poised, or tensed, for her to say those words: The Muss. But then he c'd hardly ask her straight out why she didn't, even though she always did, but always. Or after they'd made love she did. Why, sometimes it even came with a joke referring to that muscle (muss) down there, how good it'd performed. Anyrate, it next occurred that he wasn't exactly hanging out to hear that ole familiar (reassuring) term. (Cos I ain't. Not now. Muss be the activities you been gettin' up to, Jakey boy.) Grinning to himself.

Lying on her big wide bed (like her spread thighs of woman giving out a baby or her body to a man as if she knows he's a baby, too) with sheets, yellow ones, smell like perfume and soap mixed together, kinda nice, curtains hanging heavy (from the weight of all them flowers!), a wall of detailed depiction Jake now and then sniffed the air case he could, you know, like smell 'em, you never knew with these whitemen makers (and breakers) of things (and men) they mighta put sumpthin' in the material to make it smell like it looked: fucken beautiful, tell the truth. A wall of different coloured flowers across the windows, and on the drawers thing there a vase which he always looked at for the real flowers it held, this time a spray like a — like a — well it reminded a man of a lion's mane which wasn't right, not for flowers, the proud way they rose up larger than the shoulders (vase) — no, forget the lion's head, tha's jussa firs' try, make it like one a them peacocks, a burst 'f colour, a — hahaha (pea)cock display — promising himself yet again he was gonna fill his li'l vase, just the once, jus' to say he'd done it.

On his bus recently he'd got the shock of his life to see a famous fulla, John Kirwan, the All Black, holding a buncha flowers and words underneath telling (a man) the bus sitters, Say It With Flowers, sumpthin' like that. Fact it'd tole a man a bit more than jus' that, 'cept he wouldn't let it get quite through.

Come to think of it this was a nice house, nicest he'd even been in; he'd never taken any notice before (I only came here to fuck Rita, hahaha!), she musta been married to a rich fulla; Jake knew the ex was a white (a honky shet) and that she'd given him the boot, which was a never-failing reminder every time of his own former marital situation of Beth giving him (me) the boot. 'Cept he didn't leave her with no flash house, jus' kids including a dead one shortly followed by anutha dead one (jeez). Now look where she was. Then he thought: Now look where I am. Same thing. So he got up on his elbows and powerful arms and tole Rita, You got a nice house, Ri. Why thank you, Jake The Muss — oh, she looked pretty when she smiled like that — as he touched her lifted right eyebrow cocked at him. Made him want to — to make love to her again. (Make love? Ooo, now Jakey boy, aren't you becoming the one!) Inside laughing at himself his softer thoughts. Told himself it was cos it was the second time so a man was with a different drive, another kind of energy from the first (which is, face it, man, all pumping muscle and the cock is the main muscle (muss, hahahaha!) an' tha's the truth).

Not that he had any similar type of house to compare it with, not one. His whole lifetime's experience had been a singular standard of low. Low low. So how did he know this was a nice house? he asked himself. Rita, would you say this house is . . . He wasn't quite sure how to out it, but he pushed on. You know, is it a nice place to — (I know): Your honky-ex think it was alright?

She gave a slightly colder smile, told him, Don't call him that. We're still friends you know. (Friends?) I thought you gave him the boot? He was getting confused, when all he'd tried to ask was a simple question: was this a good house by most standards or fucken not? I did ask him to leave. You know why? No, he didn't, as it happens. (I never asked.) He was unfaithful to me. Which had Jake blurt out in chortling laughter and she asked him why the laugh — mate? That last word in the tone of a man saying — bud. Unfaithful? he shook his head down ater. That's right, what I said, Jake The Muss: unfaithful. He shook his head more vigorously: Well you ain't Two Lakes' most . . . you know. Then her hand came up, against his bare chest pushing him away. Told him, When I was married I was. (Oh.) Oh. Yeah, you should be saying oh. And sorry with it.

He tried to laugh it off, her change of attitude but she rolled him right off her. And told him: Know why I play the field now as it suits? Because I promised myself I'd never let another man hurt me.

She didn't say it, but he could see in her face like he was hurting her now, though he still wasn't quite sure why. Hurting her, anyone for that madda, was the last thing he wanted. ('Nless they out to hurt me firs'. Then I'll waste 'em.) Hey, he grabbed her — admittedly a little too hard, why she pulled away from him quite violently and looked atim like those sixteen years ole familiar eyes of Beth's — Mister, please don't grab me like that again. (Fuck!) This was turning from being Two Lakes' best lover to the country's biggest arsehole. Ri, I'm sorry. Okay? Jake is sorry. (Goddamit) but she shook her head. Don't say to me Jake's sorry. Why not? Thought tha's what you wanted me to say. Why not? Because it removes yourself from responsibility, if you can spell the word, she near spat those words atim she did.

He took a moment to figure it. Alright: I'm sorry. Ri, please, come and lie down again. Shit, I only wanted to know if this house was, you know, by the standards a — a — (Fuckit). Oh, fuckit. Can't a man ask a simple question w'out you jumpin' onim? And he got up. So they were both standing, naked, on opposite sides of the bed. Glaring. Well, he was, then she was, then he wasn't, but he was about to turn and get dressed and fuck off outta here, fuck this, fuck women, fuck the world, fuck wanting to know how good this house is — Next time, Jakey baby, we're doing it at your house. She smiled all ovah him. All fucken ovah.

He said, Wha'? Which in the ole days woulda meant, what'd you say, followed by the business. Fists. But here in this softly lit, lampshaded room — a kinda pale red-wine colour they were, not that Jake made that comparison, he made it with blood — a woman iner mid-forties, three grown-up children left of their mark in zigzag stripes around her lower belly, a bit of a pot there, but the whole picture held together pretty tight, the tits nice an' big an' still firm, a stripe of pubes't ran like a dark, promising tongue from up underneath her where it counted, a picture on the wall behind her of colour splashes in that modern style a man couldn't be expected to unnerstan', in here in her bedroom he meant only to express simple surprise. And now his head running with making sure he'd have the place spick and span and maybe, jus' maybe, he'd get Cody to buy some flowers for that vase sitting like a unwanted, unloved mother without her only purpose in life.

Her real tongue came out and licked the top lip. Where he'd a li'l while back had his mouth planted, but there had been more gentle moments of just lingering butterfly kiss, or whatever they called it in the books a man never read. You heard, she told him. Your place, to say it again, Jake Heke.

He found a smile back. My place, eh? Yes, your place. How many times I gotta say it? (A few more'n that, lady, if you're to reassure me.) I got no sheets. That took her back a step. She lifted a finger atim, Jake Heke, you'd better have some when I get there or . . . (Or what? She won't come see me? Is that what I want?) Asking himself was he really trying to discourage her and if so, why? (Cos I'm afraid, the voice jumped out at him before he could ready himself against hearing it. And it kept going. Cos I'm frightened of getting close to someone. I'm frightened of —) Fuckit. He got back on top of the inner voice, or enough to move this on without turning it back to the hopeless point it was at.

I don't get much pay. Really? She cocked the eyebrow with a different gun. Then you'd better ask your boss for some overtime and a raise while you're at it. Now that was a thought. But he got pictures of his rented-from-the-State place compared to this and started shaking his head. And thinking if he got his clothes on he could fight this a bit better. But then she was nude, too. I got that young fulla Cody, and mosta the time his mates, staying. Really? The fucken eyebrow again. A man felt like ducking just in case it fired bullets. (Hahaha.) He lifted his proudly muscled chest and not too much protrusion of stomach down there for forty-two, told her, I got rugby on Sat'days now. His first game yet to come. And: I tole you 'bout the pig hunting yet?

She shook her head. No. No, you haven't told me much of yourself, about anything you do or think. Why I'm giving you the opportunity, Jake, in the comfort of your own surrounds. He exploded in laughter then. What surrounds is this, lady? But she only smiled from her repertoire of them, The surrounds I expect you'll be making for my visit, Jake . . . (Jake the what?) You might like to buy pale blue sheets, they'd suit you. Ya think so? He shifted his naked weight from one foot to the other, somehow she'd got on top of him without any effort. Yeah, I think so.

He looked at her yellow sheets, at her, back at the sheets. She inclined her head, jus' the once, in a nod. And lay oner back like she was giving birth to him, that's what it felt like.

SIXTEEN

MICHAEL JACKSON CAME struttin' toward her from the screen, all skinny existence of weirdly wonderful dancing blackness, an ebony creation she was imitating — and well, too — of his every step and snapped arm and torso and legs and (hehe) balls-holding poise, I'm *bad!* I'm bad! he was telling the world whoever had a video player and the price of a hire. And she telling her world, her bedroom and those bitch pack of girls who'd beaten her up for the last time now Hu had stepped in and so had her mother and so had Charlie — but all without violence, though Mum'd got close to threatening it in her protective way of her kids. And when the chorus and Michael asked the question, Who's bad? Polly Heke danced as she shouted back, *They're bad!* meaning those girls. And she danced on, knowing in a most self-breathless way that she was good, at dancing she was, if not Michael Jackson then one of his support dancers (I could do it, I know I could.)

She flung onto the bed, quite drained, at the end of the video experience and her mirror of it; and rather in one of her strange moods, where anything went of her thoughts. Her daring mood, of wanting to take that extra step outside of normal life for no other reason than instinct told her there might be answers there

— Oh, and for excitement, too. So she got up, turned the video off with averted eyes in case she wanted to dance to Michael's next number which was already well on, and dressed for the cold outside.

IT WAS NOT only boring but getting embarrassing walking past his house, trying different acts to make herself look legitimate, like looking at her watch as she strode, one eye for the house, that window there with the vase sitting in it, empty, surprised to see a flower vase, but it was there and so was he and so was his female company, just sitting on couches opposite each other talking, the occasional — but only that — lifting of a beer glass by him and, by the glass, wine in her hand. White wine. She, the bitch (she must be a bitch if she's with him), must've brought her own wine glass then, Polly figured. In fact, it was likely she brought her own wine because he sure as hell wouldn't've thought of buying it. Boring, embarrassing, but at least it was night and cold enough to keep any smartarse sniffy-noses away from asking her what she was doing, and taking two trips to the shops and buying an iceblock (in this cold?!) first time, which she took one bite of and threw away, a packet of chewing gum the second and ignoring the suspicious look from the shopkeeper no doubt thinking she was casing his grotty little shop for some lifting, the gum chewing making her look tough should anyone want to approach her, meaning homies; taking a standing position that gave her a direct line look at that curtainless window and the two figures sitting on blanket-draped couches, so he must've thrown them over the tatty things from the last time she did this, spying on her father. Fancy him even thinking to do that; cover up his old couches with blankets which made them look not only obvious but worse in appearance since one was grey and he must think that patterned one looks classy!

Half an hour, maybe more — she'd left her watch at home in case she got accosted and it was taken off her by bullies, since this area was just one step up from Pine Block and about one, maybe two, down from where she lived — she'd hung around. (Don't ask me why.) He'd got up a few times, come back with a can of beer and, surprise-surprise, to fill the lady's glass, though once she'd waved him away. So clearly she wasn't a pisshead like he was, even if on this occasion he seemed to be on his best behaviour (the deceiving bastard. Can't she see through him?) The house behind her standing position was, thank God, without lights on so she had some leeway.

There he goes again, saw him get up, disappear, come back (whooo, he's big alright) trying to deny to herself that he was a rather handsome man even for an incestuous rapist.

Then she saw him put his arms out to the woman, herself rather pretty if a little plump, helping her up off the couch. And then they danced. Oh how (he) they danced. And she knew good dancing when she saw it. Her mother'd always said, and in that voice she gets for the bastard despite what he's done: Oo, your father could dance. Ball bearings under his feet. Which she'd changed from saying it was air.

He moved that plumpish woman around the room in one continuous flow, twirling the bitch, easing her teasingly from him, pulling her back again. A master in charge. But the woman holding her own. (Spose he'll whack her one if she steps on his toes.) Though it was far from that likely happening as it was that she could just stand here trespassing with her eyes without someone asking what the hell she thought she was doing. Another minute, she'd give it another minute.

But dammit, the tears just wouldn't hold back, so she took one last look and walked off down the street, cursing herself for being an emotional girl, a spying girl, a strange girl, an always wondering girl, even in knowing she was going another night to spy on other people, she just couldn't help herself; as if something (or someone) was driving her.

SHE TOLE HIM, You can have me ya want. Which made his heart jump but with fear, which she picked — smiling reassuringly atim. He gave awkward smile back.

Ape? Ya worried 'bout Ape? I wouldn't say nothin'. But that wasn't it anyway, not for Abe. It was her eyes: looking into 'em was like looking at two bits of glue — no, not glue, more gobs of spit, infected spit what you cough up when you're sick. That's what the whites looked like. The browns had this sheen across them, like a veil. And he'd already looked harder on utha occasions to know that beyond those veils — two quite separate ones, as if what'd happened took place at different times — was grief beyond anything even he, inside forever crying for his bro Nig and his li'l self-taken sis Grace, had known. Beyond even his every moment aching to get revenge against Jimmy Bad Horse for setting his bro up. Sure, he was hearing her sad-eyed, sexless offer of sex with fear of her man, Apeman. But then again he weren't so in awe of even Ape that he would exactly tremble in his boots if Ape up and got jealous (at my innocence) ovah Tania and steppedim out or jus' plain wastedim from behind, the side, front-on, or *tried* to wastedim, that is. Not as if a man was gonna be standing there taking it. And it did occur to Abe that if won then he'd be sergeant-at-arms. But he didn't know he wanted that responsibility, hard enough jus' knowing what the rules were around here, kind of amazing really for a buncha roughies, how complex and layered the li'l ways and rules and unnerstandings were to learn.

Nah, I'm cool, Tarns. You don't have to, you know (offer yourself when I don't even want you). But, like, wouldn't say no to a talk. Wondering why she'd out of the blue offered herself like that.

She dropped her shades back over from atop of her head, she looked bedda withem on, even though anutha layer of veil, anutha cover-up, shrugged her skinny li'l shoulders, Okay, suit yaself. Thought you might feel like some, uh, comp'ny. Which he did, any young man did. But not with her. (I'm waiting for my chance to grab me a white woman.) Abe thinking of the extra sexual purity of screwing with a white. Tarns, it ain't worth it. But — But, she cut him short. Alright, how about we go somewhere have that talk? What I really mean anyrate. And he could see she did.

Upstairs in one of the rooms would be compromising, so they settled for taking a third party out withem, Rambo The Dumbie, the deaf mute, so Apeman'd know there was no hanky-panky and Rambo wouldn't know what was being said. They made it a cigarette run to the local dairy, taking the bruthas' orders and their laughing requests to buy 'em some as they had no money. An' that was anutha thing: the word out that the fucken Brown Shits were making dough lef' right and centre selling dope, the Hawk boys in their (confoundment) lack of unnerstan'ing at the mystery of money, even illegally made money, the process of its making and never mind its accumulation into a capital fund since they, the unknowing, ignorant, untaught stupid fuckers, they thought money truly was solely for consuming. The money from the ram-raid that'd got Abe and Mookie their patches was, so the prez reported, near all (consumed) gone. On piss and dope buys when they shoulda been growing their own, some of the bedda heads thought to 'emselves, not paying out for it; the bedda heads even knew they were giving their gov'mint unemployment benefit money to the Brown Shits the roundabout way of it coming indirectly, through anutha outfit also putting their profit on afta buying it from the Shits. Might be that they had thirty and more benefits the stupid gov'mint were payin' the collective ofem, and that they ate together far cheaper than what it'd cost living alone or in small groups sharing a flat and tho there was a guaranteed surplus to spend on beer and dope, it was never enough to put out a Hawk's fire, douse his emotional flames, they had to do crimes or, bedda still, get the young prospec's to do it forem and the patched-up members to spend it (hahaha!) Forgetting when they'd been prospec's. Eighty-one thousand six-hundred and sumpthin' that ram-raid (man, it was excitin'!) had brung in, now all of it pissed and smoked up, though Abe and Mook didn't really give it a thought, where their entry money'd gone, only that it earned them their patches and an immediate much higher status, not as high as killing someone, but about the same as hurting badly an enemy — no, not that high. But the nex' tier down, yeah. They didn't think of the money being wasted so much as their chances of being arrested for it (who cares, eh Abe? Who-gives-a-fuck?) which so far hadn't even resulted in a sniff from the pigs. Confirming to the pair of the gang's near invulnerability to the law, even if that didn't add up to the numbas of Hawks doing time at any given, uh, time.

It was getting on dusk when they were walking back, an area jus' like the Pine Block Abe'd been formed in, or so he assumed: wrecks of cars sitting on front lawns, down on kerbside on wooden blocks going nowhere like the area's inhabitants, tagger-paint scrawls on the shop fronts, the sides of houses, anywhere they could apply a can of spray paint, life boiled right down to the basics, like the food cooking in near every big pot, boiled and boiled until it was a fat-flavoured, sweet-tas'ing mush of meat falling off the pork backbone, and spuds crumbling and cabbage or watercress boiled soft and mopped up with bread with plenty budda on. Rottweilers and bull-terriers and dobermanns at every second house with owners jus' as fierce and yet they could hear laughter, everywhere it broke out, spilled, emerged like haunting melodies of the theme every member knew of: we don't laugh we'll do murder. Rambo happy to be carrying the cupla dozen packets of cigarettes cos he'd get some smiles and warm touches from the boys when he handed 'em out and the change'd be his cos he didn't smoke an' nor did he do dope — the boys thought cos Rambo was afraid the smoke'd make him start talking which'd take away his unique status and who'd want that in this tough world — and nex' minute Tarns was suddenly talking like this was 'er las' walk . . .

. . . gabbling about kids growing up with fuck-up muthas and fathas, stabbing her black leather cut-off at the houses with their lights coming on, kids running around, even near at their feet asking were they really Black Hawks, made a man feel proud to be looked up to like that, but not Tarns, she kept stabbing that finger an' saying about parents not giving two fucken fucks about any cunt 'cept 'emselves. She was infected alright. And the dumbie, Rambo, silently padding along behind 'em like a muted puppy dog; 'n fact he was a stray the gang'd picked up jus' to use but, give 'em their credit, at times jus' as someone to love who couldn't give back, or not in words, what they secretly wanted which is why they found him a convenience to express 'emselves out on. Then she stopped Abe, grabbed him by the elbow. Listen. Felt the more meaningful that word at Rambo not being able to listen. Oh how he listened. So.

So he's walking back with his ears hearing the crackling of fire, as if one of those houses they were passing was set alight right in front ofem. He could hear the sounds of young voices — near unbearable it was. She'd tole him a story that explained everything, her skinniness, her haunted sunken features, her veiled eyes with all that backtale of weeping. She tole him she'd tole it to only two utha people and Apeman wasn't the utha. Abe's late bro Nig was one though; the third she did not mention. Her words spoken so softly yet like razor slices to his hearing; of looking after her kid bros, two ofem, and a li'l sis . . . their mutha away all fucken weekend, boozing . . .

Nuthin' ta eat — nuthin'! Then my bro Mark finds five bucks so we, you know, we've got a feed at leas'. At leas' we gonna get food in our bellies . . . So I'm off, tole 'em big sis won't be long, Tarns'll be back with some fish 'n' chips. Well. Well. Her li'l black-leather-clad breasts started heaving in the dying day and she wiped with the cut-offs, both ofem, ater eyes, an' a sigh hissed out'f her like she'd been punctured — again — and Rambo behind musta seen it and sensed it cos he was starting to make funny sounds like a dog whining. And all these kids running around the place, like li'l flowers drinking in the last of day, li'l potentials closer to the monsters they were gonna grow up to be, or at the very leas' uncoping fuck-ups (jus' ask Tarns here tellin the las' of her terrible, terrible story, or one awful chapter of it) all that life, and here was this female life finishing off to a man: Mark, my bro, musta foun' some matches, too . . . I came back an' the — an' the — (Jesus Christ! I can't stand to hear no more!) But he had to. Or else run off. Abe had to hear the last even though he knew what must be coming.

. . . Came back and it w'z — everything . . . everything w'z on fire . . .

HE DIDN'T THINK they'd've screamed, not at first, they'd've cried for their big sis, cried their confusion, only when the flames surrounded them like life had their sis, would they have screamed; he'd thought and thought about this; when most of that had died a bit in his head and they were standing their have-to-be distances in the gang bar, and he was knocking back beer cans like liquid dousing his own inner flames and Apeman there beside her cocking his eyebrow at Abe like the gun it was signifying — but even he had to go piss, even Superman's got to put those can afta cans of beer somewhere; she walked as though past Abe an' tole him, When you go a huntin' for Bad Horse, I'm coming. I truly liked your bro, I did. (I unnerstan', Tarns, it's your brothers you're trying to, you know, bring back, too. Plus the li'l sister, poor li'l fuckers — where was the fucken mother she could be gone so long, all fucken weekend, on this earth for herself, the fucken bitch.) He was a good kid, y' know? (They all are, sis. Or how they start out.) She paused jus' a second. Unnerstan'? And Abe he nodded, jus' the once, without once lookin' ater. Case he, you know.

SEVENTEEN

IF BETH LAY awake late thinking of her kids, the tragedies and miracles and more of each (I hope not and hope) to come, she didn't despair. Not when a mother'd lost her daughter the way she did, though it was that very event she most thought of even after six years.

That intended visit to see Boogie at the boys' home; the only way to get the family to him was in that rental car, all that saving she'd done, giving up drinking, watching every cent from the money Jake gave her, which was half of the unemployment benefit paid to a man with wife and six children — and he used to boast openly to his friends how generous he was to her, as if it was his own hard-earned money, as if his taking half of his entitled only one-eighth share was anything but selfishness — and, the first miracle, found she had actually saved her first hundred dollars towards hiring a car to go and see Boogie, real name Mark, in the Riverton Boys' Home about an hour and a half drive (and my Grace's life) distant.

Oh, how it had started off promising to be such a good day. Jake behind the wheel, surprising her that he had a driver's licence when he'd never owned a car, never even tried, the radio going, Jake as calm, even excited (child-like) as she and children'd ever seenim. A big, hours-prepared picnic feast in the boot of their late model rental, and Jake making the most of it by driving around half of Pine Block, arm out the window, waving to people, winking, laughing, making funny remarks to his family passengers; only sour note was when they spotted Nig (my poor boy Nig, he was my first born and, I have to admit, my favourite. Something about him, the love in the boy) standing outside the Brown Fist headquarters (tall and handsome like his father); Jake hated the Browns (hated half the world and himself most of all). But the moment passed without incident. Then they were out into Two Lakes proper, away from their slums, their line-ups of two-storey, ugly State dwellings, passing houses with neat, garden-scaped lawns, washing cars on driveways, nearly all ofem white but not then seeming to bother Jake, he was too happy just to be driving, being free in quite another way to his pub-going freedom, this was mobile freedom, it was the means to cover a considerable distance, see a wide spectrum of a life they suddenly saw they never knew. And he was with his family.

Was Grace suggested they go take a look at the posh part of town, Ainsbury Heights, and Jake who got all funny at that, suspicious that Grace should know of it let alone give him the directions. And when he got there? Well, his mood changed. At seeing big houses and driveways with two, three cars parked up them; at not understanding any of it. Not how or why or what the profound process was that excluded him and his lot (as if he cared about us lot); as if he was looking at people from Mars. She remembered that part like yesterday; seeing Jake's face, his mouth partly open as they sat parked up outside a posh place, shaking his head — the confoundment (Charlie's word). Like it was his very (precious) manhood suddenly held up to a totally different light and found completely wanting. She'd said, Jake, let's get out of here. Never wanted to live up here anyrate. But he'd snapped at her. So she, and children back to their tensed state in his presence, had to sit it out till somehow Jake found his way back in his mind, his (broken — it was anyway broken long before that) heart.

He made a joke about not wanting to live up in Ainsbury because of big lawns to mow. They drove out of the area. On their way to Riverton, or so they all thought including, to be fair, him. Beth couldn't remember who suggested they drive around the lake, it might've been Grace, it might've been Jake, it might have been her, it could have been Polly, but not Abe as he never said much unless it was about his idol, his big brother Nig. And Huata was too young. They stopped off at lakeside, the lake a calm mirror reflecting what lakes do of their surrounds and the unspoken knowing that they'd never even been down to the lake (nor done much else in even a small city world) but of Jake, too, his calmness. Then it was Riverton. No it wasn't, first they'd go right round the lake. Long's we get there by lunchtime, eh dear? Jake with his rare, best charming smile and since they were all enjoying 'emselves, why not?

She remembered seeing the pub sign and Jake licking his lips, her fear and knowing that he'd stop. Except he didn't. Drove straight past. So it was definitely going to turn out the day it promised (oh, Jakey!) She was so happy for all of them. Even if Grace was a little quiet in the back. They sang songs together, started by — could they believe? — him. Jake The Muss. The man whose own children always paused, just for a fraction, before they called him dad. The car a happy family chorus, even Grace's distinctly toned voice joining in, eventually she did. (And I remember the goosebumps, when he reached a hand for mine and squeezed it with the love he first used to give me — till the bastard discovered he got more out of hitting me. And still got the love afterward.) She remembered that gesture.

He wanted to show off the rental car to his mates. No, he wasn't going in, just parking outside McClutchy's pub, toot the horn at the boys, his mates, as they walked in for their all-afternoon Saturday drinking and betting on the horses. Beth'd done her share of Saturdays — and other days — drinking too. One drink, tha's all I ask, dear. That was all he asked. How could she refuse a man who'd behaved in such exemplary fashion — another word learning from Charlie Bennett. In retrospect. On that day. That memory.

Waiting and waiting. Hold on a minute, kids, I'll go get your father. The shock of seeing what she, when she was drinking before she gave it up especially for this trip, this visit to go and see Boogie (since I couldn't be at court when he got sent away, not with my face beaten up from Jake's fists the night before because I refused to cook his pal fried eggs with boiled food, in one of my moods of had enough of this fucken life) of what she must look like parked up in a bar at noon with a whole (sweet I thought) drinking day ahead to look forward to.

Many hours later, herself starting with just one drink, the picnic on their bar table being gobbled up by the company she'd joined with (my kids still waiting out in the car. Oh, I've got my share in the guilt, too). The lame, beery breathed excuses each time she went out to reassure them that dad (and now me) wouldn't be long. Finally, Grace walking off home in a fury that the visit wasn't going to take place (I remember seeing her, even in my drunken stupor, walking off across the pub carpark.) Waking up — being shaken awake by Jake — next day at the cops at the door. Going into town, the morgue . . . to identify her. Grace — (Ohhhh!) Ohh, it hurt every — every — time. There was no hurt worse. Not even when the next child was Nig, shot dead in the gang fight.

Grace had left this world with some of her mother with her. She hadn't figured, not for the life of her, why she'd done it on the Trambert property, and she'd got the courage up several months later to look him up in the phonebook, ring the man ask him had he known Grace. No, he'd not set eyes on her in his life nor had any clue as to why she ended her life, on our property, as he put it. Which for some reason struck home with Beth as meaning she didn't have a property, as if the divide was quite clear and required no further explanation. She still didn't have her own property, though Charlie insisted half his material ownership was hers, that's how good a man he was. Though she said wait and see if they ever got around to marrying, since she had filed divorce proceedings against Jake the day after Grace's letter and he did not contest the application, in fact they couldn't locate him to serve the papers on him so it was declared decree nisi. Why Grace chose the Trambert place was now in the grave with her as would the reason if Toot hadn't broken their agreement not to show the last letter she left.

It named her father — no it didn't: it said she thought her abuser was her father. But it seemed clear enough even if Beth had never seen any sign of that sort of secret desire in Jake. And a wife of sixteen years should know shouldn't she? Maybe she didn't. (Yet still I don't accept it, or part of me doesn't.)

So Beth was beyond the grasp of despair. But not thought. The second tragedy was Nig. The second miracle — the first being the discovery that even a denied, poor woman can save (I'll never forget that) — was Boogie, when he turned up with the man Beth now had sleeping beside her, Charlie Bennett, then a child welfare officer, now the general manager of the Two Lakes' division, and had sung that ancient Maori lament with Charlie alongside him directly to Grace in her open state coffin. Now, the next miracle — Charlie hurumphed that it wasn't a miracle it was as it should be — of Boogie in his second year at university, studying of all things, law. When that is what he'd fallen foul of in his troubled younger years.

Charlie was strong on his Maori culture and had converted Boogie to learning its ancient chants, the different (ferocious) haka from the days when the Maori was at war with himself, tribe against tribe (gang against gang?) and the legends, the lores, the whole deep process which Beth could see was the base of her de facto's existence. She herself took to learning more about her culture but now she was less interested and refused Charlie's one weak characteristic of insisting it would be good for her. She told him she'd decide what was good for her, that she had tried, rather enjoyed, but now no longer felt it was for her. She teased him about being like a door-knocking Christian trying to convert her to his beliefs, just to keep him in his place on that one area of somewhat blindness on his part.

It was Abe who now kept her awake with worry. No, it didn't consume her, after Grace nothing could be so bad but nothing. And Abe was a young man with his own mind even if a lot of it had been shaped by those earlier years of Jake. And, just like Jake, with headstrong — no, hellbent — notion in his head of getting revenge for Nig's death (as stubborn and set of mind as his father). She'd run into him in the main street, on her way as it happens to have a café lunch with Charlie, quite a regular thing for them to do and she comfortable with it now, driving down from the hospital where she worked in the laundry (alright, so you're no miracle of occupation, girl, but hey, am I complaining?) She knew he'd not like the approach, even from her his mother. So she just asked, Why? hardly pausing as she walked past him. Nig, he answered, without a blink of his shaded eyes his oh-so-cool posture in the company of his Hawk mates. It wasn't till she got down the street a way that she realised Abe had joined the gang whose jailed-for-life member had shot Nig dead (on this very street, my son's blood ran).

But it was all too much for her, trying to figure out the mysteries of gang rivalry and why each did what to the other and what made brothers join opposite gangs and fight each other. And she knew Abe was too much his fighting father's son to be able to persuade away from this course his life was on. It was giving without hesitating (not even a li'l smile for me, the rat) Nig's name that had her wondering, or realising, that Abe had truly loved his oldest brother. Though joining the other side was a mystery. At the funeral Abe held back his grief. In the months, which became the years, afterward, he was grieving. And, with it, developing that deep down sullen brooding that no one does better — worse, rather — than a Maori. Ask any Maori is what she said to Charlie who tried to give her his theories that all races are the same. (Though he was one, if a very different one.) On certain things Beth — still a Heke and don't ask me why — begged to differ.

Another time she was driving down town when she spotted a familiar face even though it wore sunglasses, them wraparound things the gangies wear as if the rest of us don't know what a cop-out cover-up they are (poor frightened li'l and large things) which nagged and nagged at her until she got it. Good grief. It was that gang girl. And she was in the arch rival Hawk colours same as Abe!

At Nig's funeral the girl had come up and hugged Beth. She figured the girl was trying to say she was closer than just a gang member friend of her son's. But she didn't say and nor did Beth ask. She had a mind for making Nig's last farewell with all the dignity she could muster, and much supported by damn near half the Pine Block community come out to share her and family's grief. Mavis (oh, May. You had so much, girl) had led the singing, and it and the massed neighbourhood voices answered back, it did take much of a mother's grieving load, it did. Mavis did. Best voice in Two Lakes was — is — Mavis. 'Cept not much point if you're a drunk. Not much point in your flower blossoming in seedy bars, girl.

Jake wasn't at his son's funeral, just as he wasn't at Grace's. Now, with years and a good man's guidance and much talk, she realised Jake's problem was to do with his self-esteem. Remembering on that same ill-fated failed visit to see Boogie his revealing how he'd been raised on tales of his family being direct descendants of slaves, in the old days when Maoris practised slavery, and she'd found out since that to be a slave was the ultimate in shame since it was usually a captured warrior who preferred dishonourable life to honourable death. Growing up, Jake and his siblings had been mercilessly teased for their status. What else could he have grown up into? (Not that I forgive him. Not for that, even if I've always had my doubts, even after a thousand times and more of reading that letter Grace gave to Toot. Nor can I forgive myself, I ended up with Jake in the bar, too. It was my idea to take the picnic lunch meant for my family into that bar, those animals who just consumed it on the spot. Beth, you're guilty, too.)

She saw him now and again. Usually sitting at a bus-stop and, over the years, different ones which she figured out must mean his job had him on the move. Then she saw him working on a road gang (with his shirt off, what else, on a not very hot day) surprised at the involuntary thrill at sight of his powerfully muscular body (after all these years, and what those same muscles have done to me?) Yes. After all these years, six now, still had animal appeal despite the violence. Even Charlie, anti-violence Charlie, said that Jake didn't really know any better, not with growing up with violence as his only behavioural role model, as Charlie in his welfare officer way put it. Though where did that leave the victim? was her reply. Which Charlie had no real answer to except to agree that the buck has to stop somewhere. Funny, seeing a big, formerly fiercely proud man like Jake standing at a bus-stop had him looking less a loser than when he was the Jake The Muss of old. Sure, it didn't exactly become him, his physical stature, that covering-up head lifted in exaggeration, or otherwise his eyes were down like a child's, of can't see you, you can't see me. She even thought of pulling over in her car and asking if he wanted a lift. But he'd take it the wrong way, sure to. Or he'd think she wanted him back when she didn't. (I don't. I don't.)

So Jake was working for a roading contractor, which explained the different bus-stops she spotted him at in the evenings after work. Wondered if he had another woman; he didn't have that look that he did. Did he visit the kids' graves? Probably not. Did he think about what he'd done? A thousand questions she could have asked him but what was the point? It was past now. And no, she wasn't pining for him. Happy who she was with, even if he was no lover boy *par excellence*. No complaint about the foreplay, it was the act itself (comes too quick) leaves a woman hanging. Charlie rather formal, almost prudish, about sex.

Whereas she (well, I — I was born with a, uh, shall we say healthy — hehehe — appetite. Why Jake and I lasted so long together. We were good together, at that we were.) Oh, and they danced as well as sang together well, too. But as for talk, forget it.

Charlie was intelligent, made a woman realise she wasn't so thick herself — why, he'd even changed the way she spoke, she could hear the changes herself — he was considerate, he loved her children as though his own and they, the three remaining, loved him. (He gave me life like I had only that once got a glimpse at when we drove around town and up to Ainsbury Heights. Not that we're Ainsburians, but we ain't Pine Blockers either, not now by a long shot.) And if she could perform one big miracle with her troubled Maori people then opening up their eyes to life's possibilities, its challenges, goals, pleasures, even variety of recreation, that is what (and all) she would give.

But then that was unrealistic, she knew from bitter experience. Of her friend the chief of her sub-tribe, Te Tupaea, who had come amongst the Pine Block like a Maori Jesus, preaching at them, but for them; for their failed pride and self-dignity gone into a beer bottle is how he put it, teaching them chants and hakas and getting them motivated so they built their own community hall, but now in disuse with the graffiti taggers covering every square inch of outside wall with their markings; the lesson of, in Charlie's words, not being able to take the ghetto out of the ghetto dweller's thinking. Then the chief died suddenly and soon it all just fell apart, Beth's total involvement in trying to make Pine Block a better community was useless without enough community support. And when Mavis Tatana, her best friend, succumbed, nabbed by her upbringing, a woman fallen from her pedestal, teaching the youngsters how to sing. It was then Beth started opening her eyes to what had been going on around her but she was denying: that these people, with a handful of exceptions, were never but never going to change.

At the same time she saw the light in Charlie Bennett's eyes as meaning what she thought it did, even if the physical side turned out to be a disappointment. (So what?) A person's sexual lovelife takes up but an hour or two a week. He more than made up for it.

So life now was unrecognisably better and more interesting. But a mother who has lost two of her children, she never fully recovers. Never. And now, she knew it, she was inwardly preparing for another of her children to become tragedy, all her instincts were screaming this. Which is why this night she got quietly out of bed and took herself into Polly's room: Move over, sweetheart. (Your Mum's here.)

EIGHTEEN

MORE LLOYDS INSURANCE loss demands in the post. Another chunk of land being carved off for the housing developers. A wife who'd stopped sleeping with him (just goes to show her regard for money, her desire to continue quite unrealistically in the circumstances, our lifestyle). Gordon Trambert especially bitter, perhaps getting his wife's reasons wrong, on that one. The ignominy of pulling Alistair out of his last year of private school when one could simply not pay the fees; as well the resentment that for all the money spent on the boy's education he remained the same person: lacking in confidence, overly sensitive, easily irritated and quite frankly a bloody self-pitying, inward-looking lump. For lump he was, this misshapen happenstance of the worst of each parent's genes, his father's shapeless legs (and yet I could run like the wind in school cross-country), his mother's narrow shoulders for the size of his half-Trambert, half-Heatherington head with an exaggerated hooked nose of his mother's slightly so — face it, the boy was little different to a sheep any farmer would have culled from his flock, rid from his breeding lines. (Yet he is my son and I have a duty to make his life the very best I can.) Gordon Trambert had to fight with himself over the issue of his son since the boy might, he did concede in his gin-affected moments, reflect the true failure he, his father, was. Gordon could hear his own father warning of that, of no young person to be considered a failure until he had, well into adulthood, demonstrably failed. It is adults who fail, Henry Trambert would have said. Adults who fail their children.

He was awaiting word — with an accompanying usual huge lawyer's bill — on the outcome of his letter to his Lloyds agent instructing not to put his cover in any mass employee health claim, he had even (reason for hope) specified in writing that under no circumstances was his risk to include any potential asbestosis claim. Word from other Names had it that the letter might just be his out from this never-ending nightmare. And on that ray of hope one had not sat around idly, hell no; Gordon Trambert was looking at a franchise business selling, of all things, barbecued chicken.

The figures sent out by the franchiser looked most attractive, another carve-off of land would pay for it (and that would be about it as far as remaining equity in the farm proper went. God, how quickly even inherited equity goes if one makes mistakes). It was a matter of getting used to the idea that he might, effectively, be in an apron dealing with the kind of public his life had only ever touched on at Saturday rugby games as a fanatical spectator of the game and its better players. But never closer than that. He was more worried about telling Isobel that this was almost certainly his next plan, dream — God forbid, selling pieces of barbecued chicken — him! Of telling her yet again of another sure-fire escape from these financial woes — selling fried chicken, albeit! — and expecting her to accept the subsequent (much) lowered social status. Isobel was big — though she denied it like she denied she was big on having money — on social status. It was she who had insisted they buy the Range Rover back in — when was it — 1989, when they were hardly over the new Labour Government's axing of supplementary minimum payments to the nation's farmers as a (government bribe) subsidy on their livestock. But wasn't owning a five-year-old Range Rover a sign to the very people she thought it would impress that they weren't doing at all well? But no, she'd rather have that than a cheaper late model Jap car which wouldn't give the show away. And, what the hell, from his end, being a four-wheel drive, it was a tax deductible farm vehicle even when it wasn't. (Can't be scratching the paintwork now, old boy.)

Every evening of late he played his Russian choral music with a gin and tonic twice the normal strength, thinking of Lloyds losses, the Black Hole making all the other routine monthly accounts each seem an added nightmare, thinking about the loss of the family land inheritance bit by inexorable bit, of letting the side down but yet never giving up hope — (never!) Nor a night going by (they had got worse) without thoughts of — well, of one almost forcing his wife to have not just sex again but, while he was at it, in charge once and for all, jazzed up sex, kinky stuff (without going overboard) without the leather and whips but plenty of exotically fragrant body oils and, ah, perhaps some experimentation. (Actually, just ordinary sex would do, you inexplicable woman whose body was once at one with mine, for years we enjoyed each other as if there was no tomorrow.) And now the shop was shut, he stared his nights away into the fire, getting quietly sloshed to the company of rather sombre Russian choral music, while Isobel retired to their bedroom earlier and earlier, hardly talking when she was downstairs, leaving a man another night alone to contemplate life as a seller of barbecued chicken and accompanying pottles of peas and mashed spuds (for God's sake).

SHE DID LIKE that song he played over and over again at this time of night. 'Lord, Now Lettest Thou Thy Servant Depart In Peace' sung by Nicolai Gedda. Sitting down there staring into the fire, his head swimming in gin, debts, financial failure and he, as she imagined, bobbing along singing desperately (or sadly) but, give him his dues, sometimes with magnificent fightback, except his fightbacks never worked, they always had flaws in them, the new grand plan, the latest financial blueprint. Listening to him hum-wording along with that song since it was in Russian so his words just in-tune noises. But very much in tune (unlike he is with business life. I'm afraid he just doesn't get it, how it all works.) Though she was quite sure this composition's inspiration was not taken from financial failure. Not last century Russia when most of the far-flung populace must have lived lives of basic survival, not having the indulgence of infinite choice of monetary adventure — or disaster. Nor one thing of this supposed to be better times, better lives, continued upward social mobility as they called it. But then again, everything is relative.

She wondered what Alistair thought of his father's music. Poor Alistair: born under a bad sign. A genetic mistake. In his bedroom most of the time like a self-imposed prison sentence playing that dreadful punk rock music or worse, the headbanger cacophony. He might even have mental problems. Thank God Charlotte was out of this. Though a mother did worry about her daughter living in another city going to university — with another new boyfriend so she proclaimed! with exclamation marks in her last letter home — if she was all right, if her life was not going to be one too troubled or fraught with major event. Naturally, a mother worried about her children, if they lived in the Caribbean with millionaires she still would. (I'd worry that she did something socially that would give her away as not of the rich set. Hahaha.) Mrs Isobel Trambert could still laugh at herself.

The times when Alistair was exploding at nothing and everything, and Gordon was floundering in his loaded gins and hardly any tonic and pile of bills with that Russian choral music still going, it made her smile at the irony: of it all seeming like another secretly dysfunctional (upper — we're both third-generation) middle-class family. Like a month ago when Charlotte was back on term break and expecting her father would find her paid work on the farm, and when he explained that things weren't so good financially she'd got all morose about that, spent the two weeks moping around the house, sleeping late, looking dowdy instead of the beautiful nineteen year old every young man wanted, you'd think the money losses were all down to her. Which is what a mother told her: Anyone would think it was you who had signed on as a Lloyds Name. Though Charlotte's biting counter was, her father's problems were only compounded by the Lloyds thing not the cause. And, anyway, where did that leave her, in need of money to continue the university year — I shall give you some — no, loan you — of my own, Isobel had had quite enough of this what-about-me when Charls was only here for term breaks, she didn't have to live with it, feel her physical desire for the man she loved, had two children by (and would have been more if Gordon had wanted that), that physical desire slowly die on her; Charlotte didn't have to live with a man she was losing respect for, which is what was putting paid to the love life when it had always been, well, rather good to say the least.

But what Gordon didn't know was, his wife took her eyes out their bedroom window at those rows of two-storey houses, at the closer single-storey hideosities of new, working-class subdivision, for her reminder that life wasn't so bad and that upper-middle-class dysfunctional was those people's impossible dream just going through a hiccup. What Gordon didn't know of his wife was, she appreciated what life had given her and her family, had learnt her lesson from that terrible morning of the girl hanging herself on the oak Gordon's maternal grandmother had planted at the turn of the century (something symbolic in that which I can't put my finger on).

When Gordon informed me, I was in the bathroom. I heard the quaver in his voice and thought it might be Alistair. I have long expected my son to take, or attempt since there is a distinct difference, his own life. The boy was born miserable. I saw Gordon might go to pieces or at least show a lesser side that I should not wish children or self to see. So I took over, but in that quiet way, as my own mother had taught me of this world seemingly ruled by men. Let them make the money, and let us control the life around it. One of Gordon's problems: he never let me take control of it so we could have the best of both worlds, the money and our held-together lives. We didn't have to make fortunes, just build as best we could on the small one of both our inheritances.

It was Alistair I was worried about. Though naturally my mind was in turmoil that a stranger — or at least we presumed she was; Gordon had said a Maori girl and as we, well, didn't know any Maoris other than Gordon's former employee Harry whatshisname — was hung on our tree. Both of us knew that if Alistair was denied this witness he'd dump it on us forever and a day as our indication of lack of faith in his strength. And if we allowed him the sight he'd blame us for traumatising him, or something ridiculous. So I told him straight, the choice is yours. And in that way that even I, his normally attentive mother, had no time for the smaller event of Alistair troubled Trambert. Not when outside on our back lawn was a girl who had hung herself. And outside we went. But Alistair stayed inside.

It was an aptly miserable, grey day. There can be no sight more shocking than seeing someone hanging, from a length of rope, from a tree. I felt my legs threaten to buckle underneath me. I felt, though, a terrible anger that this child had been no longer able to endure life's circumstances; and as I walked — stoically — forward I asked myself what could a teenage girl go through that would make her do such a thing. The first thought to mind was sexual abuse. The next was an ended love affair. And, yes, it did cross my mind even then that there might be an illicit connection between the girl and my husband. He had long hinted, even when our sex life had been long satisfactory, that he wished for more. Well what more can a couple do than we do — or did? Whips, chains and leather? Wife swapping parties? Good grief. Half his trouble: he's never quite satisfied.

Her face was a deep ruddy colour. The eyes protruding. (God, they were grotesque.) I observed this with a necessary super-objective steel in me; I figured the deep red was from the blood constricted in the head when she had, um, jumped. From the branch. Bough rather, since it was sturdy and thick with its age, nearly a hundred years and now (God help us all) hanging with the ended life of a girl no older than, what, fifteen. But I did have to regather myself, as well give but again necessarily objective glance at Charlotte, who was open-mouthed, naturally so but still somewhat of a surprise as she was born with a certain hardness. My husband had a hand pressed hard against his forehead, but he was not going to lose control.

The tongue was clenched between the teeth, that was the worst part; for it symbolised most of all how her voice had not been listened to, her cries for help not heeded. That final physical characteristic of death, of tongue and therefore voice, means to communicate, caught between her own teeth summed it up for me. Later that day, alone, I sat down and played several times over a hymn from Gordon's Russian Orthodox Choir, by a woman lead, 'Bless The Lord, O My Soul'. Her voice seemed to be on behalf of the hung child, it was asking, beseeching but in a controlled way. And at least it had an answering chorus back, as well an assumed listening God for the times when no one else is listening. So who hadn't listened to this poor Maori girl?

Rigor mortis, I knew from high school remembered learning, had come and gone. Her body was limp, not rigid as it must have been for the five or six hours it stiffens the body until the acids in the muscles are released, and with that the posture. I was glad for that. I feared it might be cold enough for the body to be sufficiently brittle, or at least less malleable, had rigor mortis been, to possibly snap a limb in taking her down. (Which we would of course leave to the police, this gruesome task.) The skin colour on her arms and legs was blotchy. We were glad there was not a breath of wind to move the body, I think it would have been a kind of last indignity for enough suffering, enough indignities, to be at the mercy of air she had deprived herself of.

We'd had a group of friends over that night for dinner, I had ordered in Italian from my favourite pasta shop to save myself the bother, and it went down very well. We are not wine buffs but Gordon had got a few special bottles from a wine shop as just an end of winter cheer thing. We were all right financially then. The evening had become quite merry by our normal rather quiet standards. I had enjoyed myself. Particularly the Edwards, Pete and Jenny, third-generation farmers like ourselves. Thoroughly pleasant, no side on, both with those innocent, cow-like eyes as though in exaggerated confirmation that spouses tend to reflect each other; and disarmingly frank about matters our circle would usually keep private. Like their second daughter's schizophrenia. Jenny even talked quite openly of having difficulty having an orgasm. (That I should have such a problem!) And Pete was all attentive ears for any advice on this most serious matter, but clearly not affecting their marriage or they'd have said so. They were just the type who had guileless curiosity and question, as curiosity and question ought to be.

Gordon had too much to drink that night, and so when we got to bed, well, the performance and the promise were rather far apart. The thought that this — this child should be taking her own life when one had a sexually lifeless husband, giggling and pretending he was up to the task, all over me was awful.

Her bowels had emptied, the neck was a little elongated, I took in these details on instinct, knowing that if I faced it all in its gruesome reality I'd be able in turn to take my children, my husband if necessary, through it. I also felt terribly guilty at my own existence, for I could see the clothes, how shabby and out of date they were. And I knew without needing to be later told by the police that she had come from the State house area from where we had often heard the singing from what we thought were happy parties. I knew from my golf-club cronies, those with nursing backgrounds, and teachers, that the parties were generally anything but happy affairs. For it was nurses who saw the victims of violence, saw the drunken car-crash bodies, the stabbing victims, the aftermath (to my astonishment, I hadn't even given these things a thought) of bar fights, party brawls, sexual abuse — the lot. And it was teachers amongst my friends who saw the children who came to school hungry with failure written all over them. No books, no loving parents to read to them, no structured lives with set goals along the child's way — Oh, I had my eyes opened all right. I found I had been living in this town of which I thought I played a fairly varied role, that I knew nothing but nothing of the lives the, uh, well the underclass lived. I knew nothing when I had assumed I was rather well-informed on life.

And now that I knew better all I had done about it — and intended to do, since I had given it deep thought — is look to my lucky stars that I was not to their manor(less) born. Since one could hardly cease being what she was born and raised as and become one of them. And nor was it likely many of them would have risen, or become, what we were. My mother, though frail, was still wise and sharp enough to tell me, if sadly, that everyone has to fight their own struggles on this earth.

I also dug around for information amongst my golfing friends, the women in my pottery class, the book club, of shop assistants; anyone anywhere and everywhere I'd find myself hinting on the subject of troubled teenagers, and then if I got a nibble I'd move it to casual reference to the Heke girl, in case I struck someone who knew her or knew of her. Finally I struck one who did, or she knew of the family as she lived in the same area, Pine Block — what a dreadful name. So hard and definite. Like A or B Block in a prison. Not that I know anyone who's been in one — and so I found out that it was the father who had raped the poor child. That poor poor suffering kid.

But in my enquiries as to how long the father got sentenced to prison, it came up at the book club; Mabel Peters the retired nurse matron knew a bit more about it, she said that the police had not in fact charged the father because the semen evidence did not match the sample given by the father. And yes, a picture of a man having to masturbate to prove his innocence did very much cross one's mind. Though Mabel said that that didn't prove the man innocent except on the night in question. Which I thought was rather harshly judging and unfair of her but then typical of Mabel. She had married a traffic cop, after all. With a moustache, as we knowing friends used to giggle amongst us.

I did not attend the poor girl's funeral since it was not my upbringing to go to the funerals of strangers even in these circumstances; I'd have felt exceedingly uncomfortable and quite out of my place. And what would I have said to the mother — that I was sorry? That no, I had no idea of why her daughter chose our property. And if the mother in her distraught state had added one and one and got an affair between her child and my husband, what then? Though, of course, I was glad Gordon went since it showed, or at least I presumed it would have, that he had nothing to hide. Just as I was proud of the mother at turning down Gordon's insensitive offer of money to help towards funeral expenses.

One day I was driving my golf friends on my turn for the pick-up to golf when Mabel suddenly pointed out the window, That's him. The father. The father of whom? The girl who killed herself. Considering myself a fair person I was surprised at my ill feeling toward this strapping fellow stripped down to shorts working on a road gang; I who had accepted his innocence on what Mabel herself had told us.

One of the other girls commented that he was a handsome specimen and likened him to a thoroughbred horse, which I didn't quite go along with despite his body. A thoroughbred has a certain class. This man lacked that, though handsome and well built he most certainly was. Given that it was his roadworks we were slowed and then stop-signed by, we all got a good look at him. I was reminded of white southern American women assessing a Negro slave. I felt somewhat disgusting for being one of them. I reminded myself, though, that he was innocent. But he did have a certain violent manner about him, those muscles rippling sweatingly in the sun.

Grace Heke had changed our lives. Yet in a way that left one only with a keener sense of appreciation of one's better lot in life. Which of course made her memory the more poignant.

NINETEEN

HE SHIFTED HIS feet when he knew the original position was exactly where the ball was gonna come (I'm a fighter, I unnerstan' these things, arcs and flights and bodily movements, it's like I unnerstan' the very air bodies and objects move through — and thrown beer bottles, hahaha! from the old days) and he woulda been under it to take it at chest level, pull it into him like he and the utha locks'd practised the last five weeks every Tuesday and Thursday minus the one Thursday when a man'd decided to get on the piss cos it was raining and he (I) thought practice woulda been called off — no he didn't, tha's the excuse he gave when the boys came in after for a beer and, bugger me, they jus' looked at him and said don't come that, Jake. And Gary Douglas called him a wuss. When he'd thought he'd been getting along pretty well with 'em, what with the hunting trips and drinking with 'em several times a week, too. The whole fucken team ignored him that night, as if the nights he had turned up to practice didn't count (even when I didn't want to go and who said I have to anyrate, I'm not one a you. Not really. I only came in cos fucken Gary and Kohi talked — egged — me into it.) So he'd stood by himself feeling bad and thinking how quickly men become strangers to one another jus' on account of a man decidin' it's a free fucken country — Well, fuck 'em. Won't turn up to practice ever again.

But when he thought about it nex' day and remembered the fullas he'd got to know, several of them honkies at that, when he'd never known a whiteman not in his whole (unknowing) life — not if he didn't count his brief time with the McClutchy alkies, which he didn't cos they weren't real people, not when part of their soul was sold to the drink in a big way — surprised at them, his team-mates, sorta the same as Maori fullas 'cept they talked a bit different; one fulla, the halfback, cheeky an' funny as anything, for a whiteman he was, and kinda warm, too, if a man was gonna be honest about it, the way he, Ronnie, put his hand on a man's shoulder jus' anytime and that smile right up into a man's face. Alright, Jake? he'd ask, like he really cared. Like if you had sumpthin' on ya mind he'd be the one you'd go to tellim all about it. (I might jus' do that one day, ya never know.)

It came down, he was too close, it hit him high on the chest nearly on the chin (had to snap my head outta the way like it was a sneak punch) and the fucken ref blew the whistle, Knock-on green! Scrum. Red put-in. A man hearing the Douglas mob on the sideline laughing atim. (Fuckem. I'll showem.) But he didn't. The other side showed, not just his opposite opponent but plenty others in the team showed him, Jake (The Muss) Heke, what another kind of muscle was about.

He was out-timed, out-jumped and nemine a man's height in the lineouts. (Our fucken hooker's fault, he knows I like it lofted high not those hard straight throws, I hate those. Y' timing's gotta be too right. Wouldn't mind if it was a fight, then I'd fucken make sure the timing was there alright, don't worry about that.) He pushed his weight in the scrums but then scrums for a lock were easy. Being a lock forward he didn't have to make many tackles like the backs running against each other individually had to, but the times someone broke from the play and came (thundering) at him, he made the mistake of trying to use his strength and got run over the first time, the second he drove into the tackle 'cept the fulla turned his body slightly and a man went brushing past ended up on his face eatin' fucken dirt.

When he was out of breath — and that started very early in the game — the Douglas brothers and some of the other fullas yelled atim to keep up, to *get* in there, Jake! when he was trying. But the ole lungs jus' wouldn't supply the muscles. The first time he got the ball — jus' arrived in his hands from a maul — he thought, This is it! And he charged, right into a body tackle that not only winded him he lost possession of the fucken ball (oh!)

It didn't seem right, fair, that a man who'd been a fighter all his life, who'd ruled one of the worst pubs in town, had done fistic battle with, on several occasions, three his own size and won, should not be able to play this fucken game. Yet whatever he did he messed it up or at best made hardly no impression. He was lowered in tackles by li'l guys. Pushed around, elbowed in the lineouts, sneak-punched in rucks, raked by boots on the ground, and the cunts even mouthed off atta man while waiting for the ball to be thrown into the lineout. Made him turn, What'd you sa — Shet! Distracting a man so he misses his lineout jump altogether with wanting their blood. He did a cupla good things, had one long run and made a few sorta good tackles (they coulda been better, I know like any fighter man knows in his heart of hearts. But leas' I made 'em.)

In the clubroom bar after the game, he would've drank elsewhere if they hadn't snubbed him so totally that night he missed practice (it hurt), so ashamed did he feel of playing exactly like Gary's original facial expression'd said, like a wuss, man jus' wanted to leave. But for some reason he likened it to Beth: if he walked then he was never gonna see these people, not as friends or team-mates or even to say hello to, ever again. So he downed his beers — or tha's how he started out till Kohi tole him, Hey man, slow down, slow down, we got all night, brutha. And when Jake looked (deeply) into Kohi's eyes (yeah, he'd played well for a fulla with a fat gut) looking for any smartarse meaning he only saw goodwill. And a fighter knows goodwill like he knows badwill. Like he knows bodily movement, of objects, too, and so he shrugged, and slowed his drinking to his team-mates' pace, as was the done thing. (You're a team aren't yas?)

When the coach came ovah to their stand-up elbow-lean table, Jake Heke got guarded (Gwon, tell me how bad I played. But don't go on about it, Joe. A man knows when he hasn't done well, at anything physical he does.) Good game, Jake. (What!) Timing a bit out in the lineouts, but that'll come. Few more games. Jake astonished — shocked to his shallower core — that not only was he not being hauled out for how bad he played but — Coach, I hear right? What, it takes, like, a few games? And even his own sentence, the way he'd structured the question, surprised himself. It actually meant exactly what he wanted: did he have a few games to come right? (Tha's all I'm asking, coachie.)

Sure. What, you expect to go out there and play All Black rugby? In a third-grade senior team meant to be enjoying themselves? At, what, forty-three? Jake, come on. Hey! Forty-two. Jake trying not to break out smiling cos it'd be the relief he was smiling at as well knowing coach was teasing the year onto his age. Well, you played like forty-bloody-six, mate, Joe in that whiteman way of talking, more sure of 'emselves, less mumbled. And with the eyes right at a man. When in Jake's world, direct eye contact meant challenge. Meaning fighting talk even when it was silent.

At some time during the body-tired but heart-singing — and voice-singing, when the Douglas brothers produced a gat — night, Jake got 'n idea. Of asking Cody to join the team, it wasn't so serious a level Cody would feel out of his depth, not with a coach let you have a few games to settle in. In fact, his head swam with lots of ideas, on his own game and where he could improve. On ways he could get fitter so at least he'd enjoy the game better. (Double up on my daily press-ups.) And where he could show his team-mates (buddies) his social contribution. Remembering his days at McClutchy's where he ruled, at fighting and singing. This feeling of tired elation about the same as after a day out hunting (now I got experience). He wanted to sing to, you know, express that elation; now he was jus' drunk enough not to feel, you know, too embarrassed. Got a thought then of why: why would a man be embarrassed at jus' hearin' his own voice singing a fucken song when he knew he could sing it, not as if it'd be like a man's firs' rugby game in twenny-five years, this was sumpthin' a man'd never missed a practice at — (Haha! a practice) — not one fucken week, of doing his (drunk) singing thing at the pub, at pardies all ovah — all OVAH — this town in, what, nearly the same twenny-five years.

He (I) had sung with the best. The pub an' pardy best anyrate. So he went to Gary on the gat, Hey Ga, you know 'Tennessee Waltz'? Holding his breath cos the younger players, which was mosta them, would go, Ohh, not a fucken oldie numba! Put a man off, make 'im feel stink about himself. When in the ole days they'd a only said it from a safe distance that it was a oldie song. 'Cept no one said anything. 'N fact they all went, Yeah! Jake's gonna sing us a song.

So (you know) he took a breath and sang. And no one said a word or laughed, they only joined him in the chorus: . . . *to the beautiful Tennessee Waltz*. He hadn't felt this good in — oh, a long long time. (And wait'll I play football better. And wait'll you hear my best songs. Wait, wait, jus' you good people wait: Jakey'll show you.) In this life — not the fucken next — he'd showem.

TWENTY

THE VIEW FROM her upstairs window used to change according to how much money she had. In the ole days before Mulla it was a set routine process of the fortnightly solo mutha's (I even talk like a Hawk now) benefit as it ran out, her tobacco supply as it got down to skinnier and skinnier rolled smokes, how her mind turned scavenger as she went for long walks in the neighbourhood hoping to find some money on the ground even when — when she thought about it — all of Pine Block'd be like this in the days leading up to benefit payout, hundreds and hundreds of solo mums jus' like her, the unemployed, the heaps on bullshit sickness benefits, they should call this place Benefit Block, if it could be called a benefit (fucken gov'mint, never give us enough, jus' enough to keep us scrapin' by the rest of our lives, fucken gov'mint cunts) of hundreds — no, thousands — dependent on government for their entire existences (though not as if we invite 'em, even our local MP — who the fuck's he? What Party is in office? — to our parties, hahaha! Thassa only party we care about.)

Tha's how it used t' be before Mulla. Now, utha than a cupla bad weeks when Mulla didn't get a cut from a drug deal, she felt almost rich in that she had spare cash instead of running completely out three, four days before the fortnightly ole cycle came around (again), and the kids hadn't gone to school hungry in ages, plenty food in the cubbids (I'm rich), which meant they were easier to put up with, you know, bein' a mother when a woman weren't actually, like, born to this motherhood stuff (I wasn't.) Rich, or enough to lift her sights and since it was usually out her upstairs bedroom window her sights more and more fell on the new housing subdivisions, as she imagined living in her own house, witha what-they-call-it, a mortgage (Social Security could take it outta my benefit, the fucken thieving gov'mint, give it to us with one han', take it with the utha) but she'd settle for that if she could have her own house; she'd mow the lawn, not like half the bastards round here, waitin' till someone, a mate, a rellie, got sick of the sight of it and did it for 'em, useless fucken bastards and bitches going: Oh, I was jus' gonna do that, tomorrow. Like everything was tomorrow.

As she'd got to quite like walking from the ole broke days, Gloria Jones would walk (with my eyes up, not on the ground) down to the new subdivisions, slowing down so the experience lasted longer, near watering at the mouth at wanting to have one of these homes; why, they had carports and some had garages, she could make the garage a spare room (I know: I could rent it out, that'd pay half the, whatsit, mortgage, for starters. And if I could get Mulla to move in but not officially so I wouldn't lose my solo mum's benefit, well naturally he'd pay board — and then some — and before I knew it I'd have my cunning li'l arse covered with the whole benefit to myself, me and the kids. Shit, might be able to save up a deposit and buy a car. But as the (fucken) Social Security'd be deducting and I wouldn't be telling 'em not to or they'd smell a rat, fuck me I'd end up owning the place in, what, ten years?) The thought(s) made her tremble.

Her hoping, wanting thoughts made her wet, too. For him, Mulla, who she never thought she'd get to like but not only did she — well, she was sure she loved him. (Yeah, reckon I do. Now I do.) Despite his facial tattoos, his gang membership, bein' a ex-con, he was a decent man beneath it all, better'n any and all of the men she'd been with ovah the years put together. If he could pull off one good deal on his own, without having to share it with the uthas (shit, some of 'em don't get outta bed till lunchtime) that would be the deposit they wanted on a new (our own) house. 'N fact, a cupla months back Mulla's share of that ten kaygee dope deal was four and a bit grand. He gave Gloria a thousand dollars of it, the mos' money she'd ever had in her whole life, and she went out and bought clothes, clothes, for herself — oh, forgot the kids — so she bought them a few things, 'bout two hundred's worth, the rest she glad-ragged herself to the 9's — no, the legs 11's, hahaha-hehehe, liked so many things she even had to give some back when it came to more than the seven hundred she had to spend after buying two cartons of tailor-made smokes and a bitta food for the cubbid. She couldn't believe it the cost, and how far it didn't go, not really. But boy had it been good spending it. The rest of his thousands Mulla jus' blew like they all do the gangies and the people around here, it's how they are with money, kids, love: they blow it. On drinking. On buying up the large, big noting, in the lowie bars they go to that open early (to dispense the medicine for their ailing hearts).

Mulla'd been moaning his head off of late, 'bout Jimmy Bad Horse (oo, what a mean mongrel dog that is. Yet he's got sumpthin' about 'im) not respecting his senior status by sending him out with punk kid prospects to case robbery or burg jobs. Robbery, the firs' preference, more dough in it. In an' out. Gloria was anguishing over whether to put it to Mulla outright, why didn't he turn this to his advantage, get the pros's to do a job and pull out a hunk of the dough. She had the armed bank robberies well imagined in her mind, of the prospects running in doing their desperate thing, waving their shotties around, feeling terrified and like giants at the same time — givus the fucken dough bags! — out to the first getaway vehicle — which Mulla said Jimmy's tried to say he should be driving but Mulla insulted enough by that to tell him fuck, a man his many years in the gang didn't have to be frontline risk stuff, after all the time he'd done inside, too. No, Mulla would be driving the second vehicle; the pros's'd just bundle in their bags of dough and frantic selves and want their young asses outta there. Mulla could have a plan to drop them off at her house, she could give 'em the big impression of harbouring dangerous criminals, make 'em feel good, hot stuff about 'emselves, whilst Mulla was elsewhere pulling big wads of cash (I want the slabs of fifties, not hundreds. Hundreds make people suspicious. Fifties but I'll take twennies — take fifty cent pieces if I had a place to turn 'em into notes! hahaha) and then they'd have a deposit on a house.

She thought and thought about this and today she'd be putting it to Mulla, meaning it risked everything but then, what the hell, not as if life'd given a woman many utha options. (I'll be aksing him hehehe) amused at how they said the word ask.

She'd rung Mulla at the HQ on the next-door's phone, Shirley The Early Bird's phone (fucken moaning bitch, asking me when'm I gonna get my own phone. How many times has she borrowed sumpthin' from me and never paid it back? C'd start my own sugar factory with the 'mount a sugar she's had off me. And what about the cupla bucks here, five bucks there, she's borrowed and thought I'd forget it cos they're only two-dollar coins. Nothin' *only* 'bout two-dollar coins and cert'inly not a five-dollar note when you're on the DPB. So fucker. Get my own house an' I'll have phones in every room 'cept the kids', case they make toll calls, hahaha. Though dunno who they'd know outside a Two Lakes.) Wanna come ovah, hon? Puttin' that purr on, that fuck-me iner voice. (I feel like coming.) Givim a good one. Then get the talk on his resentment at his seniority being treated like it didn't mean nothin'; maybe givim a blowjob, then put the question: Mulla, I been thinking . . .

THE LOVEMAKING WAS better'n she'd hoped and even planned. Sumpthin' on Mulla's mind that he'd mostly let go (released) in the sack. An' that was alright. (Fine by me, lover boy.) Afterward: Wha's wrong, my honey? (Dammit. Forgot to tellim how good his fucking was.) Ooo, you had some energy today, baby. But, you know, I kinda sensed sumpthin' . . . (Come on now, my tattooed, lovable galoot. Talk to Glor. Talk to me.)

As she expected, Mulla's talk was about his lack of respect, about Jimmy Shirkey bein' a cunt who used people, telling Gloria about the drug deals Jimmy put together onis cellphone (as if the cellphone in itself was important, as if it was part the complaint Mulla had) and how he was certain Jimmy was pocketing some of the profits ovah and above what he as a long-serving prez was 'ntitled to. Just what she wanted to hear. She almost rushed in there. But no, not yet. (Easy, girl. Easy.)

Mulla, from the firs' day I set eyes on that Jimmy I knew he weren't right. And then she touched Mulla's tattooed cheeks, the fern-curl spirals from the Maori warrior days of old, and the nose crossmarks like a ladder going up the bridge. Around the nostrils the design curled in on itself to the finest li'l hole in the centre. Was like looking into his universe (tiny that it is). Up onis forehead the lines went out from centre like rainbow rings on a wide arc, but curled sharply jus' past the eyebrows and went down under the eyes. They mighta looked alright if it wasn't, like, near th' end of the 20th century (hahaha). But she was used to them and so were her kids who really liked the man behind them, no denying he was generous to them (and me) and a good listener, too.

Let's go for a drive, look at some a those nice new houses down the hill. An' when we come back we c'n, you know. Flashing him a smile that came so easily cos he was good to love with; it was his caring and yet his getting right into the act itself. (Mean to say: if we're fuckin' we're fuckin', hahaha.) They went out the door and down the stairs of this shit State dwelling holdin' hands.

Making out she wasn't watching his face too intently when she was. Whaddaya think, hon? Be good to live in one a them? as they sat lookin' at one of the new houses. Or — she put on the hesitation — or maybe not, not with one a them, you know, mor'gages, eh? An' forced herself to look out her window. Whassa mor'gage? is the firs' thing he wanted to know. She turned: Thassa loan, hon. You get them from the banks, don't aks me why they call it that, they jus' do. You pay it back, thassa main thing. With interest, how they, the honky banks, make their money. Off the backs of us poor brown folk.

Took him a while to say more. Do white poor people have them mor'gage things, too? Yeah, spose they do. Yeah, they mus' do. They live in houses same as we do. So how come the honky banks're makin' money off their backs, too? Gloria had no answer for that nor cared that she didn't. All I know, Mulla, is they're makin' money from people wantin' (badly now) to live in their own houses. Mow their lawns ev'ry Sat'day morning, eh hon? Coaxing him back to the suburban dream. Would ya like that — nahh, you wouldn't, eh? Not you mowing lawns, though I'd do them. You wouldn't have t' be seen mowing fucken lawns, I'd unnerstan' that. Only thing is, ya need a deposit. Know what a deposit is, Mulls? Yeah, course I know. It's what ya put down on sumpthin' and never go back to pickit up cos you can't afford the rest of the payments, HAHAHA!

Oh, you a funny man alright, Mulls. You are (you fucken jerk. Can't you see I want a house so bad I'd near do anything for it?) You always make me laugh, Mulls, even when I'm, y' know, down in the dumps.

That brought him ovah. Or his hand, that is. What about, hon? But she shook her head. No, nothin'. Glor, c'mon, we c'n talk to each utha. Dumps about what? But she shook her head and played it to her manipulative max. Nah, i's alright, honey, only a stupid dream. Letting out a most expressively long sigh. Spreading it on with jam: Jussa a stupid dream, Mulls. 'Nutha sigh. (Now tha's enough jam, Gloria baby. Or he'll be spittin' it out.)

His tattooed arm came across her vision, pointing. What, tha' the dream? That what you want? Again she shook her head, and this time closed her eyes. Just briefly, enough to have him ask again, You talking one a them houses? And she nodded. Jus' the once. How much the deposit? Five, it came out a li'l too quick (have to watch that). Five what — grand? Or hundred? She looked at him with a sweet li'l smile: Oh, hon, if only it was jus' five hundred. Couldn't bear to look at that drop in his face but saw it anyway. (So that's it then.)

So it's five grand? That gets y' in? She turned again. Gets *us* in, I w's thinking. He started the car. She wasn't pushing it any further, the rest was up to him, since the deposit was never, but never, gonna come from her. (Even if God walked into my place and said here's your five grand to put on the house, I wouldn't make it to where you pay it. I'd have some of it spent before I got there. I'd go round to friends and ask where the Housie was, find a card school, a fucken pardy still raging in the morning from the night before, I would I would. It's how I am. How everyone I know is: we jus' don't unnerstan' how money works and to be, you know, responsible — fuck responsible. Yet we got the same wantings as everyone else.)

They drove over to the next new subdivision that still had houses being built. And though it was the same as what they'd a few streets away been looking at, it seemed to Gloria Jones that these were even more desirable. And look, she pointed at the sale signs, they're the same price! And happy that Mulla was nodding at that, with a frown on th't said he was thinking. Really thinking. Five g's eh? he said again in quite a different tone, like it was reachable (oh, please let it be!) Yeah. Lotta money, eh? Giving her faraway look like at a rainbow that didn't really have a potta gold at the bottom (which end anyrate?).

They drove to the end of the cul-de-sac of the street where it was fenced farmland. A high old red-brick wall and a grey-slate roof behind the walls ahead of them 'bout a football field distant. (I could be his, fucken richman Trambert's, neighbour.) How much t' buy that place, Glor? Mulla grinning, mussa read her mind. Five hundred, she said — grand. He looked at her and with genuine astonishment. How do you know? Well, she didn't. But it was easy to figure from them giveaway real-estate booklets she'd been picking up from the stands of late, that houses that size were a half million. A mind-boggling sum. Then she saw Mulla come forward on the steering wheel of this, one of the gang cars, frowning. What's up, hon? Took him a few moments to answer.

Tha's the house Jake's girl hung herself. Startled Gloria. She looked. Saw the top of a big spread of tree jus' starting to get new leaves. (Oh yeah, tha's right. How could anyone in Pine Block forget that? But I thought Mulla was inside then, doin' one of his sentences.) Jake, Nig Heke's ole man? Who else Jake, and when he turned, his face was with a kinda awe. Jake The Muss, his kid. Yeah, Gloria nodded. Grace wasser name. Bit of a li'l stuck-up. But that was a mistake: Mulla gave her a filthy look. Glor, she's dead. Killed 'erself. Now puzzling ater. (I made a mistake. This cunt's even more, you know, sensitive than I thought.) I never meant she was a stuck-up, not my words, only what people said about her. You know how they are in Pine Block, can't say nothin' nice 'bout no one.

She drew in breath, annoyed at herself, her nasty slip of the tongue. Why I wannna move out to a place like this, Mull. Get away from 'em. Then she stretched a false yawn, Oh well. If only, as they say. Ran long, red-painted fingernails down his dirty jeans leg, C'mon. Le's go home and do some more lovin'. Leas' it don't cost nuthin'. Givinim that smile — with interest.

All the way home he kept saying, five grand, eh. And she had a picture in her mind of that fucken big house, the Trambert place; thinking of his riches and how unfair it was the start he got, the advantage of his colour(lessness) as well whatever it is about people with dough that makes those without it see red, become blind, have thoughts of anger, and even a desire to kill. But then she was jus' a Pine Block woman, a solo mutha goin' out witha gang member who secretly wanted to change for the bedda, who would she kill except in her dreams? It was only loving a woman an' her man c'd have that was dreams you c'd make happen. Jus' good ole cock and cunt, baby. Laughing after their genital joinings ater crude comment about him leaving his deposit. Oh how they laughed at that. Or they did when he promised she'd get that deposit, too. How she laughed then.

TWENTY-ONE

SHE'D PROMISED HERSELF she'd wait till spring, but didn't (couldn't). It'd kept asking at her, asking at her, exactly as though a real voice: Go on, Polly. Just so you know.

So here she was, a trespasser on the Trambert property, eased along that high brick wall, having waited outside watching several cars go in, choosing the Friday because that was the night Grace had done what she did. (I want to know what she might've seen that last night.)

Well, what this Heke girl was seeing was a large old house well lit up inside and partly out, of a size that staggered and even frightened her, as if size alone put her at an impossible disadvantage; after what she'd guessed was the last car of friends since they arrived within about twenty minutes of each other then waiting an endless time of fighting with herself about whether she should go in or just forget this obsession with a sister who wasn't coming back, who wasn't growing into her older even more beautiful version in the grave — she was stopped. Ceased. Kaput. Polly Heke (who's gonna change her name to Bennett soon's he marries Mum), she's dead and more than six years gone and you should be gone from here.

But she stood up from her crouch at the corner of the high wall and she walked for that open gateway, thinking only of the next step. So it was dogs she thought of. But then again even if, they'd not have them roaming the place, not with guests. A grim smile to herself: Unless they got dogs trained to recognise Maori girl trespassers.

Along that wall, on the inside and quite another experience altogether; sliding her back along it, left and right and ahead and above at half a sky of stars, the blank rest must be cloud; left for that big shape of tree, top part making an outline against the faint glow of sky. Sliding along with no possible explanation should she be seen or should a dog smell her presence and give the alarm. Well, she could give an explanation but it would be one bizzare explaining even being true. And the embarrassment.

As she neared the tree she fought the mental pictures of Grace, how she remembered her, how she was that frozen image in a coffin, and — please don't — how she would have appeared hanging from this very tree. Had to stop, cup a hand over her mouth so the distress wouldn't get out.

Then she fought with the ridiculous notion that Grace's ghost might be here, which made her cold all over; a thought that her dead sister might leap out shrieking for no other reason than, well, Grace's ghost would hardly be at peace. And nor would Grace appreciate her sister going over her last night's tracks (but why, if I love her?) Just didn't seem that Grace would approve and yet that didn't stop her. She was here now.

The wind was catching up there, up where the tree cleared the brick-wall height. And it sounded quite awful; she thought she'd better call this off now. But next she was feeling for a hold above her and then she was pulling herself up. (Oh, God.)

Above, it was making quite a deep roaring sound, coming in gusts. The light from the house spilled some way out onto a large lawn, the tree quite (thank God) a distance from the room where the people were standing as though in a movie. Real people. Holding drinks. Wine glasses. (Oo-hoo.) And white people at that. Not that the race were strangers to her like for some Maoris she knew; but still, this hoity-toity kind were sort of intimidating in the more confident manner they had. And were they dressed well, specially the ladies (the lucky bitches). Thinking she was going to marry someone with money and to hell with Charlie Bennett saying she should make her own. (My mother's better life is from Charlie's main income not Mum's hospital laundry wages.) She started climbing.

She was too scared to be wondering if this is what Grace would have seen, could hardly glance at anything but the next branch outline to grab onto; but funny thing, she did feel safer with each higher level of ascendency. And feel the new leaf growth small and soft in her hands, funny thing reminding her of a sanitary pad the softness; buds yet to burst on her fingertips, and the varying thicknesses of branches she had to test for holding her weight. Her eyes had adjusted so she could pick out quite clearly the different thicknesses against the sky. And through the criss-crossing and blotches of leaf outline that room, with some of the people lost to the climbing angle.

Higher. Where was the sturdy bough (poor dearest) Grace must've chosen at the last? Why did she come here? What did she see? What last thoughts did she have? Polly knew the visit to Boogie in a boys' home that never transpired was one thing in Grace's mind. Of course the rapes. (I hate him.) Looked above her. Was that it? Is that the branch she tied the rope to? Felt sick. Had to hold onto the trunk, wrap arms around it, till the nausea passed. Asked herself: Am I here to practise? (No. For God's sake, Poll. Of course you aren't.) But then thought she might be. She might be.

Now she had the picture of Grace's hands (they would have been cold, it was a cold night) fiddling as she tied the rope to that sturdy branch above. Polly looked down. Up again. Could hear the scritchy sounds of rope against wood. Then the wind picked up and replaced that with a disturbing roaring. Now Grace seemed to be everywhere. And Polly all out in goosebumps. The gust kept up for some time, had Polly wrapped around the trunk once more, till it eased to like scores of small creatures, mice, rustling up there. Then that too died, eventually it did (like my sis did). (And how did she know what kind of knot to tie?) And what had she thought as she was about to jump? She had to steady herself from a dizziness suddenly come over with being here, the enormity of it; of where the night's last act had taken place.

Looking the other way and there was sight of hundreds and hundreds of house and street lights out beyond the wall. Took a bit to get her bearings — quite a shock to realise the higher placed lights was her old street, Rimu Street, Pine Block; and that that spill down of single-storey lights was the subdivision carve-offs of land ole Mr (rich) Trambert had sold. Remembering back that when Grace was here — and how unbelievable this is being here on the same tree — the higher lights would have been what she saw. Then Polly turned back to the house, closing her eyes in trepidation just until she was over the worst part (of being my sister).

They stood around drinking like that for some length of laughing, quite rigidly postured; the men in jackets, different browns and different check patterns, sort of smooth in an old-fashioned way, the women more elegantly modern, even trendy several of them, with the most beautiful of hairstylings. Each and every one of them. (I could stay here all night and probably will, or till they're gone, just watching them.)

She saw them leave one room and appear, or maybe half them did, in a room next door, sat down at what must be a very long and large dining table (oh, how very nace for you). But then grinning at recall of her mother's telling of Charlie taking her for the first time to a restaurant — when's my turn? — and how all her preconceptions were misconceptions: everyone wasn't looking at her. No one cared a stuff about how she used her eating utensils. The night had ended up with her and Charlie on the dance floor, and at one stage the restaurant had cheered and applauded her and Charlie doing their thing on the floor. So Polly checked herself being critical or jealous, and watched.

She heard, as they sat down and ate and drank more wine, singing and laughter from her old residential side, but hard to pick out if from the new housing closer, or from her old street. Whatever, it was of the loud merriment kind, and the singing was surprisingly clear — she could hear that there were harmonies even if they were a bit fudgy. Came with it a certainty that Grace would have heard this and seen this, this contrast of worlds either side of her elevated vision.

When, eventually, the party down there moved back to the first room, presumably the sitting room, or one of them in a house that large, they were differently mannered (would Grace have seen this, too?) more relaxed, more with laughter, and stereo music started up. Not that Polly recognised the music. Just that it was white, a white voice singing.

And it was white people dancing, too — she broke out giggling — Polly'd never seen such terrible dancing, such lack of rhythm, such awkward and ugly posturing passing itself off as dancing. Then she suddenly thought it might be just a joke, that in a second the three couples she could see in and out of her vision would break off laughing at themselves and do it properly. So Polly enjoyed the joke, too, why not, as she waited for which couple would declare the joke over.

But no couple did. Because it wasn't a joke. Well it was — to her (me! HAHAHA!) The joke was on herself. On assuming these people to be better than they were. When this was it: they couldn't dance. They didn't understand the bodies they inhabited. They had no sense of rhythm or timing. No soul. No meat, therefore. And they weren't so intimidating, such impossibly unattainable, heights of humanity after all. (Man, they're just ordinary like some of us are. And if I danced like that, I'd be ashamed of myself.)

She knew with the same certainty of earlier that Grace would not have witnessed this dancing (surely), or she wouldn't have killed herself. She would have taken hope from it, if she was here making miserable comparison with her own life back over her — Polly's now — shoulder. But then again the rapes. (How could I have forgotten about that.)

Eyes over at the Rimu Street hill-line now, window slabs of light, the background glow they all gave off, no partying sounds, just dog barks, a tyre screech, and more stars revealed above it all. Back to the house and those hideous dancers, hands up to the bough Grace's weight (she's a Weight until the ground finally takes her) might've hung from, shed a few tears for her but more than enough shed now. (That's enough now, Poll.)

And down Polly Heke climbed, with sure grabbing hands, swift, flowing descent, like her run along the lawn in the shadow of the brick wall was a flow into night with night eyes and sure feet, a flow through air, a freeing from a memory. Grace'd be alright now. And her now older sister, Polly, too (I'm alright. Now I am. Nothing to worry about. It's done but I ain't. Got my whole life ahead of me.) She couldn't wait to get home, ask her mother did she know white people can't dance, did she know that? Laughing as she ran out the gateway. Laughing she was.

TWENTY-TWO

THAT WAS IT! Fuck Cody and fuck his useless mates — Out! He lifted a snoring head from the floor (I jus' put the vacuum that's not a vacuum over it this morning, while that little cunt Cody was sleeping) slapped its face — hard. You. Muthafucka. Get the hell outta my house. And he flung the man (like I used to when I was a bouncer at McClutchy's) except this time without any punches. Not as if the fulla was fighting. And he wasn't big enough anyrate.

Over to another unconscious form, head hung over the sofa arm-rest near to the fucken floor, empty beer bottles at his feet, Jake about to yank a handful of hair but deciding it might be a nightmare to wake up to (no one ever did that to me. Wouldn't dare, either.) So he gave the fulla a slap instead — Oi! Wake up. The fulla came up like he'd been shot, mouth open, what the? Don't gimme the what-the, boy. This is get the — Get the fuck outta my house! (Well, rented from the State, that is.) Then he clapped his big hands together — loud. Up! Up! C'mon you muthafuckas, 'fore I make you clean up first!

Over to Cody, sat slumped in the corner, a beer stubbie still inis hand though he was awake now and looking at Jake in confusion and near makin' a man feel so bad he'd change his mind.

(No, fuckem.) Stuck his hands on his hips. Cody. (Shit, how c'n I say this.) Took another glance around to give him reason, at the fucken mess. Pack ya bags. Though he didn't look Cody directly in the eye. And when Cody got groggily (on the grass I bet) to his feet and tole him he didn't have no bags ta fucken pack, in that smartarse tone (as if *I* been doing this, having raging parties, all the time a huge mess, as if I lost my pride in myself when, sure, a man's had his moments. But I always came back from 'em, from being down but not stayin' down. Whereas Cody, come to think of it and I have thought about it, a lot, he ain't fucken changed one bit 'cept for the worse. So fuckim.)

When he said that and in the tone he did, Jake went, Tha' right? You got no bags t' pack? Means you only got, what, a plastic shopping bag to stick your stuff in, get you out sooner? Good. Then do it an' get. Ya hear? I mean it. Whole fucken lot of you, get.

Stood there looking — or daring 'em to return his look — at every man as he trooped out; Cody the last. Standing at the doorway, Jake . . . ? With that look. Start remindin' a man of what they'd shared, from when they were both bums, a man bum and a streetkid bum, living in the park in town. Jakey, me an' you — No ya don't. Nemine the Jakey, Code. Tole you a hundred times, I had enough. Trying not to remember that this kid'd accompanied him to his son's funeral — was Cody kept nagging a man, ya should go, Jake. Gwon, I'll come with ya. Wasn't for Cody a man wouldn't a shown his respec's to his shot-dead son (fucken Black Hawks). Fucken gangs whatever stupid name they went under.

Jake, I wanna, I wanna change, man, honest I do. Can't help how I been — Uh-uh. Jake wasn't havin' that shit. Ya can and you ain't. But not my lookout, not any more it ain't. Been cleaning up your shet for (six) years now, kid. Go get your own place — But Jake, it's three in the fucken morning, man. But Jake shook his head, looked the li'l cunt right in the eye, with warning of the old Jake. Time to go, Cody.

It occurred to him after he'd picked up most of the empty beer stubbie bottles and cans in their different shapes of crushing, dented, twisted forms, the cigarette butts — on the fucken floor if you please, even if it is hard wearin' carpet, ya don't do that in another man's house — and had to pick up spew — spew! — from a corner with a shovel and pan then scrub it with soapy water, then the kitchen mess like starving dogs'd been feeding, and havin' a scrap while they were at it, that even as he was asking himself why did they get so drunk, so out of it wasted, he'd seen — no, (c'mon, Jake) ya mean done — all this before. Seen, and yet never seen, a hundred, a thousand times before. Even as he screwed his face in disgust at cleaning up their mess, even as he asked again why did they get so drunk, it was occurring at the same time that this was a mirror of himself, or what he had been.

Another thing, awake and sober at this hour had been damn near a first, a unplanned one, mind; they were out hunting — well, illegal spotlighting for deer hahaha — with Gary and Kohi and Jason along too (fulla never stopped tellin' jokes. Had me laughin' all fucken night. Or in between the excitement of a deer stepping into our beam which Kohi was directing off the cab roof of Jason's pick-up, Gary driving, me and Jayse with the rifles) and kept coming onto them, four for the night, light-captured poses of innocence (poor li'l fuckers, dazzled by the light, can't move, ya put the gun near right up to their stupid heads and fire. But it makes y' heart go fast with excitement, and they're worth good money, a good night is like making a week's wages. We're ordinary men, the fullas't make the rules don't unnerstan' this, but fuckem, we're out doin' it anyway, hahaha!) But on the way back Gary took a corner too fast and they ended up over a bank, took several hours to get the truck out. And a man comes home to this.

He got a beer from the fridge (leas' they left me some of my own beer I paid for with my own two hands — Well, not two hands on a shovel like I used to: the boss promoted me to a machine, a front-end loader. Handle it like I'm born to it. Could drive it with my eyes closed one hand tied behind my back — least they'd left him a beer to sit on a sofa and, you know, think about things.) Though since it was Beth's face and accompanying voice kept coming back, as though she was here physically and he was pushing her out of the room but she kept coming back, it started to get to him.

Eventually he stood up. Yeah? Yeah, what do you fucken want, woman? Ain't you had enough of my blood, my pride, my (innocence) right to my own life? Standing there clutching an empty beer stubbie at this ungodly hour when today, Saturday, was a rugby-playing day and he should be fresh, get plenty sleep so he played well, which he had of the coming to a close season, really well.

Standing there in the sitting room, suddenly aware he had no curtains so people — if they were up — could see him talking (yelling) to himself. Oh, fuckit. Who cares? Though he did move closer to the door to reduce possible vision of him. But first he checked the flower vase (gonna put some in it one day, yellow ones and throw some red and white ones in. Nearly did when Rita came round) to make sure it hadn't been pissed in and if it had he'd be paying a visit to that bar they drank at in town, with their loud rap music and funny way they all dressed. That any of his kids — if he knew what they looked like now (ain't set eyes onem in years) — if any of 'em dressed like that he'd — Well. (I'd be pissed off but then again what could I say? What rights've I got with 'em?)

It was like he was confronted by Beth. He didn't unnerstan' this, not as if he was drunk or hungover with the heebie-jeebie imaginings a man got when he was hitting the booze day after day, he was near enough clean. Hadn't had a drink since after rugby practice Thursday. Work the Friday and a pick-up at the new roading site by the Douglas brothers (laughin' at bein' in my ma-chine br-rooom-brr-roooom! HAHAHA!), an' out to that (glorious) bush, not too far outta town, round this lake that you could shave yaself in, skate like one a them ice-skaters on teevee across its mirror surface, and forested hills in that mirror and birds V'ed against the fading sky, an' the ones in the trees making last call to the day; slow drive down those pine-forest roads where a man's thoughts were at one with, well, nature. No one sayin' anything, as if to let the day go to sleep nice 'n' quiet by itself.

Then the spotlight beam slicing open the night, like putting a hole in it, a big yellow/white widening hole, a magic ray seeking out game for men to kill. And that was alright, too: everything's got a fit, a place, a slot in this life. Man'd come to unnerstan' this, out in the bush he did.

Now here he was having a 'maginary row — talk? — with Beth. And first, she told him, siddown Jake. Please. Heard it as if she was right there (Oh, Bethy, I done you wrong I know that.) Which he did. But, you know, witha scowl 'n case she thought she was the fucken boss now after all these years (of bein' apart).

By the time this imagined (turned out to be) heart-to-heart was through, Jake was quite emotional. The things he'd done, been reminded of. The pardies he'd thrown (and ruined with my fists, my temper, my wanting to all the time be the tougharse). Feeling kind of sorry. (For what I did?) Not that he admitted that, not aloud nor in his mind. It was jus' a feeling niggling away there. It was knowledge, it was facts that weren't quite any of that (not if I don't want 'em to be. So fuck you, woman.) Fuckit, have another beer, to calm this knotty ache in his stomach. These unsettled, maybe challenged, thoughts.

And another beer (musta worked up a thirst having my firs' beer-free Friday in, what, years? Forever of my youth and adulthood?) as his thoughts churned; all the memories of himself were unpleasant, like this scene he'd walked into (stone col' sober!) those kind of memories, of rage-up pardies a man'd never given one thought to but of enjoyment — why ya have 'em isn't it? — weren't as if every one ofem ended up a fight, if ya don't count backhanders and jus' one-punch over-in-a-sec ones. So he kept downing beers to expel them (stupid fucken thoughts. You'd a thought I been the only wrong man in fucken Two Lakes, Beth.

Did the same as every other man I knew. Tha's right: same's every other man I — knew?) Yeah, knew. Now that struck him (like I punched myself) that he *knew*. Including from his childhood.

Cos he sure's hell didn't know a one of 'em now. Not Dooly, not Sonnyboy Jacobs (who hit me a beaudy, firs' one was in the guts took my fucken wind. Nex' one was flush on the jaw, when it was always me who hit like that.) Sonnyboy who'd been in the kitchen drinking with a man, not long back in town from wherever the fuck else he'd been living, when Beth'd burst in, with that (fucken) letter, from Grace, (wrongly) accusing a man of doing what'd been done to her (my own kid?) and he'd got so wild (who wouldn't?) he up and banged Beth. No he didn't. He upended the table and he was going for Beth. Tha's when Sonnyboy Jacobs stepped in. Who a man used to know. Like Jackie, Denny, Monty, Matiu, Bully, and 'specially Dooley (was my best mate) they were all used-to-knows.

But hadn't a man won his own respect with a new set of friends? Hadn't he shown the Douglas brothers he was made of the same stuff as them (and then some, once I came to unnerstan' what was goin' on, the rules of hunting, that it was patience and enjoying for itself, be it a creek to cross fifty times or jus' the birds, carryin' a pig, deer backquarters, even the biting mozzies, a man'd learned to become one with the experience; and once I learned how rugby worked and my part to play in it an' unnerstood the coach, even though he w's smaller than me, meant what he said when he told a man don't you ever punch a man when you're playing for me unless he punches you first or unless I give you specific instructions to take out a man with a reputation. Once I unnerstood that, and once I learnt the hard way that if a man ain't fit then the game's a fucken nightmare not a pleasure), and now a man was as if he was Jake The Muss all over again but yet without the Muss part cos — cos, well, it didn't really madda. Not really.

Not that Gary and Kohi were wusses. They just used violence if there wasn't no other choice. Which'd happened only once in his witness at their pub and Kohi had put one fulla out one hit, bang, Gary took his man one-two-three and Jason's punch was so quick — an' hard! — Jake'd missed it. Nor had that left any of the would-bes for Jake to show how good he was. Nor did they speak but one word of the fight afterward. Just a shaking of their heads (like that dream humming, as one) as if they regretted having to do the bizniz but boy don't be fucking with them Douglas Brothers. In big leddas like that, too. Well, di'n't they not only respect a man but *like* him? Hadn't they invited him on many occasions to their home, to their family gatherings where everyone got drunk but a nice, happy, singing, joking, laughing drunk that stayed like that and men went to sleep on it, not with grazed knuckles and tingling all over of (sweet) violence just been done (again)? Hadn't they?

But fuckit, why should he be letting Beth's memory tell him he was an arsehole? He cracked his sixth, or was it more'n that, bottle of beer; feeling bedder. At one stage yelling out of his thoughts, Shut the fuck up, Beth! Wondering why he'd separated her out from his angry outburst. (Why, Jake?) Who cared? He'd had enough her trying to tellim sumpthin'. (I'm alright. I done my time; it don't have to be jail. Jail can be how you live on the outside in so-called freedom. Weren't no fucken freedom having t' live with that over me: even when I gave 'em my sample. Fuck Beth. How much's she want of a man?) She, Beth's ghostlike presence, kept trying to tellim sumpthin' more. But he was many beers past listening (fucker. Done my suffering.)

CUNTS SPOSED TO be his team-mates were moaning at every turn at a man. Alright, he wasn't playing so well, would they if they'd drunk till, what, ten this morning? Then hardly asleep when he got snapped awake by sumpthin' (I think it was that fucken Beth, harp-harp-harping at a man even in sleep.) He didn't know how it'd happened, hadn't done a session like that for ages, and now he was paying — dearly — for it by not being able to get into the game.

The other team'd loaded up with young bloods from their gun Colts side, hungry fullas wanting another game having already played earlier. Young, fit, fast, mean and lean. Made a man feel his age.

He heard cheering from the sideline at someone coming on as a replacement, for a bullshit injury Jake was sure; halfa Two Lakes woulda heard the cheer, Jake told himself this was jus' bluffing shit, to make his side think this was a real gun come on. Caught the smart cunt's eye when he ran on and took his place at the side of the scrum, on the flank, openside. The hatred in the kid's eyes. Quite got to Jake. But then so did it spark in him a desire to get his shit together.

Lineout ball sailed straight into his hands, other fulla didn't wanna know, which suited Jake Heke. Like the gap opened up did. And he started his engine on full revs and went into it out into open country. Now he'd showem. The goalposts not that far away.

Felt like he'd been hit by a truck. On the ground, ball gone from his grasp, his team running backwards then after the ball going out along the other side's backline, in time to see them score. (The fuck happened?) He'd been running out in wide open spaces looking for the support to pass to (and thinking I was gonna go all the way, so only making out I was gonna pass. Fuckem, criticising me earlier.) Then out of nowhere an opposition blue shirt and then the truck.

The replacement flanker was all over the fucken paddock (like he's got them Energiser batteries inis boots!), tackling everything that moved, tidying up the loose ball, and making long, advantage-line breaking runs himself. Jake Heke, the fighter (the puffed fighter) in him admiring the man's fine form, reminded him of Michael Jones, the All Black. Or Zinzan Brooke, the All Black number 8 but he'd played at 7 and 6 as well. This young fulla might be one in the making, so Jake was thinking as he ran belatedly to a breakdown which was won for once by his side and so the ball came out, one player, another then him (me?) — a lock not supposed to be receiving it out this wide, he was sposed to be in there in the tight, but what the hell — He ran. (Shit!) His (fucken) legs got taken out from under him. What the?! — Sure the tackler'd spat in his face.

He asked one of the boys, Who was it tackled me? Who else, but the flying flanker. Okay. Jake The Muss'd show Mista fucken Spitter, next ruck. Then who should come screaming past but Spit, elbowing Jake aside, calling him Cunt! while he was at it. So the young punk wanted a war did he? Now war Jake The Muss was good at.

Except playing his part in the war proved difficult; he was just not there in time, he didn't have the skills, the speed, just this lung-screaming desire to get one big hit on the flanker fulla so at least he could say he gottim back for the spit in the face, the reminder of which enraged him and yet at the same time seemed to have the effect of making him even shorter on breath. (F' fuck's sake, Jake — *get*tim!)

Halftime, the three-minute break and all Jake could think (feel) was the shaven-head tearaway flanker's spit — oh, an' his insults (call me names). Listening with less'n half a ear to the coach telling him sumpthin' about the lineouts that he should turn and let his forwards drive him forward steada taking the gap — Fuckim. (Ain't his face running with another man's spit. How'd he like it bein' called a cunt? That bal'-head's mine. And my spit's got knuckles on it — big knuckles.)

Took an age, though, just to get near to the ball in the second half; and when a man's got the ball it's hard to throw a punch even when the fulla ya want to throw it at's smashing you ovah in a tackle. Not with coach on the sideline. A man'll be stood down with only two games left in the (very enjoyable, thank you very much) season.

He got the ball in yet another clean take, thinking his anger at the flanker'd so psyched out his opponent the gutless wonder wasn't jumping against him no more. And he kept leaving that gap for Jake to run (man, I could sail a fucken big ship through) into. Alright, a try'd make up for a lotta things. (V-room, v-rooom!) He got his Mack truck engine going.

Woke being asked where was he from, what was his name, where did he live. Anyone'd think I'm a criminal, he tole the St Johns ambulance guy down on his knees asking these stupid questions. You a cop? Then he realised he'd been carried off and the game was still going — without him. He asked, What happened? You got taken in an illegal tackle, mate. This funny li'l whiteman fulla in his white shirt and red things on his shoulders. Stiff arm? Jake wanted to know so he could get the fulla who did it. Yes, stiff arm. He struggled to get off the ground to his feet but felt dizzy. The li'l St Johns pushed him back down, Now you stay right where you are. Fuck off, I'm playin'. No you're not. I've told the ref you've been concussed. You not only can't continue playing this game, but there's a stand-down period — (No!) The season only had two games left in it. How many weeks you say? Three. It was three.

IN BETWEEN THE singular distraction of the Lloyds matter looking like it was going his way on the letter he'd sent with the specific instructions to exclude his insurance cover on the asbestosis claims, which would at least mean the money would stop bleeding him to death, and having decided he couldn't see himself selling fried chicken on a franchise (but I do have something else which I should've thought of years ago) — he always had plans b, c and d — Gordon Trambert was enjoying a rather amazing rugby spectacle. Of T. Nahona — or Toot! as his sideline supporters were wildly proclaiming of his magnificent prowess — cribbing an extra Saturday game for the senior B side and seeming to have a particular target, the big, rather fine-looking lock; which had ended in Nahona being sinbinned for the high tackle (he should have been ordered off, but still, what a player) and the big fellow carted off to the sideline to recover. Clearly this young Toot Nahona had something in for the big lock who himself looked a few years too old to be playing this game, but not a bad player, if a little on the lazy side to start with. Perhaps he'd put in some dirty work with Toot and found Toot a willing replier to that.

He was surprised that the lock didn't see the set-up of the lineout gap being deliberate, with the opposition lock stepping back and strapping young Nahona peeling off from the tail and running a loop to get his speed up to make his hard, driving tackles as the lock took the ostensible gap. Gordon Trambert did see Toot Nahona rake the lock's head in a ruck, hardly honourable rugby and something which Gordon had yelled his objection to. But still, Nahona's general play was pure pleasure to behold.

He heard the big lock addressed at one stage as Jake The-something or other, Gordon didn't catch it. Whatever, this Jake fellow had certainly got a pasting by young Nahona. It was — almost — all Gordon Trambert could think about driving home, though he did have his moment of wishing he could take Toot Nahona aside and offer him both encouragement as well as advice that he could go a long way in the game if he'd get himself fitter. On today's inspired — or possessed — performance such advice would have been unnecessary.

Just before home he slowed down to look at the newly staked-out land for a planned twenty-house subdivision which he had almost sold as bare land until he suddenly realised he could have developed them as sections ready to build on, with roading and drainage put in by his own hired sub-contractors and make the land developer's profit for himself. (Why the bloody hell I didn't see that before I'll never know.) Rueing those parcels of bare land he'd let others make big profits on. Now it was his turn. Perhaps his turnaround of financial fortunes; he could feel it. Though he had to admit to himself, if no one else, that he'd had this sure-thing feeling before. So, you know, one would not declare it a guaranteed success. (Oh, but then again I haven't felt this sure about anything in business I've done for some considerable time.)

His other major worry in life was personal: Isobel and he were drifting apart. She had lost respect for him, he knew it; it felt worse than had she out and out hated him, for whatever reason. But her scorn for his business management — which he thought rather a harsh judgement — became her disrespect for him the man. (She's stopped even giving me my, uh, selfish screws. The ones an understanding, well-bred upper-middle-class woman has been subtly raised to, well, understand as her, uh, duty. As long as a chap doesn't abuse it.) He felt she had lost her way on that; that she had taken a stance without sufficient thought and been, well, sort of swept along by it, her emotions at everything being clouded by the money woes hanging over them. Unlike himself who had fought for all he was worth, the proof of it now in taking over control of his land (and with it my own destiny) even if he'd had to borrow from the bank to pay for the subdivision costs. (I'll get it back two-, possibly, three-fold if the economy keeps picking up as it has done. It can't possibly go wrong.) And even should there chance (chance, Gordon? These downturns come with approaching signals don't they?) an economic downturn he still had equity (just) in both the land and, as soon as it was done, the section development, too. The rugby spectacular solo performance by Toot Nahona brought a little smile. At least till he drove through his home gates and found himself hoping, if rather forlornly, that this latest change of plan might start the process of winning back her respect. And who on this earth didn't desire, even crave, respect? Not Gordon Trambert. Hell, just a good session in bed would do. One is human after all. It'd been some time. Perhaps one ought to have appreciated her better when the respect was there.

TWENTY-THREE

MULLA WAS SLUMPED ovah the steering wheel damn near in tears if she hadn't been there — looking atim. The hell's up with you? when if she didn't know she wouldn't've aksed like that. So he leaned back, sucked in breath (Fuckit, I'll teller the truth, why.) Glor, I can't do anutha fucken sentence in jail, I can't (I can't).

Tha' right? With eyes that said she di'n't seem to care one fuck. Eyes't the black stuff, mascara, di'n't suit, made her look too — I dunno — slutty. As for that black lipstick when she had brown skin, it made 'er eyes look bloodshot, even though he couldn't make the connection between lip colour and eyes, it jus' did. I thought you was a tougharse Brown Fis'? Yeah, well I am. (I'm in the fucken gang aren't I? I been a member for goin' on, what, seventeen, eighteen years.) Something struck him then. Eighteen years? Tha' how long a man's been a kid, wouldn't grow up, eighteen fucken years? Made 'im feel even worse about himself. What, with how Glor was lookin' atim (wi'out respect. Man, she's lost her respect for me.)

All it is is you sitting in a stolen car half a mile from the action — th' action-jackson's the pros's' job — they pull in here, get out, run ovah to the stolen car you'll have here, throw the bags in the boot, jump in, goin' crazy with wantin' outta fucken here.

An' you, Mulla the fulla, all of a sudden's their only hope, their only one chance a gettin' their li'l black arses outta here cos all they wanted is t' earn their patches — all you do is drive 'em to my place, Glor'll look after 'em, whilst you're helping yourself to some a the money. Now, how hard's that? An' how's that gonna put you back inside? Don't you want a house wi' me no more? That what you're tellin' me, that it's all ovah between us?

And it was no act her staring furiously out the windscreen in the parking area they were sat in round the back of a building in town, commercial premises, with an alley jus' one left turn of the wheel escape away for the day't now was never gonna come. (Fuckim.)

Glor, I never wanted sumpthin' so much in my life — Liar. Fucken liar. Don't gimme that shet, Mulla. You a-greed. Or'd you for-get? Spoke it like that: broken up like her dream was. (It's all broken. My dreams're all gone down the fucken toilet.)

Now he was crying. Which disgusted her. Not a Brown Fist crying. Jeezuz chrise, man, you been peeling onions under your lap while we been sittin' here? Wha's wrong wi' you? I aks you to build a twenny-storey building in the main street?

Can't do no more time, I keep tellin' you. Hon, I — Fine. Fine by me, Mulla Rota. Alright? Tha's jus' fine by me, now take me home. To my State home, that is. If you don't mine.

Driving through his tears and misery, Mulla wanted more'n anything to teller, alright he'd do the armed rob with the pros's then, if she'd only unnerstan' his position, if she'd only know that if they got caught and went down for it, he was's good's dead cos he couldn't do no more time (I can't I can't can't can't). He had no more lef' inim. No more of the necessary what-for, of supply of hatred, of mongrel-dog cunning and rabid-dog bite for any cunt tried a man on, as every man got done toim, even the toughest; it was the way of doing jail time: ya suffered twice, first in losing y' freedom, second for havin' to put up walls of steel, concrete, clamp a big lock on yer heart, seal up yer tear ducts, shut down ya soul, and think even less than what you anyway never thought 'fore ya came in, 'fore ya was so fucken thick ya got caught again; ya mind had to be even more mindless 'n that. And Mulla Rota jus' wasn't like that no more. An', funny thing, it was this very woman who'd helped bring about the change inim. He wanted that new (I been in cells not much smaller!) house as much as she wanted it. And he wanted her kids to share in it, the dream come true. But.

Glor, i's ten years with my record for even *dri*vin' in a armed rob. Yeah. Yeah, she looked across atim. I 'gree wi' that. I agree. But then again, think of it this way: y' get parole don't ya? So ya make that, what, a seven? And afta seven years you come out an' you gotta share of a house to come home to. A *house*, Mulls? And me. An' me. I count, don't I? If ya don't mine a lady has had, like, a li'l fling now and then. Seven years isa long time. Smiling atim. (The bitch is smilin' at sayin' she'd be unfaithful to me?) But then her logic made sense. But no, seven years, a man couldn't do anutha seven weeks (I can't I can't.)

But then as he got closer to her place and knew this was prob'ly gonna be it, he got an idea. A good one. Surprised he hadn't thought of it before. Listen, he said as he turned off the engine of the shared mean machine. But she kept on climbing out. Please! Glor, please. (He di'n't remember ever having said please to anyone.) Said it again: Please, hon. Reaching for her — gently. Sit back down for a minute. I got this idea . . .

And she did quite like it. Yeah, she did. (If the stupid crybaby cunt c'n pull even that off.)

MOOKIE TOOK TOO long to load the shottie. Too long to get in the stolen car. Too long in givin' chuckle about the guns. Too long in startin' the engine. Too lo — Mook! Man, you gonna take us on this job or what? Too long a knowing frown for Abe's liking.

They drove over to Pine Block, just the extension of the suburb their pad was in, just a spillover like a toilet overflow what difference, it was all human shit; the State houses said so, and the car wrecks, the broken, rusting hulks of bodies and shells in the streets on the lawns said it. Abe, when he was a Heke — and he was having his occasional doubts on bein' a Blackie, lately he was — remembered Grace's friend, Toot, (used to call Grace G) lived in one, it was sat right outside his own family's front lawn, they didn't like him his parents didn't, so he had to sleep nights in the car wreck, he had to eat after they'd eaten, sometimes on their scraps if the parents'd pissed up more than usual. Abe often wondered, and tried to spot, if kids lived in the wrecks now. He'd heard Toot'd ended up a real good rugby player (like I coulda been if I hadn't got this idea in my head to be a Hawk).

The shottie on the seat between 'em, both anxious about the stolen car cos this's where the pigs started their searches and, hahaha, ended most ofem. The sawn-off sittin' there like it had life, not a thing gonna end it; maybe the thickness of barrels and the effect of being shortened, and how darkly warm and inviting the timber stock looked (jus' to hold, to run ya hand ovah and feel how smooth — hey, like a woman's body, her arm, or startin' ater knee — yeah, how smooth it was to the touch) as they turned into Rimu Street (my ole street. Man . . .) lookin' at it and realising it was not as similar to the street his gang resided in, sumpthin' about the associations (maybe it's the layers of memories, like grime, built up) and his being formed here. Jake The Muss and his mother conceiving him here. (When? After a party, when he was drunk? In the morning, with his breath still stink of booze?) Yet he remembered she said they'd had a good, uh, love life (well she is my mother).

He touched the shottie handle. An excuse to shoot (hah! shoot) a look at Mook, they'd grown up together and even after Beth took her family, minus Jake, Grace and Nig, out of the area to live with Charlie Bennett, Abe met up with Mook every day at school and they shared each other's streets after school. And here's a man — who'd been one since, what, fifteen, with havin' Jake as a ole man made him one before his time — and Mookie back on the street they'd waddled with shitty nappies while their mothers (his stayed like that, leas' mine changed) played cards and got steadily drunker as they drank beer at a practised, easy pace. (Like exquisitely drawn-out sex ya think, Abe? Seein's the sex they got wouldn't a been, like, out of a love-story movie.)

They went with corner eyes at the Brown Fists' barb-wire topped, high sheet-iron fences, the big gates there the side door, the top of the two-storey rearing up like direst of threats but of trembling, fury-rising challenge, too (and all them inhabitants inside on the utha side of the gates to Hell). How they hated them. Without even thinking why, though Abe felt he had his brotherly love reasons. They were just two forces, blindly opposed to each other. The same race, the same youth, the same growing up circumstances, same town, same country. Same blind hatred.

They went past the Shits' HQ and made unintended quiet sighs the same in passing, on down to the shops, now like ghetto pictures from America, graffiti scrawls, steel shutters, that decayed look, and did a u-ey and came back up Rimu. Gun it, Mook. Why, man? I said, gun it. So Mookie gunned it and they went past the Brown Shits' HQ at speed. And Mookie was asking, How we gonna do a driveby if I'm goin' a hundred and sumpthin'? You gotta laser on your shottie?

But Abe didn't say anything. And Mookie knew him well enough not to push it too far. Keep goin' and head for the hills somewhere, man. I wanna talk. Mookie shot a glance at his friend. Man, we don't have t' drive to no hills for me to know you're, uh. He didn't need to say it and nor would, not Mookie. Abe only looked across at Mook to see how far his contempt ran, how bad it showed. Instead, he saw his friend looking about the same as he felt. Mook?

Was Mook shaking his head and saying, man, man, ovah an' ovah. You know, the ram-raid was bad enough but leas' we did it, eh? Leas' we did it. But a driveby? Even if it's him, Jimmy Bad Horse himself, we saw, it's — well, man, mean t' say, shootin' a man is . . . Mookie driving them through the streets with the wrecks of cars sat kerbside, graffiti sprays like ghetto hieroglyphics, like messages from hell, rottweilers that'd eat a baby one gulp, and owners that produced and dumbfoundedly proceeded to try and raise (abuse) all the Block's babies, or most ofem anyway. And these two young dudes in a stolen car cos they were gonna abandon it soon's they'd done the biz, get back to the pad and boast cool about it, about a driveby like adding to their job CVs, unable to go through with it.

Mook, I was worried you'd, you know — Man I w's worried you were. Neither was gonna say the word: scared. No need to put the boot into 'emselves. Abe, you tell any of the bruthas what we were gonna do? Fear in Mook's voice. No man, I didn't. 'D you? Yeah, I did. Sorry, bro, but I tole someone.

Abe looked away, out his window at the fucken straight, uncomplicated don't-have-ta-prove-'emselves-all-the-damn-time or'n'ry folks. Mosta them white (lucky bastards). He looked at Mook: Y' think honkies have to do drivebys to, like, prove 'emselves? Do ya, man? And Mook shook his head, Nah, I doubt it. And both were shaking their heads, both a li'l bit tearful (from the relief of realising they weren't that fucken crazy). Man, I remember this trip with my ole man, Abe began. We had a rental car, eh, my ole lady'd saved up to get so we could go and see my bro — the one I tole you about's at, thing, uni-versity, well him — though he was in a boys' home, eh, cos they thought he was bad when the brother we knew weren't bad, he was juss, like, mixed up (like us), people didn't unnerstan' him, eh, specially the cops, only my — Well only Charlie understood him. And so he was in this home. And we were going to visit him; ole lady had a massive picnic in the boot. She'd wrote to Boog to say we were coming. My ole man was drivin'. You knew him, eh Mook? Yeah, man, everyone knew your ole man. Jake The Muss. Though he never said one word to me, Abe, not in all the time we grew up together. Nor me much either, Mook, and I was his son. Jake The Arsehole, man, tha's what he shoulda been called.

Well, the trip started off choice. Jake in a good mood, happy he was driving this bran' new car even though we had t' give it back nex' day (which didn't come for one of us. It didn't come.) I remember we were in the back seat singing up large, me and my li'l bro and two sistas, Poll and — He had to stop. It was like her very soul had rushed up from inside him, Grace's (my sister's soul). Grace, eh? Mookie finished for him. Yeah, Grace. A moment of silence, as though just for her.

Man, I was freaked, Abe, when I heard 'bout her. I was. Cryin' for you, man. I was cryin' for you. Cryin' for me, too, Mook. For the fucken lot of us. (I felt sumpthin' go in me that day when we were told by Mum Grace had, uh, killed herself. Knew straight away in my heart, even though I was only fifteen, I knew why she'd done it. And when it came out a cupla weeks later it was cos of my ole man she thought, her letter said, had been doing really bad bizniz to her, rape, I was the only one who didn't believe it. Sure, she was being raped by someone — had my suspicions it was Bully, sumpthin' about that man. But I think she killed herself for a heap of reasons, not just that. I think because she all the time went on about potential and why shouldn't she and us her sibs have our potential realised, what was wrong with us that we weren't allowed to reach our potential as like a birthright. She used to talk like that. And I think she woulda told me if dad'd done that to her. Which I don't think he did.

Dunno why. I think cos I'd never seen that side inim, me who useda be thinkin' about him all the fucken time, half in fear, the utha half, funny thing, with, like, love. Cos he was my ole man afta all. And the man I knew wouldn't've done that. I had observed him too closely; I woulda seen a sign, an indication as our next father, good ole Charlie, woulda put it and encouraged us to put. (Sorry to let you down, Charlie, and Mum, too. But I felt I had to do this. I'm thinking I mighta made a bad decision.) I would've seen an indication somewhere in his range of behaviour I was always observing cos I was always trying to figure out where I fitted, what I was, who I was, and man, even what was bein' made of me from having him as my father. I sure as hell knew it was doin' something to me.

But he wouldn't've touched his own daughter. If everyone sayin' he did had given it some thought, they mighta said different: cos he hardly ever touched his kids, as many times as he beat up Mum, thrashed her sometimes, he hardly laid a hand on us kids. To him that wouldn't a been manly. Yet comes to a woman, he was like every — every — man we grew up knowing: he thought it was — whassa word? — acceptable. Acceptable to beat a woman cos, well, cos she was a woman. But he never had nothin' against — nor for — kids. To him they were like they existed somewhere out of his reach or care, out in neutral territory. Not territory he ever thought of invading, it was just neutral. Didn't mean anything.)

We never got to visit Boogie. Yeah, I know, Abe. You tole me. Tha's right, I did. Well, when I was sittin' in the back when he pulled up outside that pub he used to drink at, I said to myself right there an' then: He ain't coming back out. Not till he's off his face pissed and with his mates headin' to our place for a pardy. I wanted to say this to Mum. To tell her don't hang around hopin', he ain't comin' out, it's his real home in there, those people're his real family. But I didn't say it. I wanted to tell Grace, to talk it over with her while Mum was in the pub the firs' time trying to gettim out. If me and Grace were one voice sayin' the same thing, we coulda jus' gone on and visited Boog. I c'd drive, was your big bro taught me. Right, Mook? (I need his friendship more than I need anything right now.) Right, Abe, 'member you jerkin' my bro's car down the road — ughh-urgh-urgh! Abe taking the relief of laughing along with his friend.

But I didn't say what I wanted t' say, Mook. Same as back there, tryin' to be a driveby. To be what I ain't, even though I been wanting that Jimmy's blood since he set up my bro, I ain't a driveby . . . A silence between 'em, of friendship, of being confused in this world either never gavem the answers or they came too late.

Man, an' nor'm I. Tell the truth, I di'n't wanna be in that rammie. Abe toldim, I know you didn't. And here's me making you cos all I wanted was in with the Hawks, eh bro? Yeah, man. What gave me the what-for to do it, thought of bein' a patched Hawk. (But now they weren't so sure.) Mookie pulled over. As it happened there was a piss-up goin' on at the back of a house, gats goin', fire goin' (kids running round the front, on the street, down the road). Laughter, mos'ly fat people standin' around drinkin', it's what they do when they ain't eatin', they're gettin' drunk. Singin' to the gats, sounds that't reach down to the lower new housing areas if the wind was carrying that way, and maybe — Abe had caught a glimpse earlier, of the grey slate roof — to the Trambert place and their hearing (and judging) and living free of worries, woes, bad influence fathers, failed drivebys, the daily hourly call on a man's manhood (and only a young man, too). Only to be found wanting when most it counted, or did now that Mookie had told someone.

So what're you gonna say after we ditch the car and're back at the pad, Mook? Say what, to who? Well, whoever you tole what we were gonna do. Who was it anyrate?

Uh, was Apeman I tole. *Ape*man! You tole him? The sarge-t arms, you tell him and now he'll be — man, Mook, what've you done to us? Abe, I tole him for you. He was bad mouthin' you, man, to a few of the bruthas. So I piped up and tole him maybe he'd change his mind after we'd done the driveby. Shoulda seenis face, Abe. He looked sick. (Yeah. How I feel right now.) And Abe sighed, took his eyes out the stolen window and for yet anutha time of doubts on who and what he was. No one to go talk about it to neither. Not even Mook. Was sumpthin' a man had to do onis own. Yet he couldn't help feeling so much of this (shit) had been already pre-decided for him. It hit Abe Heke (fuck the Blackie nonsense) in a thunderbolt flash of revelation: I — we, me and Mookie, all of us — got made to what we are. We di'n't have no choice. It felt, though, anything but a revelation; it felt like knowing every robbery job was guaranteed to have a man caught.

He reached out for Mook. Man, please, Mook, I'm freakin' out. Mookie's instincts were to grab his friend; so here they were, two sposed-to-be-tough cunts, patched-up Hawk membas, holding each utha in a stolen car. From the swift current of his startling thoughts, Abe said: What if we di'n't want to be how we are? And Mook said What? What you say, bro? I ain't gonna laugh at ya, jus' wanna know what you're sayin'. Still holding Abe.

But the feeling passed; he felt as if he were up on the bank with contemplating eyes down at the water mirroring himself, and Mook, too. He eased away from Mook, patting his mate's cheek as he did. Bes' friend I ever had. What we mighta been, eh, Mook? And Mook got that. Yeah, Abe Heke: we mighta been — he frowned. What would we've been, man, if we'd, you know, hadda different life? A bedda life ya mean. Yeah, a bedda one. Man, then I would say (I would say . . .), I'd say fucken near anything. My dead sis used to call it . . . She used to tell everyone in the Block. Potential. Yeah, that's the word.

But then their almost-mirroring looks changed yet again, Abe with sigh, Mook echoing it. Oh, well, Abe ran black leather cut-off gloves over the dashboard of a car too suspiciously modern to be likely their lawful possession. Ain't ready (not now, man) to be the jailbird found his, uh, potential. Nah, fuck that, Abe. Who needs that at our age? Hahaha. (Gotta laugh or we'll cry. Or do sumpthin' people, Real People, will not know the reason for.) Hahaha . . .

TWENTY-FOUR

HE THOUGHT IF he had a few beers first that'd do it and he could walk in not feeling stupid. But then he thought having beer jus' to buy some lousy flowers prob'ly been sitting in the Hindu's shop for days was a bit stupid — who'd buy flowers around here even if the area was one better than Pine Block? — and if he focused on gettin' the price down he'd be glowing about his li'l victory over a Indian and halfway up the street before he was worried about being seen carryin' 'em and before he knew it he'd be home, and they, the (lovely) flowers, would be sitting in some nice cool water in the jar there on the window-sill. An' a man'd be grinning and sayin', There there, my li'l lovely flowers, Jakey'll look after yous. But if he didn't hurry up and make up his mind, Rita'd be here and he wouldn't have the surprise for her.

But then, he thought, Nah, I got her one a those wine cask things last time, she should be lucky I thoughta that. But standing there in his sitting room some weeks missing of Cody's messy, always drunk, stoned and pilled presence multiplied by six or ten or sometimes twenny of the bastards, though he kind of missed the li'l cunt, Jake had eyes only for the blue vase and in his mind it had yellow and white flowers pluming from it. So he clapped his hands against his nicely pressed jeans and decided fuckit, jus' go an' buy the fucken things, man.

In the shop, Yes Mr Jakey, don't see you much in here? Where you take your business, not down the road, I hope? My prices very good. (No they aren't. You're a fucken black thief.) Yeah, well, I go to work early, home late. How late, Mr Jake, we stay open till very late, ten o'clock here. Open before you go to work. (Alright so I don't buy stuff here, only when I'm desperate. Buy my groceries at the Four Square down the road, a lot cheaper.) But Jake had seen — been taken by — a particular bunch of flowers in a big plastic bucket outside the Hindu's shop (smells of curry — don't mind a curry myself, but not too hot). He'd got a takeaway curry once, from his regular Chinese shop in town, and it was so hot he marched back to the shop and asked what the hell they'd put in. Only few chilli Missa Jake. Li'l cunts, they were jus' havin' a laugh at a man's expense. But they did givim some free rice to make up and ladled some other kinda juice into his foil container that would help make curry no' so ho'. Li'l slit-eyes, live here a hundred years and still can't speak English prop'ly. Know how to say money a hundred different ways though, li'l money-hungry bastards. And these Hindus aren't no bedda.

How much those ole flowers in the bucket? Old, Mr Jake? They are fresh in. But Jake didn't miss the blood-shotty eyes assessing him. Fresh when — las' week? No, not last week. Yesterday, I think. Ya think? Or you know? You buying, Mr Jake? 'Pends. On what, Mr Jake? (On if I c'n get 'em for a good price but mos'ly if I c'n walk out of here carryin' 'em. Fucken flowers!) On how much, Mr Patel, he had the name from waiting for the bus across from the block of shops and seeing it (proudly) lettered on the window running the outside perimeter of a red circle: PATEL'S DAIRY OPEN LATE — the longer to take the people's money, Jake's notion of the Indian man's entire outlook.

For you, because I see you every day 'cross the road, big man, proud man, waiting for his bus, I will drop from five ninety-five to, let us see now . . . Regarding Jake with those eyes't looked like the man got on the piss every night when he knew these Indians didn't. (Mus' be the curries they eat has their eyes on fire, haha!) Shall we say very special price of thrrre ninety-five? Rolling the r like a li'l Indian blackbird trilling, if they do trill. Even Jake could figure that was a good discount, but first he stepped outside and grabbed the bunch he wanted (firs' time I ever held flowers in my whole life. Now ain't that sumpthin'?) and held up close for inspection. And in just holding them, the stems wet (and crisp) and green in his big hands, he knew he was going to walk home with them. And the idea he'd got earlier that he'd have them wrapped up in newspaper so people wouldn't know now came to him as almost an insult to the flowers (Y' sweet li'l lovelies, Jakey never meant t' hurt ya feelings.)

So he pulled out a ten and asked, How much the discount if I buy two bunches? Oh, Mr Jake, the one discount was just a favour, for you the proud man, the big man, when I see you there, so handsome, so — he made a bicep gesture — ooo, strong (so what's he meaning by this, of me standin' at the bus-stop?) But you see, if I sell you two bunches at my very special price I am myself, my family, out of pocket. (His family? What's his fucken family got to with the price of fi — of flowers?) So Jake said it: I ain't asking the family for the discount. Ah no, you are quite right there, Mr Jake, you are not. And yet you are. You see, this is a family business. My wife, my children, my brother who buys our vegetable — and flower — produce from the market, you see how it is never my decision? (No, can't.) Jake shook his head, he didn't understand. If I make a sale, in this particular — he said the word as though starting with a b, why Jake was trying to stop himself grinning, as well at the li'l cunt tellin' these lies about his family — case I am losing money that belongs to *all* my family. And, you know, I am being a *good* family man, Mr Jake — Yeah, alright, alright. Nex' you'll be tellin' me their names an' how old they are an' that, Jake cut in. I never asked for your home (and your flash car you change every year), jussa couple a bucks discount. I'll still take two bunches though. (But leave me out on the family lecture stuff, mista. That's your lookout not mine.)

Walking home he was thinking not about the flowers but Patel's words, and his parting question. Big strong man like you, Jake — he'd dropped the Mr — no good wife to bear your children big and strong and handsome the same, no? He hadn't answered — couldn't answer. If he told the truth he'd be telling his (private) life story. Wouldn't surprise him if the black cunt knew half of it anyrate. He sure knew his name when Jake hardly ever shopped there. Little reason if a man no longer smoked. He might run out of butter, milk, bread, but thinking about it he had rarely done that. The only times he was short in the grocery department was if Cody and his mates got stoned and pigged out anything they could find, tinned stuff and toasting the bread from the freezer. But mostly Cody knew there'd be serious trouble if they did that too often, so they managed to live within their budget. (Hadn't thought about it like that. I just lived.)

Another funny thing, he got in his bank statement that he had one-thousand nine-hundred and two-dollars something cents. That was last month. He got such a fright he borrowed the firm van and went the next day lunchtime into town and withdrew the lot in cash in case they'd made a mistake (not my lookout). And every night after work checked the mailbox for a letter from the bank saying they'd made a mistake. But a week and no such letter. So he put it back in his account, less a hundred to go out and celebrate, and not before giving it a good look all spread out on the kitchen table and seeing, just maybe, the start of a car sitting there. Put an end to the shame of catching a bus. He'd worked out it came from his pay automatically going into the account and him drawing a set amount every Thursday lunchtime to buy groceries, the rent got deducted automatically, and he'd draw for the electricity bill when it came, and with a couple of wage increases with his change of job off the shovel onto a machine, then being made a charge-hand which he at first thought was cos he had the muscle power if any man got stroppy, till the boss told him, You've got good communication skills, Jake. You get on well with the men and they respect you. Well, that'd made him think, as well brought him out in the flushes of such praise, to know that he was respected and it had nothin' to do with his fists, which in turn led him to realise the Douglas brothers who he very much liked and admired, well they respected him, too, and yet they hadn't seen him have one fight. (I seen them fight, just the once when those smartarse dudes, a rugby team from outta town, thought they'd show how tough they were.) Maybe, he thought as he gave the flower vase a good wash in the sink and then towelled every square inch cos he knew the flowers wouldn't like the detergent not even a hint of it, didn't know why he knew since they were his first flowers ever, prob'ly instinc', maybe a man's changed a li'l bit. Maybe.

He (I'm) was (so) glad he'd got the two bunches, even if the other bunch he'd only got a buck off the price, because one wouldn't've been enough. He had the flowers individually laid out on old fish-and-chip wrap newspaper (not as if I read the paper. What would I be interested in, 'cept for the sport? The world out there don't include me in it. I'm on the outside lookin' in — well I'm not lookin' in, I ignore it, mostly I do. I'm jus' on the outside and that's it. Like most of the people I used to know, maybe most of my race) having filled the vase with water, and started placing them in, jiggling them about and smiling at the stems jamming up and his impatience, so he slowed himself down (calm down, boy, anyone'd think this was sex you was urgent for).

He slowed himself down and placed each one carefully and with consideration into the vase, alternating the colours, white, yellow, white. But they didn't sorta like fit. So out they came and he tried a more random combination. And as he added a flower the water started to spill over the top so he had to empty some of it out. Another flower in, careful-careful (Jakey ain't gonna hurt ya.) There. That was better. One flower left over.

Stepped back to admire his handiwork. This blue vase transformed by yellow and white bursts from green stems like bird plumage from its head. Smiling. Jake Heke was smiling. Well. Well how about that, exclaimed aloud in his li'l tidy kitchen. Rita'd be here soon. He took the vase, carrying it very carefully and more than that, with a kind of emotion-niggling reverence, to the window-sill. Stopped halfway across the sitting room floor. I know what. I'll keep 'em on the kitchen table while I'm sittin' there havin' a beer and when Rita knocks I'll take 'em to the sill then. That way he could sit and gaze at them.

After three quick cans — to get the rush and maybe the flowers — he sat down again with the fourth from his well-stocked-with-beer fridge and began to think about beauty, since it wasn't actually something a man spent his time giving thought to, except when it was in women, and not as if the woman now late coming here was beautiful and yet she was. Alright, how's she compare with those flowers? She doesn't, was his first reaction. Well she sort of does, if flowers're natural and this arrangement being his is not sophisticated, it just is, which is pretty damn good, and so is she, Rita. Stripped off she's plump, got them ripples in her upper thighs and a bit of a bump in her gut. But she doesn't make a man sick as soon as he's had her and nor does she think she has anything to be ashamed of when she stands around naked after they've done the business and always it's good business, so is she beautiful? No she's not. But she has beauty. But then what is beauty? What if a person's born with ugly features but beautiful inside? All these questions of, suddenly, great importance. (It's like the question of what meaning are stars to sea dwellers or those who are blind?)

Well, next thing he was in the bathroom, looking at himself in the mirror. And asking himself what it was he saw, without knowing why he was doing this having never done anything, not even a thought, like this before. Jake, what do you see? Couldn't tell himself he was looking for beauty, couldn't tell himself he was looking for sign, or proof, or absence of its existence inside him. The looking he'd done inside himself was on that question, of did he rape his daughter when he was drunk and just couldn't remember it or didn't want to remember. What he'd come up with was, there had never been a time in his life of not remembering a major incident no matter when he had been drunk out of his skull. When a man was in more sober recall the important, the big, the disastrous, the violent things, always wrote themselves up on the blackboard of his mind. Always. Like a teacher starting the lesson with a list of the bad things he'd done so the blackboard never had an empty week. (But was never the name Grace there. But never.) But what he'd found there, inside himself, was the truth, some tiny bright burning of himself that he could hold onto and keep him strong enough to withstand the wrong people thought of him until the light became, as it had now, bigger. Not that it declared a man innocent in people's minds, nor gave him back his standing; it was just a strength to keep going and make another of himself even if he didn't know such a process was happening. Nor even now that it had happened. (I feel the same, more or less.) But looking at himself in the mirror he thought, just for a moment, that he saw more. (Ah, but then Jake The Muss Heke you haven't been shown *how* to look at yourself.)

Those days living like a tramp in the park, and the days afterward of life's everyday needs proving to be huge, confusing decisions, of not knowing how to go about getting a State rental, of filling out a form for a job, even shopping for groceries, or ironing, washing clothes; it was like growing up, and not all over again but for the first time. At what, thirty-six? Shit. (*Shit.*)

When the knocking on the door from Rita came he kept standing there before the mirror, as if there wasn't too much of this (the story) to go before he'd be covered in light glorious light. (Not long to go, Jakey.)

But anyway she was the one who finished it off, after first she expressed delight at seeing the flowers he shyly inclined his head at in grinning hint. Oh *Ja*-key, she'd said. Aren't you a funny one. I wondered about that vase the last time I was here. And when he told her he'd filled it for the very first time she got a bit teary eyed and hugged him. Just hugged him. Then he went and got the wine cask, left over from her last visit and remembered the instructions of how to set up the (cute li'l) tap, and tapped it into a wine glass he'd bought specially for her that time. He cracked another can. Had got a squeeze of toothpaste in his mouth while he was in the bathroom so she'd not smell he'd been drinking beforehand. He put a record on his stereo he'd bought second-hand, thinking next he was going to buy a CD player, but this'd do, some Dusty Springfield, white woman who sang like a black woman, and asked Rita, Wanna dance? And she told him, Ask me again, Jakey. And he didn't ask why she wanted him to, he just asked again: Would you like a dance, Ri? Oh yes! she said as if he'd asked for the first time. And up she got. From the sofa he had the blanket over, well he had a blanket over both them, but she had the flash one with the criss-cross patterns. And they danced.

To the bed where he'd bought his first ever sheets, straight out of their wrapping onto the bed. Next time he was gonna get one a them proper covers, a bedspread. In the newly sheeted bed she was all her best controlling self: Easy now, baby. Nice 'n' slow. We got all night. You're like a stallion, honey. Ooo yes, big and strong and so fucking handsome (what the Hindu said, without the fucken), but just hold yourself, alright? And he joked, Hold my horses ya mean? Yeah, tha's what Ri means, honey. Hold your horses till you hear the call.

And it was the best loving he'd made, even better than the best with Beth (oh Bethy) even though they'd done it good. You have to have the other person (meaning me) in the right frame of mind too for it to, uh, be so, uh, complete like this. Her moaning as she came was like Dusty's bes' singing in his mind, his pounding heart, his surging loins, which the sweet melody moanin' was calling to him same time, you come on now, Jakey. You let go of that stallion steed in yourself. And how she did open herself like giving and taking (potential life seed) birth of him at the same time. How she did that.

She finished in leaving him with the parting, troubling words like Mr Patel did, around midnight; he was going hunting in the morning, with his new purchased rifle (after the cops did a check on me for criminal convictions and I was surprised I didn't come up even though I hadn't been to court, I just thought with all those fights I had, cupla hundred, they must show up somewhere. But I was clean, which made me feel cleaner than I felt before that, and they gave me my firearms licence and it had my name on it which pleased me, it was like a statement that I was actually worth something, that whatever I'd done wasn't so bad it was on their records — but it's bad enough, Jake Heke. You better be knowing that — I went to the bank and got the money and bought a second-hand .30-06, what the Douglas brothers advised me to buy. My own gun. Like having my own woman.) Even though it'd been, well, a wonderful night, a word he'd used for the first time; just before she got in her car and he out under the moonlight, a half moon up there, which reminded him of spotlighting for deer, saying goodnight, thanks for a — but he had said the word, wonderful, only in his (silly proud) mind — good night, Ri, she'd said: You're a good man, Jakey. A good man. (Why thank you.) If only you thought about your kids, if only you mentioned them, if only you just now and again wondered after them, I'd — why I'd seriously consider living with you, I would. Which is what he'd asked her tonight, after the loving as they basked in that nice silence of tingling skin, emptied loins but fulfilled hearts, the very soul. Now he had his answer, or his reason why.

She — her words — were just disappearing red eyes in the night, left him standing there, under the streetlight now not the moon, the moon had removed him from its pale glow, it was just streetlight, and a man feeling like everything of meaning got lost, got taken, snatched away from him even when he was trying. Even when he was really trying. The beam of truth's light on the matter of his children just did not reach him. (A man has to learn these things, don't he? Like a man who is loved in his childhood grows up to be, at worst, a person capable of loving in his manhood, even a failed manhood. Isn't that how it must work?)

He found sleep still grinding his teeth and tears yet again welling up in his eyes. And he dreamed of children who were strangers to him. And they weren't with that unified humming of the unforgettable dream. Sound they made was crying. With him, the dream figure, quite unable to know what to do how to do, it was like being asked to build a building when you didn't know how to hold the hammer. Even when another voice (sounded like Beth) was whispering to him in the dream, Just pick up the hammer and start. He just couldn't hear it could (poor) Jake Heke. Every male growing-up figure, every male friend he had, had more or less mirrored his standards, his values. That was why he couldn't hear even the best (my own) intentioned voice.

TWENTY-FIVE

HE WOKE UP from a dream of him in a roaring mean-machine gang car painted undercoat grey with black smears (cos they make it look tougher), smelling of the bruthas body stink, even in a dream, and himself firing out the back window, like he shoulda been able to get himself to do, at a whole army of Brown Shits — to arguing down the passage, when he hadn't got to shooting Jimmy Bad Horse and, now he was awake and with the real world, probably never would. (I failed. I woulda fought with the man, fists, no hol's barred. But soon's I put the gun in my hand I lost it. My courage fell outta me like my guts'd spilled.) Arguing between a man and woman. Not that arguing was a new experience, here or anywhere else 'cept those few years living with Charlie Bennett.

Looked straight out at the night from his sheeted bed — he'd bought them thinking if his mother ever heard he was sleeping sheetless when she hated sheetless, from Jake, and anyway it wasn't very clean, she'd be the one doin' the shooting; the night was clear, with stars, yeah man, and that immediate voiceless yet great echoing claiming of all men's (irrelevant) souls, even angry, now much troubled, young men like him. Maybe especially like him. He contemplated stars and claiming and inner questions for a moment before the arguing voices made claim again on his awoken ears. (Fuck them. Man never gets any sleep round here.)

Yeah, and fuck you, too, mista! — *Phlatt!* Say that again, bitch. (No, don't say it.) Whyn't she jus' shuddup? Alright I will: Go fuck yaself. Ya hear? Do what you want, think it *worries* me? Man, it don't even *hur*t me.

Abe could picture her li'l thin frame standing up to Ape, bettin' she'd haver shades on even at this early morn hour; admirin'er but thinking she was a fool to be standin' up to Ape's manhood cos he was gonna find out what did hurter, seein's it weren't slaps. So he braced himself for what was to come. Old memories, childhood ones, came trickling back the opposite of the trickle of sleep that comes ovah a man. This was a waking, as sharp as sleep is sweetly (usually) dull. As keen as a cold wind coming off the lake, or the forested hills in winter of his imagining since he'd never been out there. (Ain't been nowhere. None of us have. Ain't goin' nowhere neither. None of us are. In this house or even outside it. We just sit, waitin' for a bus that ain't gonna come.)

Of his ole man and ole lady and her, Beth (my mum), saying to Jake (The Arsehole): You go 'head, mista. Do your fucken worst, mista. That's what she used to say, calledim mista, like Tarns was sneeringly calling her man, Apeman. Heard her now: You go right ahead, mista. But I still ain't backin' down to you. I — Bang! Ape's fist and Abe's memory went off like a shot. (You fucken arsehole cunt . . .) Thinking he might just up and do sumpthin' about this. But then again, his courage not back to normal yet.

He started shaking instead. Same time his own old memories were making a claim on him, of being a kid huddled on the bed, the bottom bunk, and Nig going back and forth to listen to progress on their father beating up Mum, back to the frightened kids (you'd a thought we'd've got used to it) and giving each his or her turn of comforting (strong) arms and half-whispering voice ('cept I don't remember what he used to say. What could he have said that would take away what was happening, what could he say to have us believe that the world could be and was a better place?) If Nig wasn't there then it was Grace who dished out the comforts, to Huata and Polly she did, like it was her got the house back in order if Mum was too beaten or herself too drunk and uncaring to do it, cos Jake sure as hell never cleaned up the mess, the chaos of his causing. He didn't remember what Grace used to say either, her memory had a kind of veil over it, he remembered only her last few years.

That sound wasn't a slap it was a punch. He knew punches when he heard 'em, so did most kids he knew (ask them). Now it was like God or sumpthin' had asked him a question of was he with fear of this now he was older in its listening witness? (Yeah. I am, man. I am. It hurts and disturbs me jus' the same.) So then he hated his father for what he'd done to their growing-up witness. But then he got the thought: What if Jake's growing up had been that? Wouldn't he, like, grow up and do the same? So where does it end? No, fuckim. No excuse. Someone's gotta break the pattern, the cycle. (I wouldn't hit a woman. Even if I wanted to, my mother'd kill me.) Alright, so it was like these questions and half answers were from God, so where is He now in this HQ hell at deepest (dark) hour of Sunday (churchgoers to come) morning? Where is He?

Abe got up. Tarns gave a shortened scream as he was pullin' on his black-leather pants. He stopped; like listening to a song he knew well, off by (broken) heart: *bang! Uuh* — knew that line, too: she was cutting her cry short to deny the bastard satisfaction. Just like his mother'd done. Fuck you, Ape! Aloud, as he dived into his black jumper, same colour as the night, but not as black as the throbbing like the arrival of some terrible presence was just now come. Like something in the process of the inhabitants of this night, down that hallway, had made a (dark) decision.

Ooooff-mmm! sound of air punched out of a person — *that* person. The li'l patched-up member carrying all lowly women's sadness. The li'l sexless, broken-hearted, infected gangie bitch with only a much-fucked body to offer as sign, gesture, of her impossible friendship when even half a decent man would see sex was the las' thing she was offering, it wasn't even love she wanted. Li'l thing jus' wanted her life back. For it to start again, afresh, anew. With highways and byways she could choose to go down. (When she offered me to go to bed it was just her fucked-up unnerstanding, of man and men that she'd figured out from the cave she lived in iner mind; that men firstly wanted the deal to have sex in it; which is why she took, allowed, resigned to grunting, glassy-eyed cock insertion, times countless, of men and man their selfish terrible singular need (wants) uses and abuses taking 'emselves out on her (poor lil') body, never assuming she had a soul.)

Whack! of the li'l body now bein' punched, that had to be in her face, but still she cut short her cry to show the cunt pain didn't hurt her, her hurt'd already, long ago, been done (oh Tarns, Tarns . . .), Abe Heke trembling. Abe Heke (fuck the Blackie name) betrayed by himself, down to a reduced state of not being able to go to her rescue.

So his mind went through another change, of asking why didn't she jus' say sorry, why didn't she jus' shut her mouth and then it'll stop, she should know a man is a man in our world, specially in a gang, it's all (he thinks and therefore is) he's got. It was the world each of them'd come from before here, of woman, women gotta lie down, trap shut, to a man's manhood, to his PRIDE (when where's the PRIDE in smashing up a woman? Where's the pride in that?) As Abe lay on top of his bed pretending the beating was going past him.

Then another change: mind suddenly snapped awake, or the curtains yanked across, as clear as that star-filled night out the window, every li'l pinprick, stab, wink, burst 'n' spread of separate light, of separate entities of heavenly bodies in space was like a person's — this person's — (universe) mind; the thoughts that'd made him, unmade him, shaped him, warped him, disfigured, sculpted — same thing. Same thing. (Same fucken thing, stars in space and memory grooves bein' pinpricks, stabs, winks, bursts 'n' spreads: isa same thing. And-so-is-what-is-happening-down-that-passageway: it's the *same thing*.) It's life turned, made into ugly, disfigured shaping, acting out itself. Trying to break free of its ill-cast mould.

He could hear it, that presence, as though a ghostly soft whoosh of quietly arriving air come in and settled in a corner. So he waited in terror for what wasn't the same, since what he was hearin', what was coming to his ears, what was dark and came with now a certain smell (like a low slut's sex) like something gone rotten, something beyond life even as he, Abe Heke, had known it and nor would his father, not even Jake, as the boot went in, and in and in. And he standing on the same shuddering, sympathetic (to the sound, the vibrations) floorboards she, Tania, was on, and then . . . footsteps, a voice't said, Shut the fuck up, woman. Kicker again, Ape, she won't shut it. He didn't shout his words, the prez. He just said them, but in a tone. Of last warning.

(HIS FACE, LOOK atim, isa p'ture of Man, all men, or mosta the men I knew. Oh, but not Nig Heke, I never liked a man so much, if only he hadn't fucked it with Horse, if only Jake his ole man hadn't made a fool outta Horse in a crowded pub, then Nig'd still be alive and I wouldn't've put myself on the block for all the fullas t' fuck me in showing my disappointment in Nig — or so I had been told — letting The Family down. But his making up for his disgrace (or so we thought it was) by being one of the gunmen in the shootout with, well, this gang, which is why I joined it cos of Jimmy Bad Horse setting up Nig to lose his life and me being Nig's girl, his one an' only, tricked into thinking badly ofim, he'd still be alive now (alive-alive-oh. But what's alive, Nig? You must know that bedda now. What's alive, man? Is this alive?) And his li'l bro, Abe down the passage there prob'ly out to it not hearin' this; a nice kid, though dunno about the name change to Blackie, it's what my man Ape did, and now look what he's doin', I think he'll kill me (so what's bein' killed? What is there to be afraid of?)

Changing his name from a Heke? The — the re*spec'* that name had, like or hate the man, when he was Jake The Muss Heke. Oo, even I got damp thinking ofim. Only utha man I got that for was his son, Nig. Mus' be I like the Hekes.

Lookit this man's face: it's a mask they pull out from behind their backs, their real self, then they start beating up the woman (me. If woman is what I am. And somehow I don't think I ever made it to one. Un-made, that's how it happened for me.) *Bang!* Now shuddup. No, I won't shuddup. Bang! Funny thing, they don't hurt, not really. Ya get used to 'em the blows. Ya even feel kind of superior, yeah. Ya fucken deaf, mista? I said, you go t' fucken hell. Ya hear? (Course he hears, why he's jus' hit me again — ohh! — Now that one did hurt.) Ya cunt! I'm a cunt, he says. *So-are-you!*

Walk up toim, can't hardly see out my lef' eye: Happy now, mista? Wan' anutha whack? Gwon, have anutha one, on the house, callit Tarns' chrissie prezzie. (Ohhhhh!) Now I'm on the floor, the dirty, unwashed boards seen a million los' footsteps on the stumbling way to bed, sheetless beds, seenem in every stoned, drunk, pilled state, but yet kinda clear-headed about 'emselves, their true state, the hell they know they're livin' in when they thought bein' here was sposed to end that, they know every night of their life that no madda how much dope and piss and pills are down and inhaled it don't change the life made 'em, brought 'em here. I'm on the floor now lookin' atis feet. Well, his boots: Hey! That's goin' a bit far ain't it? Even for you, a fucken ape from the fucken jungle! Gotta mouthful of my own teeth.

Now I'm bein' hauled up — fuckim. In his face: Ooo, you so strong Mista Apeman. You been doin' WEIghts? (Haha-fucken-ha.) Spit out bits of my physical existence (who cares? Weren't much of an existence anyrate.) Had bad teeth anyrate.

Is all slow motion to me. Ever since that day of the burning, whenever the crunch comes on the reel of life slows down. So I can see it bedda (HAHA!) — Urghhhhhh! Stupid idiot thinks my laughter's at him when it's at me, my funny li'l mind. Ya would wouldn't ya? (Take that. And this.) You're so screwed up you think the world's down to jus' one person who counts. Yeah, you heard right. *Bang!* Do it again, mista, I'm still tellin' ya. You think your hurt is the only thing't means anything in this worl'. But what about mine? What about kids asleep down the road, in this town, this country, who're hurtin', what about them then? Or're you th' only person on the planet. I know: the only ape in the jungle! HAHAHA! Laugh inis fucken face. Laugh-in-his-fucken-face. (Oh, now lookit this: he's pulled out a gun. Been sittin' tucked into the back of his (filthy) jeans all this time. I knew he was beyond his normal wild t'night.)

Thata gun? (I wish I remembered that line the movie-star woman said. Oh, well, nemine. It don't madda. Nuthin' maddas.) He's got it out now, it's a commitment. To his manhood. As if I'm a threat to that. Huh? You wha'? I am near to laughing inis face again. You wha', wha'd you say jus' then? Justa make sure I heard right.

He says: How'd ya like a bullet up your cunt.

How would I? HAHAHAHA! Mista, I had *worse* up there, know what I mean? (Oh, he knows alright. Jus' lookit his face now.) Ape, ya bedda not explode before your gun does, bro. Here it comes — bang! 'Nutha whack for the road. Feel bedda now, Mista Bullet? No, Mista Bullet doesn't, why he sticks the gun down there, at my bizniz (some bizniz. It's bankrupt!) my cunt, my hole, my box, my snatch, my twat, their and his bitta (dry) meat. It never belonged to me, not from when the firs' uninvited man helped himself to it, not since the moments in time my life disowned me, dispossessed me of myself. Funny that, how violation of my vagina should be my entry card, my passport to the gang countries (to hell) when I never had ownership of any sexuality, no actual feelings that were the same sweet shivers I dreamed they could be, and Nig Heke a few times took me close to knowing.

So. So I look at the *real* cunt and askim: A bullet up my cunt? Like I said, I had worse an' I had *bi*gger. And then I laugh: Ha-ha-ha-ha-hah!

Uhhhh! this one in the guts, taken my breath but not my spirit but still fall to the ground, can't help it, my wind's gone, can't breathe. God, men. Fucken men. I shoulda been a lezzie. Women don't hurt each utha. Prob'ly the, uh, sex side woulda been bedda, too. Softer. Like Nig was. Oh how I '(n)joyed with him. He was gentle — gentle — with me. Apeman, hell, he caught me same time as I caught him, we was both on a downer, it sure weren't his li'l cock I enjoyed. I jus' up and accepted him as my man and took what came. All the cocks I knew, had inside me, in every hole 'cept my ears, only one evah gave me feeling down there was Nig. I think cos he was loved, by his mother; she'd given him a base. He pulled me up onto it. (Oh, Nig. I'm so sorry, man.) The rest, they was jus' weights, like live corpses humpin' up and down on me, flippin' me ovah on my back like a dog, *uh-uh-uh-uh*, wonder they never started barkin', cos plenty sure had bite soon's they had their way; they done it this way that way any which way when I couldn't feel it hardly any.

Oh, but a man in his state's got no mercy, he's got no eyes to see, he's left even our world (he's the forming stuff of mankind, star stuff, stardust, violently marrying matter) it's why I'm coming up off the wall and now slammed against the wall (all the atoms of himself his terrible inner core are banging against each utha). And now even the prez is joined in, he's jus' tole Ape to kick me if I don't shuddup. Ya can't be standin' up to a man. These are *real* men, or so they truly think, I dunno about believe, there is a difference. But really, you guys, you're jus' fucken children. (There, take that.) Ya never grew up. Ya can't. (You can't.)

Shut-your-fucken-mouth, sista. The cheek to call me sista when he's sayin' that. Or — But he doesn't say what. Or what? I ask him. Or what? But he's not sayin'. He c'n see Ape's got the gun. Ya can't hurt me — But dammit, in sayin' the word I up and fucken cry. Me. When I hardly evah cry. Tears are a woman's way of saying she's weaker than a man. But I ain't weaker than these two arseholes. I think I'm cryin' cos there's a third party but yet I can't have my say. I'm cryin' because he's sided with Ape, he hasn't heard my side of the story. Ape's got it inis head that I wanna go with Abe, says I got the hot eyes forim all the time when I don't. I jus' keep seein' Nig inim, I keep lookin' at Abe and thinkin' he shouldn't be in this gang, he should be at home with that mother they got who gave 'em their love base even witha ole man like they had. (And take me outta here with you — please.)

Prez, where's the rule says I can't look at anutha brutha or talk toim? I thought tha's why we joined, cos we're a family. Aren't we? Aren't we? But his eyes are cold. Cold like that gun barrel is. They don't like women, I shoulda known that. They hate us. We're their fuck-up mothers they c'n take it out on. If they liked women they wouldn't think nigger men in America're so fucken cool and hotshit callin' their women bitch and ho. (Oh-oh. I think he's gonna use that thing. It's his cock: he's pulled it out and now it's gotta be emptied.) From looking at someone sposed to be my man I'm lookin' at my executioner.

. . . WE WAS HANGING around this music shop in town, me and two of the sistas, two bruthas (to pro-tect us women, hahaha, whadda fucken joke), shaded up so people, Real People, wouldn't know how much we hate, envy, admire and don't unnerstan' 'em. But mainly to hear the music cos Maori gangies love their music. And we were there, even if we'd never admit, not hardly even to ourselves, cos of a need for people, even Real People. To ourselves, out loud, we'd go, Real People? Man, they suck. Makin' out our daily strolls down the main street are only to scare 'em, snarl at 'em, show 'em how bad we are; truth is, it's the broken connection we're secretly hangin' out for, our end of the wire is still severed on the ground hissing and crackling, whilst they've repaired theirs, connected it up with uthas bedd'n us, who try harder. So fuck 'em, is what we say when we mean sumpthin' else.

Cos we were a group we got our guts, our (false) courage to walk on into the shop (gwon, stare) take our sweet fucken time lookin' at the CDs ovah at the Rap section and the S for Soul beside that. Then a brutha, emboldened by being a gangie withis mates to back him, goes up to the counter and asks the white fulla does he have a CD by a singer called Speech. Pretty weird name but how it is; weren't our li'l baby to name, hahaha. The brutha thinkin' he was pretty smart to be askin' for a singer called that. Well, the honky looks it up on his computa and fuck me if he doesn't have it. Well, I'll be, we all say at once. Good, says the brutha. Play it. Track two. Which was titled (aptly so) 'Ask Somebody Who Ain't (If You Think The System's Working.)' Long title. Very apt. But then in anutha way, I was thinking, the system was workin' for us by the fulla agreein' to play it on his stereo.

And we stood there in our glad, sad an' dirty rags, behind, unnerneath, armoured by, our shades, or bold enough to have 'em up on our head but poised to come down like shutters at end of a shop day in the ghettos we came from and lived in; strangers in our own town, our country (to ourselves), thinkin' how staunch we were gettin' 'em to play our music without sayin' please, and yet feelin' very uncool bein' in here, their shop, their stereo, their CD selection, their money, their everything that we weren't. After we listened to it there was this feeling, we dunno, of somehow feeling bedda about bein' in here. The music'd not only fluke-united us but it took away so many of our fears. I think cos it put us on familiar — very familiar — territory where we knew, even us scumbags, we ruled.

So Angel goes up to the whiteman, Can you please play track seven. Please, if you will. Angel. The man goes back, Are you intending to purchase this, uh, madam, when we knew he wanted to say bitch. And Angel goes, Yeah, sure. Course we are. When we weren't. Or not that I knew of, not when we had Speech at home that't come from a burglary somewhere.

Well, Angel gets it started by picking up from the opening line. It was about flowers, petals, how that hippy generation was into that sorta stuff. (Like ours could've been too. I like flowers.) But then Angel got shy and dried up. So I took it over and she came back in again, so did the uthas. The song w's called Let's Be Hippies, which is the las' thing we wanted to be, even secretly. Hippies are white people. But what we wanted was to sing this song and as close to the original as we could, tha's what we wanted in our hearts of aching, yearning hearts.

We dunno what happened what took ovah us. We did know that the White Folk in the shop maddered less and less to us as the song unfolded and we, like flower petals, like sunshine, with it. Guess the smoke in the car on the way musta helped, musta sparked sumpthin'. By the time we hit the chorus with Speech and his own chorus we were soarin', baby. Man, we've hit with all the practice Speech himself musta put into it and we had, too, at our pad, our long idle days of bein' (government-paid) gangies (it ain't a glamorous life, as most'll well imagine it ain't, but not us, not to start with) unemployed, nuthin' to fucken do and no do anyrate to do it even if it walked up to us with a (beautifully) written invitation. But the nights were ours, we raged at nights, our li'l petals came out in the blue cellophaned light, and now Doodie took the high harmony in his beautiful — man, jus' beautiful — falsetto like a — like a lake, if a lake could sing, if something clear and shining, deep and well with its own peace was capable of converting to voice then Doodie was a lake.

The timing was everything in this powerful chorus. But we were there. We were right there. And we all knew, the five of us, that if we were never to get nothin' right again in our lives we had to get this right. So we lifted our heads, closed our eyes, pulled down the shutters to our shopfront faces, but only so we could sing, to make fuck-sure we were gonna pull this one off. Hell, was only a few sung lines of all our lives we had to get right. Jus' a few lines.

The words were about release and how just one lousy day of it'd do. (One lousy minute, honey bunny, is what we were talking — well, singing. Yeah, singing, baby. Us, a buncha Hawks who once were li'l sumpthins that didn't and couldn't work out. Us.)

With phrasing that was big, tight and difficult. But (God) we got it. We goddit. We sang it the second time with even greater confidence than the firs', as much as we did amongst ourselves back at the pad, but shit that didn't count, that wasn't like this, witha audience of Real People (Suck on this, People.) Havin' ourselves and bein' stars front of our own audience, our own mirrors. We were knowing performing excellence outside of our, uh, comfort zone. And when the lines came about the guy not wanting to sex with her, I thought, Wow. Tha' right, a fulla who don't want sex he just wants to spend one perfect day with her (me)? And he asks is that OK? Baby, Mista Speech and any man who thinks like that you'll not only get your perfect day you c'n have the sex withit, too — afterward.)

Then we walked outta that shop. Out onto the main street (where I was when Nig my beloved got shot. We were line-ups across the street, Maoris and fuck-ups the same, but against each utha. Stood there with some of us tooled up, hatin' each utha without ever knowing why. Shots rang out, they echoed in the canyons of human construction, in the canyons of a few of us our minds, and Nig got catapulted backwards, blasted by a Hawk came running across the road witha shottie and let rip.) Now we were a new batch 'cept me walking lined-up across the pavement not to fuck People off but cos'f what we'd done, the place we'd gone to, the music released from us. We were jus' kids enjoying a perfect day.

JUST ONE DAY to release . . . the line coming back to me with a gun stuck not in my place down there where men took false refuge, or jus' plain shot their (heavee) loads into, but at my face which they ignored, where the real story was. (And scoured into my heart.) Only a few understood me, Nig and oh, tha's right, Mulla Rota. Poor Mulla, still in the utha gang, still in jail even when he was out, briefly, supposedly free. I told him of the fire. I told Nig and I told him down the passage, Abe. Oh well, won't be tellin' no more to no one, not witha gun stuck in my face 'bout to go off.

Gotta gun in my face and the mind behind the face is with one word from that song: release. It's why I'm smilin' and he's frowning, he wants to see fear before he pulls the trigger, but I won't be givinim that. The smile's from my heart, when heart was pure and untouched, a po*tent*ial, when it was a potential to be anything it wanted, anything this pretty li'l girl from Mangakino, middle of nowhere but still a somewhere, an anywheresville of this big world, this tiny world, anything I wanted. One perfect day in my life.

I ask the Ape: You sure 'bout this, what you're gonna do? Not to save myself. Not at all. It's cos I'm sure he can't do the time for it, not a life sentence, a minimum of ten years. (Even my life's worth sumpthin' to the justice system.) That what he thinks he's saving of his soul, his man-pride, his (tattooed) face, the very manhood he thinks he's doing this for is what'll desert him. One night — it won't be day — in his cell, it'll be a night like this, early hours, he'll wake up to a thunderstorm goin' inside him. Then he'll be in anutha place, a cold frozen place shivering, shaking all ovah and all his lies and falsehoods he's wrapped himself in'll shed from him like clothes. Nah, he won't be able to do the time.

Oh well. His face isa p'cture the same as the prez's. I never spoke the prez's name not even in my mind, cos Prez is all he was and is, a title, a membership he hides behind like Jimmy Bad Horse does, real men, real leaders wouldn't be presidents of gangs of fuck-ups and monsters. Real men'd be presidents out there in the wider world. Or of good gangs. I'm smiling at them both, it's a wonder they can't see how pure the smile is. Go on then, I offer softly. Do it.

I see his hand trembling, so's his jaw, his hurt he's building up for himself — himself, not me. I'm just another cause — so he can do this. The filming in his eyes. And still I smile. I smile. He takes a shuffle closer, he wants to say something, to justify himself. (But what can he say?) He wants me to beg for what he ain't gonna give me. I smile. I just smile. Everything's so clear now. Words, faces, meanings, but not my life. No, I don't think what I got dished up was a very fair call. But, oh well, how the cards fall, as they say, for some.

I see it leave the barrel. But first of his eye. I see the trigger squeeze register in his eye. Now I see it leave the barrel I do (I do. I do.) And they're the words I'm hearing, not the thunder of death hurtling for me. I hear them as marriage-vow takings, one to the other, one in echo of the other: I do. I do. That's what I've said to that force, that thing, just left its beautiful dark cave, that opening to my next and last world: I do. Tania says: I do. I'm saying so the bullet, when it takes me, takes me good. Forever in my perfect day . . .

Light. Light. Light, ligh', li'lies and this softest of darknesses on the fast way; with it the mother I knew and the father I didn't saying goodnight and sorry so sorry, but it's alright. It's alright, now it is. This's so much better than I thought and hoped it would be. Got my own sorries to say to my sister, my two brothers. That's alright, Tarns. Wasn't your fault. We're here where everything is forgiven, and there's Nig. Hello, Nig. Smiling my pure smile atim. Tarns is home.

HOME! (I GOTTA go home!) The shot is one echoing, reverberating word in Abe Heke's mind: Home! Home.

Right by the door, light a yellow spill slicing his feet, waiting to hear a moan, a sound to say she was alive. But all he got was a stream of words, a whispered exchange of voices he knew well enough when at ordinary level and yet didn't know (these aren't my bruthas, these are mongrel-dog cunts). His teeth coming together so hard they coulda cracked.

Shit, man. Man, she pushed me too far. Yeah, I know she did, man, but man you fucken *kill*eder. Look ater. Man, I c'n see that, not fucken bline, what we gonna do now? What we gonna do, man, is fucken life in the can we don't getter outta here. The fuck you puddit iner head for? Man, I tole you: she pissed me off. I tole her to shut the fuck up. Yeah, I know you did. I tole her the same. But fucken hell, Ape . . . she's — Well, maybe she ain't? See anything movin'? Nah, man, she's wasted. Ape, you killeder. How many times you gonna tell me that 'fore you think I know I did? Alright then, now what?

Now what? Prez, what about him down there, fucken Mista Smoothie? Finish it off while we're at it. While we're at it? Man, while you're at it. I never killed no one. But yeah, if he's gotta go he's gotta go. May as well finish off what ya started.

They whispered his name. They've killed her and now it's his turn! He rushed for the window, but part of him left back there, with her, Tania (who else would she have? Never even knew her surname. Never knew her, except the story of her two bros and li'l sister burning to death. Well now she's dead. She's a Weight until they stick her in a hurriedly dug grave. They'll come for me, find I'm gone, that'll make 'em panic, but I'll keep, that's what they'll be saying, that cunt'll keep; lug her downstairs, into one of the car boots, take her out to the forest somewhere. Out there they'll be arguing over who digs the hole: Man, was you shot her. Yeah, tha's right, why I shouldn't have to dig the fucken hole. But I'm the prez. An' I'm the sarge-'t-arms. Even in concealing a murder, no one wants responsibility.

They'll pull her out of the boot, drag her through the bush in the dark, it won't be a very deep hole, too fuck-lazy to do it properly. She'll be dropped into the shallow hole, dirt over her poor li'l face, her final indignity, of bein' poorly buried by fuck-ups.

They'll be shakin' when they get back in the mean machine, nowhere to look, nowhere to escape the deed jus' done — Hold on a minit: there *is*. One or the other'll cry in joy as he remembers a joint. The prez'll give his cold-hearted smile, those snake eyes'll glow in the dark, so'll the joint passing between 'em, the smoke'll do its work fast, it'll have to, but at first it'll magnify the deed to its enormous awful height, but it's a matter of hanging in there till that passes. And when it does nothin'll matter, specially not the life just taken, specially not that. The weed'll turn murder to the dust the victim'll eventually, in the by and by, become. The smoke'll give the mind reason upon reason as to why it did what it did: righteousness will set in. They won't be but ten minutes into the journey home when they'll be considering the next righteous deed to be done, against him, fucken Abe Heke — he's forgone the right to the name he took, Blackie — and the pain he'll suffer first. Oh, yeah, the pain.

Out the window, hanging by his fingertips, letting go, falling into eternity, but ground not long in buckling him. (I'm alright?) Hurt an ankle bad but that wouldn't stop him running. For home. (I'm goin' home.)

TWENTY-SIX

THAT HE NOTICED the big, wall-enclosed house they were working close to was the Trambert place (and that must be the tree sticking up, all lush with summer growth and yet with my kid's last moments somewhere with her presence) was troubling enough. They were the road and sectionworks contractor, his machine had to turn every few minutes into the view of the house and that damn tree. So in the end he switched his mind off from it or he'd have not been able to do his job properly. Which is what he prided himself on since his boss had told him those good things about himself, made him a charge-hand and now he had a van to take home even if he had to get up half an hour earlier to pick up the three men under him.

Then the man developing the Trambert land turns up, dressed how they do these white men and always looking confident, cocksure of 'emselves even when they're li'l runts. Not that this fulla was a runt, but he wasn't nothin' special neither. Then one of the boys says it's Trambert himself. And the first thing Jake Heke thought was, how much more fucken money does the man want? Then guilt that the man would know everything he thought he knew about him, Jake, the hanged girl's father. And Jake seriously thought about quitting the job. Especially that it was the very next day he caught the man staring at him. Felt he couldn't take going through it all again. (I done my time. Here on the outside.) But lucky for Trambert he nodded at Jake, though Jake wasn't sure why the nod if the man knew what he thought he did.

But fuckit, he thought of the hunting times to come with the Douglas brothers, how different the experience'd be, they promised him. Which is why on Fridays he brought his rifle to work in the van, when it used to be his second favourite night for drinking and partying, Saturday being best cos it could start at around noon, but now Fridays, or if the weather allowed, were for hunting after their work; he had his hunting gear all ready to transfer to their four-wheel drive (and my gun). It was the job that afforded the hunting, his share of the vehicle petrol, share a tyre replacement, food and bullets even if the deer meat gave the boys a bonus, it still cost (like everything does, right Jake?) So he told himself forget Trambert, just keep focused on the job; and as he didn't eat lunch he worked his machine through lunch and that way didn't break his fixed focus. Job was only a two monther anyrate. He could last that long — couldn't he? — if he'd lasted all this time with what people (wrongly) thought about him.

Every day Trambert would be there at some stage or other. Tall and a bit of a smoothie in that well-dressed way, one a them silk things around his neck, sometimes a brown-flecked jacket and tie, nice shoes, walking over the sections of worked soil starting to take shape out of where sheep'd grazed. Stopping every so often, a man in thought, as if this was the most important project of his (money-hungry) life. Car he had was a bit past it, for a fulla rich as him. Must be a tightarse as well. Prob'ly why he was rich. And there wasn't a visit when Jake didn't catchim looking his way, just glances, but, he had to admit, friendly enough; with that li'l nod they give, white men like him. Not like the boss who was also a honky but rough as guts, big moustache, big and strong and didn't take no shit from no one. Not that

Jake'd ever had reason or desire to give his boss shit; he was a good man. Worked alongside his men, could drive any machine and had several gangs on different contracts around town and a couple of highway jobs out of town. He spent a lot of time going from job to job, which made Jake's position more responsible and one he took seriously. No particular reason why, other than it just seemed fair to the man that being a chargehand meant what it said: he was in charge. And if they didn't like him not having lunch with them they never dared say, just gave a man looks and even they wore off when they realised he just didn't eat lunch. He wasn't trying to be a suckarse to the boss. (Who likes a suckarse?)

One day Trambert came walking over to Jake as he sat in his front-end loader waiting for a late truck to dump dirt into. Jake found himself a little bit nervous at the approach. But he could hardly say anything. Just be ready on the defensive. Good morning. Morning. I'm Gordon Trambert. (So fucken what?) And you'd be Jake, is that right? Jake just nodded and got ready for some crap about Grace.

I saw you on the rugby field some months back. (Oh? And?) That right? You playing on the other side? (Take that.) Trambert laughed. No, too old and anyway not good enough. But I'm a very keen fan, very avid. (Avid? Keen?) Jake not used to these sorta words, not that he didn't know their meaning. He just never used them and hardly ever heard them used. Wondering when the fulla was gonna bring up Grace. Bracing himself and hoping for that fucken dirt truck to turn up and save 'im.

Ended up talking for about ten minutes. But only on rugby, who was senior-club champion, what did Jake think of the All Black selection and how the game being professional had changed the game itself, made it faster, of higher standard. That sorta talk. Then he shook hands and went on his way. Nice fulla. 'Nless he was just being polite. (Unless he saw me stripped down in the heat and thought better of saying anything about my daughter. Alright, Rita's right, I never gave my kids mention cos I never thought ofem. Dunno why, I just didn't. But she said a few weeks ago, the first time I'd heard from her since we'd had that good night, best one of my life as I remember, or it was till she said what she did, she said I'm like a lot of men from shit backgrounds, I didn't know how to be a good parent. Didn't know how to be one fullstop. So how was I gonna learn all of a sudden at forty-three? Never too late to learn, Jake, she told me like I was a kid, as if you can just say it and it happens — when it don't. And if I up and took a interest in my kids where would I start? I asked her that. You start like you start a road job, Jake: a little bit at a time. Yeah, easy to say. Hard (impossible) to do.)

But at least Rita had turned up of her own accord and at least she said she'd been missing Jake. And at least he didn't ask her jealous questions of who else she'd been seeing in the meantime since she'd taught him, in no uncertain manner, that her business was her business and until such time as she agreed to share it with someone, with any man be it him or who knows how many others, then it bloodywell stayed her business. Bitch was stronger than Beth. And they'd made love near as good as the last time, and he'd said afterward, Spose you expec' me to say sumpthin' about one a my kids? Well, I can't. (Even if I'd wanted to. Been too long.) Been a long time, Ri. Since I even seen one a them. Wanting her to take back what she'd said and he'd make any other change she asked of him, even cut down his drinking, anything but the impossible.

She wouldn't have it though. Said again, he had to start somewhere. He asked her where, how, what did he do? But she shook her head and toldim it had to come from him, from his own within. Which took him a little figuring out how she put that last. (From my own within? Well who else's within would it be?) But he did get it, by and by. But it didn't come with any answers.

Few days later he sees a car slow right down on its way down the Trambert private road, a coupla football fields long, lined with skinny trees but nice cone shapes and pale green of leaf, but only half a field distant from the new carve-off of land they were turning into building sections. This woman in it, must be Mrs Trambert, stopped and looking out her driver's window at the site (bitch is checking on her family money growing before her eyes. Lovely eyes at that, or the quite distinguishable face suggested they'd be. Very classy.) Snooty, to Jake Heke's eyes. Then he realised she was looking at him. And she gave this li'l wave. And was that a smile? Drove on leaving him sitting on his machine feeling confused.

The next day when Trambert made his regular inspection, this time with another fulla in a suit carrying plans and both doing a lot of pointing, Jake was sure Trambert's greeting lacked something. It did from earlier times when he would come over to Jake if Jake wasn't on the machine working it, and talk rugby. Last time he asked about a young player called Toot Nahona. Said he'd seen the game when this Nahona fulla'd — well, gave you a hard time, Jake. Jake remembering the flanker, and how he'd really got one in for Jake no doubt about that. And won the confrontation, hands down. Well this visit if Jake'd walked up and asked about a specific rugby game he got the feeling Gordon Trambert would have been colder of attitude. So someone'd been talking to him. Turned a man into his shell. And why shouldn't he?

SO IT'S HIM? Yes, it's him. Jake Heke, they said at almost the same moment, which got a little smile from her (for a change). He's big, isn't he? I don't know, I've seen bigger. Every Saturday senior rugby I see them even bigger than him. It's not so much his size as a certain presence. Well, that's probably what I meant, Gordon. A certain crude charisma. Yes, I think it would be fair to describe him as that; I've talked a few times to him on the site. Without ever realising of course. And then Gordon Trambert realised something else.

Do you remember I told you of returning past the cemetery after the Heke girl's funeral and — Don't call her the Heke girl, Gordon. She had a name: Grace. Alright, fair enough. Grace. Well at Grace's graveside was this rather astonishingly moving sight of a young man with wild, frizzy locks, lurching his way to the grave, myself parked up at the roadside, two sextons frozen poses of eating their lunch. And this grief-stricken kid, this teenager as though out of a jungle, as though some tragic part in a melodrama, fallen to his knees and — And there he was like a dog howling inconsolably to the — well in this instance a rather grey sky. An unforgettable sight. Had me in tears. You in tears, Gordon? Cocking that eyebrow how she did at him. But at least this was communication and brought about, as happenstance would have it, by the father of Grace, tragic Grace Heke.

Then he told his wife of one day seeing an outstanding rugby player as being one and the same youth but several years, a shaven head, older. And now it was explained why Toot Nahona had so ferociously targeted Jake Heke on the rugby field, he had been Grace's friend. And of course Jake had come under suspicion that he had sexually abused his daughter, until tests showed it wasn't him, according to one of Isobel's golfing friends, a real ferret for private information on near anyone. Estrangement or not, they sat there in the living room with drinks he'd got while they were at it (actually sharing a moment together), a quiet astonishment at how this funny old world sometimes turned out.

So how are your costs on this development? Why Isobel, you're actually interested? I'm interested to know if it's you-know-what. Go on, say it. You mean another disaster? Yes, I do mean that. Is there reason I shouldn't? After all, there is a track record. I agree, oh pessimistic wife of mine — No, not pessimistic. Cynical, Gordon. Cynical.

Our costs, my dear, are exactly as they were contractually fixed at. And you may be interested to know that Lloyds no longer want our blood, they'll settle for a few pints shall we say. Gordon wondering in his heart what his wife would settle for to put end, or at least start the process, to this estrangement. But he didn't ask. What, and there are pints left to give? Just, dear.

Just. Oh, well, that's a relief. I'll have another drink while you're up.

She talked about their son, Alistair, and how he appeared to be taking a somewhat dramatic turn for the better. Perhaps it was a case of late maturing. Whatever the reason, it was enough to cheer a father, indeed a husband for having his wife at least share this with him, feeling the better. It might have been the drink, or what he thought he was seeing, or hearing, in her eyes, her tone, that stirred a sexual urge in him. But dammit (no), he'd not grovel for it. Put it out of his mind, he'd not let it show. He might, if he had the strength, ignore her hint if that was what he was seeing increasingly as he made her a third gin and tonic. (Yes. I shall ignore her overtures. Then we'll see about my being a man to respect.)

And they kept returning to him, Jake. Jake Heke, well well well. Innocent, Isobel? Or guilty? Oh, definitely innocent. Are you sure? Of course she was sure. What, are you worried he'll come here with an eye for me? Gordon couldn't help himself: He'll have to line up behind me then. Don't be disgusting, Gordon. Yes, yes, I know it's been a long time. No, he lifted his hand. Don't even mention it. It comes when it comes. Is that your crude idea of a pun, darling? (Is this your idea of a long awaited hint, my darling?) The first time she'd used any form of endearment in some long time. He changed the subject. He wasn't that easy.

ONE OF THE bruthas, drunk and stoned, had cut a big hole in the wall upstairs so it looked down on the main floor area of the Browns' HQ where everyone got together and got nightly, daily if there was bread enough, drunk and anyway constantly stoned on dope. He did it, he said, to remind him of being in jail looking down from a landing, HAHAHA! using a Stanley knife which some of the bruthas carried for cutting faces not lino, but cut through the gib-board like cake been sittin' in the sun a few days.

And he'd yelled out from up there: *Num'a one landing!* in an imitated screw's voice. *Down f' breakfas'!* And the boys and sheilas down below beside 'emselves with laughter and aksing was it bacon an' eggs or just fucken porridge sludge? And over the months utha bruthas'd cut a piece out so it was a length of viewpoint a good eight studs in width and enough to show from below, if anyone looked up, of head and shoulders lookin' down jus' like in a jail. 'Cept there wasn't a net like in jail for the jumpers, the commit sideways wannabes who'd had enough, couldn't do no more time. It was jus' straight dirty floorboards and elbow-height tables like in a public bar for everyone to lean on as they got drunk (again). Yeah, jus' missing a net for those fullas who couldn't do no more time.

Like Mulla Rota couldn't. (I just couldn't, man.) Not one more week. A day in the copshop lock-up, a week on remand, yeah. A man must expect that. But a sentence? Hell no. A man was all used up inside. And nor did he laugh at the pun. Not now.

He was looking down reminded, as always, of being on the firs' landing of a jail, hearing inis mind those echoes of grilles opening and closing, screws' keys jangling, the constant voice explosion and all the bad expressin' that sounded worse echoing in a concrete-walled chamber. He was lookin' down then suddenly eased back from view at sight of Chylo, mad, murder-potential, achin'-t'-happen Chylo. With Gloria. And fucken Jimmy Bad Horse. In a talking huddle. And Mulla peeping down on 'em his heart breaking in two. (She's dropped me cos I didn't wanna do it. The job was *my* idea. Now she's gone for Chy cos he'll do anything.) Including, it was also clear, having her, as Chy's hand went on her hip and she turned into the touch, oh, yeah, he could hear her sayin', and Mulla could imagine Chylo's eyes glass ovah cos sex weren't just sex with him, not with Chylo. It was what he and every man wanted but it frightened him, or it was inis head as sumpthin' a normal or even a half fucked-up gang member'd not recognise. He'd be the type to beat up a woman in the middle of fucking her. Or pull out his Stanley knife and giver a cutting. And now she was unwittingly offering herself to Chylo (cos I wasn't havin' none of her do-anything to get a deposit on a new house). And when Jimmy Shirkey put a hand on her tight-jeaned arse and her laugh echoed up to Mulla, he felt like diving ovah landin' on the floor dead at their fucken betraying feet. Specially *her* feet. (Man, I *loved* you.)

Confused, even suddenly nauseous and dizzy in his terrible hurt and betrayal, Mulla Rota lurched back to his room, shut the door behind him. Had thought of only wanting this feeling, this awful sense of himself, this fucken whole existence that'd been lived through, endured — just — and then thought he'd come out the utha side only to end like this, of it may as well bein' a true end. Wanted to kill himself. (May's well die, man. May's well end the fucken thing. Whassa use? Whassa use of even bein' a good person and you get shat on?) And he lay down on the bed, a tall man, a facially tattooed man with Maori warrior designs, same patterns same pain of bearing silent electric needling as them two down there plotting with his woman, and wept like a man stripped of his warrior status, stripped of meaning, stolen of love, taken of life jus' when it'd started to be and mean sumpthin'. That's how Mulla Rota wept.

Though there remained, or came, one last spark of life in him. Which did inform his broken self of its presence. You got one more spark lef', Mulls, it said. So who's it gonna be? When the cryin's done, when the life can't be no more, who's it gonna be to give it some sorta las' meaning? And he did have a face clear in even his distraught mind.

TWENTY-SEVEN

THE CAR DIDN'T fit, not down that drive. Not 'nless it was here to visit one of the boys under his charge. But if so, it'd be news to him: he knew what sorta car it was. What kinda people it carried. So he watched it carefully, turning his machine straight on at it, as it came at speed down the tree-lined tarsealed road, flashing undercoat grey through the gaps, in summer sunlight, summer blue sky, air with birds, them poplar trees with birds, he'd taken the trouble to ask Mr Trambert what they were, now Trambert was friendly after all. Poplars, Jake. At first Jake thought Trambert said populars — the name he repeated — till Trambert chuckled and corrected him, so Jake'd laughed, too. Puzzled at Trambert muttering sumpthin' about not being exactly popular in his own home. But then Jake thinking he can't've heard right, like he didn't the tree name.

He watched as it slowed down, pulled over, sat there only for a few minutes, turning his engine off in case he could pick up something, though the distance probably too far. Only enough to see it was two fullas in front, driver this side, hard lookin' dude even from what, sixty, seventy feet, and looked like a woman the back, her arm pointing over between the fullas' shoulders. Another fifteen feet Jake reckoned and he'd be able to get a close look, so he started his engine and went forward, which risked his being noticed because the section he was on sloped down to him so he'd be up on the slight rise. But then they wouldn't think, even if they saw it, that a ordinary fulla on a front-end loader'd be interested in them.

(Well, I'll be. If it ain't . . .) when they did a u-ey and he got a view of the passenger fulla in the front. But he couldn't quite pull the face, the name to go with it from memory. Damned if he could. Even long after their smudgy grey-painted mean machine'd growled back to where it came from.

He drove back in the company van that evening, makin' out, should anyone want to know, he was checking the portable lock-up tool shed and just the site in general, the machines left overnight, like a responsible employee. Now he had the name of the one dude he recognised, Jimmy Bad Horse. (Who blew his arse when I fronted him in my bar that time. Who came to my son Nig's funeral under police escort, the convoy of their stupid fucken cars you can spot a mile and what they do half their stupid crim business in, before the main group of mourners — fucken hundreds ofem) and so many faces of Pine Block residents he recognised, him and Cody concealed behind bushes cos he just had to go to this one's, as he'd missed Grace's (got so drunk I slept in and it was all over when I got the taxi to take me to the cemetery). It was Jimmy Bad Horse who himself got sent away for his part in the main street shootings and now, how the years pass, out and about and unchanged. Once a cunt always a cunt.

He hung around the site, wondered about going over to the Tramberts', warn 'em, but what to warn about, that some Brown Fist jerks were casing his place to burgle? How'd he know they weren't pointing out where Grace'd hung herself, seein' Nig was one ofem. And so what if it was a burg being planned, what's Trambert ever done for a man? Thinking about it, Jake sort of added the one of Grace hanging from Trambert's tree (that tree with its big broad top sticking up) and the three of these lowlifes to make the four of sorta justice, in a way. In a way of a white man bein' what he was, rich, secure, whatever else they are, and the gangies, even though they're arseholes, bein' what they were, Maori, poor, not secure, jus' fuck-ups. But he did wait around a bit, in fact till the dusk was nearly done with. And he did drive right down by the Trambert gateway, saw it was open, and Trambert's Range Rover in the forecourt, or whatever they call the driveway when it loops around a circle of lawn with a tree in the middle, house behind, and he didn't see no gang car. So he'd done more than his bit that no one'd know about, well, maybe he'd mention it to Rita, if she still wanted to see him again, hard to tell with her, got her own mind, and that stuff about his attitude to his own children. (How can I help it?) He'd more than done his duty as a — as a what? he suddenly got to asking himself, and with a smile forming as he drove the company van back home. As a citizen. (A what?) A straight citizen clean in the police's eyes, with a granted firearms licence, is what.

SHE TOLE HIM she wanted, since he wasn't gonna do a armed bank job with no prospec's, a job those fucken white cunts'd never forget. Talked like a gang memba herself now, even said aks for ask. She wanted not jus' the cash she was without doubt in her mind certain they'd have lyin' around like they'd have them ole paintings in fancy frames hangin' on the walls, 'emselves prob'ly carpeted, yeah, walls carpeted tha's how Gloria Jones had it (carpeted walls? Man, no honky's place I ever burgled had carpet on the fucken walls.)

She wanted not jus' the cash they'd have in their safe but for 'em to know they'd taken their money from Maoris, even rubbish Maoris like her whose families weren't ever nothin' in the eyes of the grander scheme of things, of genuine ones who'd been stripped of their land and too much of their dignity withit. In the ole days Gloria woulda been a slave, or a slut for the warriors to help 'emselves to. They were gonna be wearin' masks, balaclavas, she had it all figured out, so naturally if they had masks they could, well, do jus' about what they liked couldn't they? Or they could if he'd been agreeable but he wasn't. And she wouldn't hear it about him not bein' able to do the time. Nor when he aksed what did she have against them people to wanna do the things she was wanting to do?

Like trash the place. Kick their muthafucka white heads in, she'd snarled like she w's the wildest patched-up memba bitch goin', not jussa solo mum down the street used to put her smokes before her kids' food in their bellies. You c'n fucker, the lady of the house y' wan', Gloria Jones said. *I* won't care, *I* won't be jealous — which only told him, Mulla, that she mustn't think enough of *him* to care, let alone 'bout the poor woman she was wanting him to rape — long as I don't have to like *call* you off, Mulla Rota, HAHAHAHAHA! He thinking her brain was becomin' scrambled eggs from the dope she jus' loved to smoke now near all the time.

But no, he'd decided once and f'rall, he wasn't doin' no crime that was carryin' a sentence and tha's what he tole her.

HE HAD HIS prob'ly only true friend in the gang (everyone's got one, ain't they? Even me) Hector The Honey Nectar James to keep his eye on 'em, Gloria, Chylo and Jimmy. Knowin' it could costim his life if Hec had changed his loyalties. But Hec reported back on Chy and Glor as thick as thieves, those were his words, and prob'ly they're — uh, sorry, Mulls — doin' the bizzo together, too. Hec meaning she was prob'ly two-outin' Chylo and Jimmy, one in each hole, cos man, Hec reported faithfully, the three ofem were thick, drinking together, smokin' together, and dancing together, too, even Jimmy, blind to his lack of dancin' talent out on the HQ floor with Glor. Actin', Hector reported in disgust, like a gang slut.

An' when Hec came up to Mulla's room Mulla'd had turned onim like anutha prison cell, tole him it looked like Jimmy was goin' true to form as he'd heard Chy boastin' how he and Gloria were gonna do some bizniz together and Jimmy'd aked 'em to bringim back a trophy, some kinda prize, Mulla knew Jimmy'd done his part, sucked the uthas into thinkin' what they were doin' was a very good thing to do. So Mulla knew he'd picked the right face inis mind. He aksed his good friend one more favour, could he go and buy or borrow him a Stanley carpet knife?

I DUNNO WHY, but I couldn't stop thinkin' about it, that fucken car with fucken Jimmy Bad Horse in it. They could only've been, what do they call it, casing the Trambert place. I thought I should ask Trambert when he came on site the nex' day and talked the Super 12 rugby with me, how much we enjoyed it and as for Jonah Lomu, well, what was there left to say, but we said it anyway, that rugby'd never known a man like it. And Trambert said something about the world needing heroes and role models and stars, but I didn't quite get his point. Firs' time I spoke to a proper Pakeha man in my life like we were better than just — wha's the word? — acquaintances. I think cos he loved the game and he understood it. And I'd only started playing again from my younger teenage days but I understood he'd've liked to have been a better player. So we were, you know, even. Me playing, he wishing he had. Both ordinary.

The same morning he came and after we'd run our talk on the Super 12 and Jonah and Zinzan Brooke and his dropkick by a forward in the test against South Africa in the World Cup Final, I wanted to ask him then if he had burglar alarms. But didn't know how to put it without him thinking it was a suspicious question. He's still standing there himself, as if he senses I got something to say, or so I was thinking in my not knowing what to do about the gangies casing his place. Then he said, I know who you are. You're Grace's father. And made my blood run cold. And my concerns for his fucken house's welfare from them thieving arsehole Browns gonna hit 'em any day now die on the spot. And I feel he's betrayed our, uh, acquaintance.

But fuck me if he don't next say — before I can give him the mean eye and tellim to mind his own fucken business what would he know about it — and we know you were blamed for it unjustly.

Unjustly, he said? I just nodded, trying to keep my fucken dignity, my pride, man. I knew what I'd been, and what kinda father I hadn't, now Rita'd told me, pointed out the, uh, error of my ways. But man I was no fucken rapist of my own kid and any man ever brought that up with me, even in declaring me innocent, better know that: Jake Heke did not do that. Had to show him the true face of innocence.

He (I) did a lot of other things, sure. (I) he did things he didn't know no better not to do. And things he did know better but went ahead and did anyway. He knew inis heart of hearts even as it happened, even inis blindness to himself, he'd been a bad husband, a terrible husband, and just as bad a father. And he knew now from Rita's relentless — her word, not mine — time and again occasions of late of showing a man to himself that he was partly made by what he grew up seeing and thinking of himself, that slave thing, that Heke family inheritance of being descended from lowly cowardly slaves, that made me — even with that, Rita? Yeah, even with that — only partly not responsible for the things he did. But mainly you're at fault, Jake, because a man has to face himself no matter how hard it is. At some stage in his life he's gotta face himself.

I did them things. I harmed my own family. I gave 'em witness they should never but never have been given. Like Rita said, I owed 'em a better birthright than witnessing 'em to their father's violence, why not his love? Why not my love? I had it in me, even if it was for my mates, my buddies, 'emselves like me. It was there. I just never spread it. But the face I had to show Gordon Trambert when he declared the one deserving injustice I suffered, it had to be of dignity. Cos that's all I had left worth saving of me what I'd been. The dignity of that one, single act of innocence. And even then, even then Rita never let me off the hook, Jake you got what you deserved. You were an innocent wrongly accused. Just like your child, your beautiful daughter Grace was an innocent born into your household.

I told the man thank you. Couldn't say no more or tears'd spill. He said we must get together and have a talk, he'd like that. Yeah, and so would I, I heard coming from myself. I did manage to get that out.

I worked my machine with an eye on the Trambert drive, as I did wonder how he knew this information. Still thinking I shoulda told the man of the Brown Fist cunts. But I thought if I saw these cunts I'd warn 'em off, be another chance to show that Jimmy what a bad horse he wasn't. I came back that night and sat in the van till two-thirty in the morning. Funny thing, all the thinking I got done passed the time as if I was needing to be there anyway. Thinking about Beth, my kids. Not that I could do anything about it.

I figured, too, that they'd not hit the place on the weekend cos these people would have friends over prob'ly. But I told the Douglas brothers leave me out of the hunting Friday. That I had a date. Which I did. Who says it's gotta have nice legs and a skirt?

Maybe it was my way of makin' up just a li'l bit for Grace; that tree there her shrine I had to look after. Maybe that's why I stayed on after work on the Friday. By habit, anyway, I had my rifle in the van bein' a Friday. Asked myself did I really want to shoot someone to make myself look like a hero or to satisfy my violence I knew'd never been cured, more eased with age. (But it's never cured, once you got the, what-they-call-it, the virus.) Lot of my dreams're violent. Though one thing: not once did I ever dream of raping anyone, let alone my own daughter. Jake The Muss, even when he was a Muss (and, you know, pretty blind to 'imself) wouldn't've done that. Nor would Jake Heke, not in all the years of his teeth-grinding, violently landscaped waking thoughts and sleeping dreams, not even (I) he would do that.

Then I thought I been listening to this woman Rita telling me every damn thing I don't wanna hear about myself all these months, so why not tell her about this, see what she advises?

But they showed up.

I saw the lights enter the driveway then they went off. I was out of my van my ears to the night and sure enough, the progress of a vehicle coming my way. But no lights to say it was legitimate. Just stars up there. And me down here with my rifle, my manhood picking a time like this to ask what it really was. That fucken lightless car coming slowly on. Lights on at the Tramberts', but no visitors on their list this night. Not invited ones.

TWENTY-EIGHT

THEY WERE COMING into the court room like big jugs of humans being poured, each from a different container, with the formally dressed ones, the court officials, and the lawyers, already with their permanently reserved places in Two Lakes' newly opened High Court, but the rest of quite different flavour.

Jake telling himself to stick to Rita's instructions now that the gang arseholes started their sunglass-wearin' dark oozing through the side door. She'd said, give 'em an even stare, Jake, like this, not this, showing him what he looked like when he was giving the meanies. But it was hard seein' 'em in the flesh, they riled a man instantly, made 'im want to fight the bastards, but no, an instruction is a instruction, and there was a lot more than the old-day pride at stake here. Now there was.

So he gave back a steady stare, keeping his blinks near to an eye-hurtin' minimum. (I have to. I just have to.) But so hard to keep up the act with the way they swaggered in, fucken big galoot kids hidin' behind their shades and numbers and bullshit reps. Fuckem. No, don't even be thinking like that, he told himself, or it'll be you losing it, the only thing that'll count in this trial: dignity. And courage (guts).

Rita hadn't arrived yet; he wondered if she was putting him to the test, of leavin' him on his own to face this like she'd persuaded him to face all the other things. Not that he was through with that. But progress had been made.

The lawyers he thought wore wigs like you see on teevee, but these ones didn't. He got quite a startle to see Beth when she walked in, how she'd changed, how damn good she looked, how smartly dressed she was, like the man with her, whatshisname, the welfare fulla, Bennett, that's right. Big fulla but kinda paunchy. Had to tell himself don't be lookin' at the man like that: he's the one ended up with Beth not you, and fathered your kids how they shoulda been fathered. Got even more of a start when she saw him and nodded. Ever so formally he felt. (Oh, well, what's past is past. I don't feel so ashamed now.) He gave a little nod back that woulda been a little smile if he didn't have the gang cunts in front ofim.

The kids with Beth and her man, well he didn't see them at first. And when he did as they took their seats up there in the higher public gallery he didn't at first recognise them. Was that Polly? Why, she'd turned into a very fine-looking young woman. And talk about confident. Guilt then forced him to look at the other. Hu? Is that Huata? Kid was fucken near a man's size now. And he'd be what, twelve, thirteen, fourteen at most? Truth was, Jake didn't know not to even a couple of years how old his kids were. They did look well, though. Someone looking like Boogie was nowhere to be seen. (Hell, what if he's died, been killed, too?)

He averted his eyes, couldn't bear to get cold blank stares, he was lucky Beth'd even nodded his way. (Got to find my own sources of strength. Love, too.) Which is the feeling he got when he saw another file-in through the same side door as the gang cunts: it was love he felt. Kohi, Gary, Jason, Hepa, Haki Douglas, and a few others he didn't know, a whole bunch ofem, walked in and each man giving gesture to Jake, and eyes at the gang cunts sitting with tattooed arms folded trying to look tough, wearin' their shades inside. Oh, how the Douglas brothers and cousins were giving them arseholes the unshaded eye. And about the same as Rita had told him he should give, with not too much aggression, just with all your fearless heart, Jake Heke. Tha's all you have to give those bastards.

So he did. He looked over at 'em and felt his head lift and he didn't move a muscle on his face and knew the Douglas's wouldn't be either, hard men that they were. And he could feel that humming coming from their direction, like they were trying to send it out to him, lettim know they were withim all the way.

Then an official voice toldem all quiet please and be standing for his honour the learned judge. So they all stood, even the gangies knew to or they'd be ordered from the court-room. And this old fulla, white of course, comes in but looking very dignified but in a different way to Jake Heke's unnerstandin' of dignity. The judge took his seat, nodded to the beautifully timbered room of a mix of the town's, the world's, inhabitants, from the fullas who would've felled the trees to those who'd read those thick books lining the shelves behind the judge made from the trees. (It's all kind of the same.)

They sat down, everyone but the gangies who slumped and dropped their sullen, burning weights down. And names were called and charges read. Murder. Which made Jake Heke shudder, but not enough to move him one inch in staring still at the gangies in a bunch on their own, several spaces around them cleared. He shuddered but differently at hearing the name — his name — Heke amongst the droning by the court official, as spoken by a whiteman which was different to a Maori voice sayin' it.

And he wanted more than anything in this moment for that face to just look his way seeing he'd shifted his defiant but dignified gaze from the gangies to him (my son, whether he acknowledges or not). Just to know is all a man asks. Inside, no different to a silent prayer: Just look at me once, boy.

(He's frightened. Don't be frightened, son. Jakey's here. One look is all I ask.) Your honour, the crown's witness will be, as just declared, Abraham Jacob Heke. (Tha's right, we named him Jacob his middle name.) Your honour will appreciate the stringent security measures to protect this witness giving evidence against the defendant Montgomery on the gravest of all criminal charges, murder, and the other defendant . . . (blah-blah-blah, just look at me, Abe. So you know I'm here. Like I shoulda been.)

Beth's eyes caught Jake as he shot a glance at her, asking with his eyes what next, what next? (I never knew what was best in this life, I just didn't. But I'm willing to learn. Gimme a sign, Beth, of what to do about our son.) But her eyes went to that son without giving Jake any sign.

Proceedings were some way on, the name of the woman those two in the dock'd murdered, or one had and the other was charged with being an accessory, had been mentioned several times: Tania Martins. Age twenty-six. Jurors were warned that photographs of the murdered woman's body would be — well, whatever the word they use for very bad to look at (poor kid). And those Hawk filth trying to intimidate Jake Heke's son Abe but getting plenty of looks from him and the Douglas brothers. Plenty.

But he did look my way. Got a shock to see me. Looked away. I was desperate. But leas' I'd done my best. Then his eyes started coming back to me, not all the way, but part. Eventually he gave them to me. And I just nodded. No smile. No nothing but the look — of support though — and the nod. My son inclined his head back. And then it lifted and never dropped again not for the whole days and days of giving his evidence against that murdering bastard whose name Abe called Apeman but was Montgomery, of all the names, a war general Jake's old pub mates used to talk about they called Monty.

I WAS GONNA shoot them. Or I would've shot him, the driver. I was waiting for them at the side of the house. With this choir music going that woulda really got to me if it wasn't for the, uh, circumstances. Their car came ghosting in, engine off, and the doors open and two people get out, walking fast for the front door where under the light I see they've got balaclavas, like we wear out hunting when it's cold. 'Cept one was a woman. A woman.

I would've shot him because he wasn't Jimmy Bad Horse he was the driver whose crazy eyes I'd seen for a man who doesn't talk, he fights, and he fights dirtier than dirty. I would've shot him because a part of me, maybe of a lot of men, would like to do it, to the bad guy most of us would. But then who'd believe me if I said I did it because he was burgling the home of a rich white family where my daughter had hung herself?

So I just stepped out where they could see me in the spillover of light: You get the fuck outta here. Then I saw he had a carpet knife. So I lifted my rifle at his head, angry. You were gonna use that on them in there? He didn't say no, nor did he look so surprised it took away any of that murderous look in his eyes in that opening of woollen head-covering. As for you, a woman, you're lucky I don't make you take those things off. (In fact, it then came to me, I better. Case I had to identify them. Might give me an advantage if they were thinking of backing up on me. Because I toldem, I'm Jake Heke. Case you didn't know.) Now rip them things off your fucken heads. (Or else.)

I could still hear that sad chorus singing faintly. So the Tramberts'd never know, not if these two pieces of shit now exposed to me didn't do sumpthin' stupid. Oh, he was a hardnut the fulla was alright. A murder waitin' to happen for sure. Her, she was no surprise, a slut who looked like she was a bit old for this sorta carry-on; and her mouth opening and closing as though she recognised me. Maybe she did. It didn't matter.

Now you get in that car of yours and don't you ever come back. I was about to say about the tree what it meant to me. But it was like telling my own, old self: it wouldn't mean nothin'. When you're deaf, when you're blind, with no ears eyes to your own life, then that's what you are.

Walked behind 'em to their car. Told her to get in and steer it, him to push. A bullet up your arse you try anything smart, mista. I didn't want the engine starting to warn the Tramberts. They'd known about me without my knowing. Now it was my turn. Made the bastard push it way clear of the gates, till he asked how far I was gonna make 'im do this. I thought of Rita and how she pushed me. Way to go yet, kid. So shuddup and keep pushing.

I stood on the Trambert private driveway watching the gang car disappear its red eyes into the night. I thought if a visitor happened along to catch me in its headlights standing there holding a gun, be me for the high-jump. So I scrammed back to the van and drove, unannounced, to Rita's, telling myself that if I found her with a man I was to accept it and walk. But she was pleased to see me. And naturally very surprised but proud of me what I'd done, as I told her of it finishing with me hearing that music even when I was so far away I couldn't have heard it. In your freed heart, she said, that's where it was coming from. I think I unnerstood what she meant, that I did.

MY SON ABE'S evidence the way he told that girl's life, of her kid brothers and li'l sister burning in the house after their mother left 'em with no money, took it for herself and went boozing, and when they found the five bucks down the back of the sofa, the li'l brother did, the older sister Tania went to buy fish and chips and when she came back the, uh, the house was burning, it had the court-room in tears, women crying, men, too. And even some of those gang cunts had lowered heads in shame that such a life lived should end up murdered by one of their own. I realised he'd told that part of her life story to get the jurors even more against that Apeman piece of filth. (My) Abe never wavered, not even when Apeman at the jury finding them guilty as charged screamed out The Family's gonna get you! It had no punch in it, not with us big fullas, me and the Douglas real family staring our contempt at the arseholes who didn't look they could get 'emselves home after this. Oh, not that I had anything to boast about. And what I did who'd believe it, that I'd stopped two of the other gang from doing what they mighta done to the Tramberts. Nothing else to boast about. Nothin'.

Rita didn't come near me, not the court-room, till it was all over. We heard there'd been another gang killing while Abe was giving his evidence. Apparently, a Brown Fist cut the throat of Jimmy Bad Horse and had shot himself. Did the deed with a Stanley knife so the lawyers and court officials were reading and whispering about in their newspapers.

I shook Abe's hand after it was over. But that was all. We didn't have anything to say to each other, I understood that. But at least my other kids, Huata and Polly, came up and shook my hand and said thanks for supporting Abe and were those my friends in support, too? Polly wanted to know that. Yeah, they're my friends. I thought she looked a lot like Grace her smile. But then again what would I've remembered of Grace? I asked Polly where was Boog these days. Nearly fell over when she said university. A kid of mine, a common ole Heke, at a university? I just had to ask, studying what? But she was turned and walking and prob'ly didn't hear.

I had a dream one night, of that strange, unified humming. It was the Douglas family, and in another smaller (reduced) group was my kids with Beth and their real father, Charlie Bennett. Humming the same tuneless note that held 'em together. I had thought, I remember thinking it, at my son Nig's funeral, in my shamed state concealed in the bushes, that Nig and me'd showem in the next life. In the next life we'd showem. Well, in this dream it was showing me it could be this life. Yeah.

Well, Jake Heke's sorry. I am sorry to all of you. Rita who I live with keeps telling me, It's alright, Jake. Now it is. Now it is. But, you know, it needn't have been.

Men Love Sex
edited by Alan Close

Australia's and New Zealand's leading male writers and most exciting new names lay bare their feelings about love and sex.

Painfully honest, confronting, hilarious and poignant, *Men Love Sex* reveals what men really talk about when they talk about love.

Venero Armanno
Ian Beck
John Birmingham
Peter Carey
Tom Carment
James Cockington
Matthew Condon
Alan Close
Christopher Cyrill
John Dale
Julian Davies
Robert Drewe
Jonathan Griffiths
Mike Johnson
Steven Lang
Gerard Lee

Damien Lovelock
Roger McDonald
Lex Marinos
Frank Moorhouse
Mark Mordue
David Owen
Eric Rolls
John Stapleton
Angus Strachan
Chad Taylor
Clinton Walker
Archie Weller
Peter Wells
Tim Winton
William Yang

Eating Fire and Drinking Water
Arlene Chai

My name is Clara Perez. I am a reporter.

This is the story of my country whose people eat fire and drink water, and of an oppressive regime whose decline is foretold by the singing of a river.

It is about how one man's act of kindness changes the lives of many, and of a woman who bleeds from the wounds of Christ and a man whose name is Pride; a leader corrupted by power, a colonel who is an artist of pain, and a charismatic young man who dies only to live again.

And it is about me.

For on that fateful morning of the fire when I went to Calle de Leon in search of one story, I found myself caught up in another. I discovered my missing history.

But to learn how two tales become one, you must follow me back to that burning street, to where it all began.

Praise for Arlene J. Chai's *The Last Time I Saw Mother*:
'a remarkable first novel . . . filled with family secrets and the intersection of personal and world histories.'
Amy Tan